THE EX

AN UNPUTDOWNABLE PSYCHOLOGICAL THRILLER WITH A BREATHTAKING TWIST

ALISON KEANE

CHAPTER 1
ELLIE
SUNDAY NIGHT

jerk awake. It takes me a few moments to remember where I am. The couch in my flat. I gasp in a breath and tell myself to calm down.

I'm safe.

My plan worked.

I look around as I sit up. It's still dark. Disappointment washes over me—I'm impatient to get going but the first trains don't leave until six in the morning.

How long was I asleep for? It feels like I've only just drifted off.

I yawn and reach for my phone, groaning when it's not right in front of me on the table. I must have thrashed around in my sleep and knocked it off.

I lean forward and feel around on the floor beside me. When I don't find it there, I try the narrow space beneath the couch. It's not there either.

My heart starts to race. I know I'm being silly, but I have the strongest sense that I'm not alone in the flat. I take a deep breath and exhale slowly. I'm just being paranoid. I reach for the lamp on the side table before I remember that the bulb blew a few weeks ago and I still haven't gotten around to replacing it.

I stand up and move to the other side of the room where

the light switch is. I've walked around the flat in the dark often enough to know its layout from memory, but I keep my hands out in front of me just in case—I can't afford to trip over something and injure myself; not tonight.

I only make it a few steps when my fingers brush off something. At first I think I've gone the wrong way and walked into the curtains, but that thought only lasts an instant because whatever I'm touching is warm. My flat is a lot of things, but warm isn't one of them. What's in front of me isn't a wall or a window.

It's him.

No.

It can't be.

That's not possible.

But then I remember my doubts from earlier. Didn't I wonder if it was all just a big double-bluff? I told myself I was being paranoid, but now it seems I wasn't. I should have known I could never outsmart him.

I hear the slightest snort of air and my heart hammers. He's enjoying this, I think, and that only makes it worse.

I want to scream at him. I want to lash out for all the pain and misery he's caused me, but I hold back. I need to be smart about this. There's only one way out of the flat and that's through the front door.

I'll have to get past him first.

How am I supposed to do that when I'm struggling to catch my breath?

He still hasn't said anything—it's completely unnerving.

I launch myself in the direction of the door, hoping there's enough space to get around him and get away before he can stop me.

It doesn't work like that. The floorboards creak and I collide with a wall of muscle. Fingers close around my upper arms.

He laughs cruelly as he throws me backwards. My head smacks against the edge of the table and erupts in a world of pain.

CHAPTER 2
ELLIE
FRIDAY: NINE DAYS EARLIER

My phone buzzes on the table. I glance down, expecting to see Dad's name. But it's not from Dad: the text is from a number that's not in my contacts; just a series of digits that I don't recognise.

I slam my cup on the table and almost spill my coffee. A familiar wave of dread washes over me, made worse by the fact that I thought this was behind me.

It can't be. I want to cry. My life hasn't exactly turned around in the last few months, but things had definitely died down—or so I thought.

Opposite me, my friend Steph is oblivious to the turmoil in my mind. "Check it if you want—I don't mind."

I close my eyes. How do I explain to her that this isn't something I want to see? I'll ignore it. I'll pop to the shops after we leave here and buy a new sim card. Dad and Steph are the only people who ever contact me anyway. I can just lie and say I've changed providers or something.

"Go on," Steph says.

I shake my head. "It's fine. I'll check it later. It's probably nothing."

She watches me through narrowed eyes with a suspicious smirk playing at the edges of her mouth. I realise what she's thinking. I'm just about to tell her she's got it wrong when her hand darts forward and grabs my phone off the table.

"Steph, no."

She doesn't understand. She only moved here a few months ago and even though we've become quite good friends, I haven't told her about what happened last year. I can't: she's the only friend I have and I don't want to lose her too.

But she ignores me and taps the screen.

I bury my face in my hands. She's going to know now; she's going to know that I've been hiding the truth from her.

It doesn't even surprise me that they found my number. Nothing surprises me anymore.

I keep waiting for Steph to react. When she doesn't, I look up and find her grinning at me over the top of my phone.

My stomach lurches. Why is she smiling? She's only ever been nice to me since we got chatting a few months ago after yoga. Why would she take pleasure in reading something nasty?

"You didn't tell me you'd met someone," she says.

"Eh?" My stomach lurches. I lean across the table so the older couple next to us can't hear. I don't want to talk about it, but her reaction has thrown me so the need to know outweighs the urge to run back home and barricade myself inside. "What the hell does it say?"

She looks at me funnily before taking a breath. "Hi Ellie, it's Nathan. We met in the supermarket. Was wondering if you'd like to go for a drink sometime."

"Oh my God," I gasp, leaning back too far in my chair. The front legs slam against the floor tiles as I correct myself, but I'm too relieved to care. Of course! Nathan! I'd forgotten his name because the truth is I wasn't expecting anything to come out of our brief chat in the supermarket.

Steph watches me, waiting for me to explain.

"I met him in the supermarket," I say weakly. "I'd completely forgotten."

Her eyes bore into me. "Who did you think it was?"

"No-one." I can't tell her. How can I? She wouldn't believe me.

She stares at me for a few moments and then seems to realise I'm not going to say any more. "So are you going to meet him?"

I smile. I've been too busy worrying about hiding the truth from her that I haven't really thought about it. Not that there's much to think about. It's been a long time since I was last on a date. The truth is, I'd given up hope of finding a boyfriend until I can move to London or Manchester and get away from this place. Manchester, most likely. I'll never be able to afford London rents.

"I don't see why not," I say as casually as I can.

I can think of a thousand reasons why not, each of them valid. What I really need to do is keep my head down and live like a hermit until I've saved enough to rent a flat some-where else.

That's what I've been doing for almost a year—and I'm still nowhere close to having enough money.

"You should," she says. "It'd be good for you."

"I should get back to work."

"But we've only just sat down! God, Ellie, they work you too hard there."

"You work far longer hours than me."

"I know, but…" She flushes.

I shake my head. I don't know why I'm defending my job. BE Call Solutions is the sort of place you work short-term whilst you sort out a better option. I've kind of gotten stuck there. I was planning to leave and had even done up my CV to apply to new jobs before it happened—now nobody else would hire me and I know I should count myself lucky that work hasn't fired me.

"Should I text him back?" I ask, chewing on a nail. I defi-nitely fancy him: there's no question about that. I just never expected him to get in touch. Most people around here have heard Mikey's twisted version of what happened between us.

"Of course! I just told you to. Do you want me to do it?"

I shake my head. "No. I'll do it. I just don't know what to say."

"What about the Builder's Arms? That's usually busy."

I recoil. There's no way I'm setting foot in that place again. "It's a nice pub," I mutter, tapping in a reply. I suggest a drink tomorrow evening around seven in one of the new bars on Bridge Street. I hesitate for a moment before I press send because I'm not convinced this is a good idea.

In the end, Steph leans in quickly and presses send for me.

"Sorry," she says sheepishly. "I just think it'll be good for you."

I can't be annoyed at her—she didn't mean anything bad by it. "What about you? Have you been seeing anyone?" I ask before I can stop myself. We've never talked about past relationships because it's obviously not a subject I want to get into. I kick myself for saying anything, but it's too late: it's out there now.

Steph's features tighten. "It's complicated."

"Oh?" That's news to me. She's such a straight-forward person that I can't imagine her being involved in anything that's not straight-forward. That's naive of me, though: I should know better after what I've been through. I change the subject quickly before she can turn my question back on me. "Come on," I say, wearily. "I'd best get back to work."

We put on our coats in silence—mine's a tatty Primark one from a few years ago; Steph's is soft black wool cut so well it has to have been expensive.

I shiver as soon as we emerge onto the street—the temperature has dipped this week and it's supposed to snow this weekend. Steph links her arm through mine, but instead of feeling comforting like it should, I'm gripped by a terrible sense of dread.

I've kept my head down like a frightened rabbit the past year. I'm excited about the prospect of a date with Nathan, but it scares me witless too. I've barely been out after dark in all that time. I've been living in the shadows. What's going to happen to me if I put myself out there again? How will Mikey react?

I become aware of Steph tugging at my arm and realise at the same time that she's yelling at me. I turn my head slowly.

"Ellie! What is it?"

I shake my head. I can't tell her. I swore I wouldn't. Everybody else I know walked away from me because they believed his twisted lies, even when I tried to tell them the truth. Everybody except my Dad—and that's probably because I've never been able to bring myself to tell him what happened.

"I just got a bit lightheaded, that's all. I probably should have had more to eat."

I can't tell Steph. I can't.

I need her.

CHAPTER 3
ELLIE
SATURDAY

What was I thinking?

I look around again. It's dark out, but the streetlights overhead feel like they're spotlight beams, highlighting my presence to everyone who walks past. And that's a lot of people. Nathan suggested we come to the night market instead of going to the pub and I happily agreed because it seemed more anonymous.

Now I'm regretting that decision. We agreed to meet at the gate to the park where the market is on. There's not a whole lot to do around here and people have come out in crowds to wander around the stalls.

I grit my teeth. I should have thought of this. It feels like everyone's looking at me and there's no sign of Nathan. I rummage in my handbag, pretending I'm hunting for my phone when I know exactly which pocket it's in. It's more for show; for something to do.

I take out my phone and activate the screen. He's late. We agreed to meet at seven and it's almost ten past. That wouldn't normally be a big deal, but I feel like I'm in a goldfish bowl right now. I don't know how much longer I can stand here on my own, wondering who's out there lurking in the shadows.

Two girls around my age walk past. One says something

to the other, who glances at me and smirks. I pull my coat tighter. I always used to trust my judgement. I can't do that anymore. It's impossible to know whether I'm being paranoid or whether they really are talking about me. I don't know which is worse.

I shiver and look around at the dark windows of the buildings that surround the park on all sides. A horrible thought strikes me.

What if this is a set-up?

It's just too much of a coincidence that a single guy around my age hasn't heard those lies about me.

I shouldn't have come. I should have stayed home where it's safe.

"I left my phone at home. Sorry I'm late."

Nathan appears in front of me just as I'm working myself into a frenzy. I'm so on edge that I recoil.

He frowns. "Sorry. Didn't mean to scare you."

"You didn't," I say, working hard to sound relaxed.

He nods and, amazingly, the tension inside me starts to ease away. "It's cold. Shall we go look around?"

I nod. As we walk through the gates, I try to force down the sense of hope that's rising inside me. My palms are sweating. I don't want to mess this up if he's sincere, but I've got to know if there's more to him than meets the eye.

"When did you move here?" I ask as casually as I can, even though my heart is pounding. So much rides on his answer. If he's from out of town then maybe, just maybe…

He glances at me. "I've always lived here."

"Oh," I say. My heart sinks. I hope my disappointment doesn't show on my face. "Right. How old did you say you were?"

"Twenty-four."

I frown. He's only a year older than me. This isn't a big town. "Were you one of the geeky lads who couldn't bring themselves to talk to girls?" I ask playfully.

His expression darkens and I curse myself for saying that.

"So where did you go to school, then?"

"I didn't go to school here. My father taught at a private school in Bristol so we stayed up there during term and came back here for summers."

I feel a weight lift off my shoulders. Maybe he hasn't heard.

"Look." Nathan elbows me. "They have mulled wine. Do you want one?"

I say nothing, frozen by indecision. I haven't had a drink in almost a year. I swore to myself that I'd never drink again, but I can smell the spices wafting towards us and I can only imagine the warm fiery sensation on my tongue.

"Save us that bench," he says, pointing up the path. "I'll grab us two."

My protests die on my lips: he's disappeared into the crowd before I can tell him no; that I'm fine with tea or juice or whatever else they have.

I shiver as I make my way to the bench before anyone else can take it. It's fine when I'm with Nathan, but when I'm on my own like this the fear returns. Maybe it's good that he's insisted on getting those mulled wines: the alcohol might help me relax. There's nothing to fear—I've got to convince myself of that if I'm to have any hope of a normal life.

I can just about see Nathan towards the back of the snaking queue. I can't help but smile as I watch him look around and fidget. He can't stand still for even a moment. Am I flattering myself by thinking he's impatient to get back to me?

Adrenaline surges through me. I watch him slowly make his way further along the queue and I can't stop my foot from jiggling too. I'm impatient for him to come back, but it's for different reasons.

It gets darker all of a sudden and I look up to see why. My dad is hovering over me, blocking out the light from the nearest street light.

"Dad?"

"What are you doing here, Ellie?"

I point at the stalls. "The market. What are you doing

here?" That's the bigger question here. When I go to his house for lunch every Sunday, I don't even bother to ask what he's been doing anymore because the answer is always work.

"The market," he grunts.

"What, really?" I stare up at him. "I didn't think this would be your scene."

Nathan appears behind Dad before he can respond. He gives me a funny look and jerks his head towards Dad. A ball of anxiety starts to form in my chest. Am I supposed to introduce them? It's only our first date.

In the end, Nathan breaks the silence. He holds out one of the takeaway coffee cups he's holding. "Here's your mulled wine."

Dad spins around, having not noticed Nathan until now. I swear he looks Nathan up and down before he turns back to me with a disapproving frown. "What are you doing, Ellie?"

Irritation bubbles up inside me. Isn't it obvious what I'm doing? Why is he speaking to me like a child in front of Nathan? "Enjoying the market, Dad. I'll see you tomorrow?" I say, hoping he takes the hint.

He doesn't move. He stands there watching me with a very odd look on his face. My cheeks flush. What's he doing here and why is he trying to make me feel awkward? He's the recluse, not me—though I suppose that's changed recently.

"I'd better go," he says, not looking at Nathan again. He storms off into the crowd, dragging his phone out of his pocket and punching at it. He looks furious.

I sigh. "Sorry about him," I mutter to Nathan. "I don't know what's gotten into him. He's a recluse. He's obviously forgotten how to act in public."

"Are you an only child?" Nathan asks. He taps his cup against mine.

"Yeah," I say, still staring in the direction Dad went even though there's no sign of him now.

"Me too."

I smile, warming to him even more. "Does your Dad still treat you like you're thirteen?"

He shakes his head. "I wish he did. He has no interest in me whatsoever."

Sympathy bubbles up inside me. "If it's any consolation, Dad shows no interest in me when he's not judging me."

"I'm sure your mum will lecture him when she hears what he's done."

I sigh and take another sip of my mulled wine. I should have expected this to come up. I savour the spicy flavour on my tongue as I try to think of the quickest way to get this over with. "She died when I was two."

"I'm sorry," he says immediately. There's no awkward pause like there usually is when I'm forced to tell people. "Mine died when I was four."

"Really?"

He rolls his eyes. "No, I'm just making it up so it seems like we have something in common."

I can't help but laugh. "Do you remember her?"

"Just bits and pieces. She was in hospital a lot so I don't have the normal childhood memories of her at home."

"Oh," I whisper. Tears come to my eyes before I even realise what's happening.

'It's okay," he says, hesitantly putting his arm around my shoulder. "My aunts and uncles have filled in the gaps. I feel like I know her even though I really don't." He smiles. "I'm sure it's the same for you."

I shake my head. "No, not really. I don't have any aunts or uncles," I say, wondering how I can change the conversation to something a bit more positive.

"What happened to your mum?" he asks, before I can think of something else to talk about.

"An accident."

"What happened?" He winces as soon as he's said it. "I'm sorry. That's personal. I should have thought before—"

"It's fine, honestly." I smile up at him to show him it's true and I'm not just saying that. "She was in an accident when she was away touring."

"Touring? Was she in a band?"

"No. She was an actress." I smile as long-forgotten images float back into my head. They're not memories—I know that now. I told Dad about them when I was a teenager and he was dismissive, telling me they must be daydreams because I'd never seen her on stage. But to me they're real.

"Oh wow. Theatre, then?"

I nod.

"What kind of stuff was she in? Was it here in town?"

I shrug. "I actually don't know. I've never looked into it."

"Doesn't your father have old posters and stuff?"

I shake my head. "He doesn't really like to talk about her."

"That's a bit selfish."

I baulk, unexplainably stung by the fact that a stranger has just criticised Dad—even though we're not that close anymore.

"Sorry. I didn't mean anything bad by it."

"No, it's okay." I frown. I've never thought about it like that before, but he has a point. "You're right, actually."

I've always thought it was fair enough that Dad didn't like talking about her, but don't I have a right to know more about her? All I have are a few pictures of her buried in a box somewhere in my flat. I feel a rush of guilt: what kind of daughter makes no effort to learn more about her mother?

"Maybe you should push him. It's your story too, not just his." He pulls his arm away and the full extent of the cold hits me again. "Your drink is finished. Shall I go get us two more?"

CHAPTER 4
ELLIE
SUNDAY

I wake up and blink, smacking my lips as I try to figure out why there's a slightly sour taste in my mouth. Last night comes back to me in snippets as I squeeze my eyes closed and take slow shallow breaths in the hope that the hangover doesn't come.

It doesn't, to my surprise. Maybe it's because my liver has had a chance to heal itself. After the market, we moved to a cosy bar just off High Street. I'd never been there before—I'm not sure I'd ever even noticed it. We chatted for a few hours over drinks. Nathan was the perfect gentleman and made sure to put me in a taxi before he left. I would have liked to ask him back for a drink, but I suppose I should be glad we left it the way we did. I don't want this to be a casual fling.

I stare up at the ceiling and replay the date in my mind. I'm soon distracted by the little spots of black. Mould. It's coming through the paint again like it does every year, thanks to the damp and my flat's unreliable heating system. I'll have to scrub it with bleach when I get time.

I can't complain. There aren't a lot of rentals in town and the rent hasn't gone up in years. This place is a bit of a dump but I'm sure if the owner maintained it better he'd put the rent up and it's already more than I can afford. So who cares about a bit of mould if it means I can get out of this town sooner than if I lived in a nicer place?

There's only one way my life is going to improve and that's by moving somewhere else. And the only way to do that is by putting in as many hours as I can at my call centre job. I begged my dad to loan me the money to get away from here, but he doesn't believe in handouts. Things haven't been the same between us since I dropped out of uni—that was just one disappointment too many for him.

I sigh and throw off the covers. It's Sunday, which means I'm due over at Dad's house for lunch. I'm not sure either of us enjoys the small talk and long silences, but I don't have anything else to do. Besides, it'll stop me from sitting at home waiting for Nathan to text.

———

Dad's house is on one of the better streets in town. It's lined with detached houses on either side, with well-manicured front gardens filled with tall trees put there to keep prying eyes out. Everywhere you look it's pristine. There's no worst house on this street: they're all perfect. I walk quickly. This is the street I grew up on, but there's no pull of familiarity. I never felt like I belonged here.

I stop with my hand on the gate as last night's conversation with Nathan floats back to me. I know so little about Mum it's embarrassing. I could tell Nathan thought that was weird. What's wrong with me? Why have I never been curious to know more about her than the few scraps of detail Dad has told me?

I pull open the gate and hurry up the path. It's a double-fronted house with ornate pillars holding up the porch, a huge place for just one person. It's a beautiful house, but for some reason I despise it. I always have.

I press the doorbell.

I do have a key somewhere, but I've not seen it in ages.

Besides, this is a routine. It's not like I'm going to turn up at noon on a Sunday and find he's not here.

Although…

The memory of meeting him last night comes back to me and I frown. It's just not like him to break his usual routine. What's going on? Is there something I missed? I've been so caught up in my own problems that I haven't paid much attention to Dad lately.

"Ellie. Good to see you."

I smile. There's nothing forced about it. It's not like I don't love him—I do. No matter what happened, he's still my dad. He's strict with money and set in his ways. Refusing me a loan was nothing personal—I know that logically even though I can't help resenting him for it sometimes. My life would be a whole lot different right now if he had put his principles aside just once and lent me the money to get out of here. "Hi Dad."

I follow him into the house. There's a delicious cooking smell in the air and my mouth starts to water.

Dad walks through the house and into the kitchen. It's a stark space, just like the rest of the house. No photos. No artwork or trinkets.

"Why do you have no photos of her?" I ask suddenly. I'm not even aware of forming the question in my head: it just came shooting out of my mouth.

He turns. "I beg your pardon?"

"Why do you have no photos hanging up? Of Mum?"

He tosses an oven glove from one hand to the other a few times before he answers. "Because I gave you all the photos I had," he says with as much emotion as somebody might use to tell you that the weather's been changeable today. "Come on. Sit down. I did the carrots with garlic and honey. Your favourite."

———

Dad stacks his cutlery neatly to the side of his plate. "Don't you like it?"

"It's lovely. I just…" The truth is I was miles away. I'm not really sure what I was thinking about—all these thoughts are swirling around in my head and I can't really make sense of any of them. Maybe the mulled wines and beers from last night hit me harder than I thought.

"Come on. You've barely touched your food."

"I'll try and eat more in a while." I look at my plate. The meat is perfectly cooked. The roast potatoes are fluffy on the inside and crispy on the outside. I'm hungry, but I'm struggling to even get a few morsels down.

I swallow. I can't avoid it any longer. "Dad, can I ask you something?"

"Yes." He says it warily, like he knows he's not going to like what I'm about to ask.

I think about telling him it's nothing and changing the subject, but then I remember what Nathan said last night. I have a *right* to know about her.

"It's about Mum," I say, clearing my throat to try and distract myself from how nervous I've suddenly become.

"What about her?"

"Well, I don't have any memories of her."

"Of course you don't. You were two when it happened."

"When *what* happened?"

He shoves his plate away. "You know what happened. We've talked about this before. What's this about, Ellie?"

The temperature in the room seems to drop several degrees. I know I should change the subject, but I can't. I need to know.

"Do you have any videos of her performances? Or home videos of us?"

His eyes widen. "No. No, I don't."

"What about posters or programmes?"

"Posters?"

"From her shows," I whisper.

He flushes. "No. I'm sorry, Ellie, but I was never one for

fancy cameras or the latest video equipment. If I had known what was coming, perhaps I might have done things differently."

I squeeze my eyes closed as a horrible feeling of guilt washes over me. It's not fair to stir this all up again. "I'm sorry, Dad. I just… I feel like I know nothing about her. Maybe if I knew more about her I'd have a better sense of direction."

He scowls. "That's nonsense and you know it. You can't blame your failures on your mother. You only have yourself to blame."

I flinch. "I'm not trying to blame her."

"What then? What possible benefit could there be to dredging all of this up?"

"*All of this?* It's my past. I have a right to know who I am."

He sighs. "The past doesn't define you. You were a little girl. I didn't want your childhood to be all misery and mourning."

"Couldn't there have been a happy middle ground? We didn't have to talk about her every day, but pretending she never existed?" My voice rises to a high-pitched squeak. "It's embarrassing, not knowing anything about where I come from."

He shakes his head in a way that I've become very familiar with. It's the look that says he's disappointed in me. "Ellie, does this have anything to do with the lad I saw you with last night?"

"Do you think he went back in time and convinced you not to tell me anything about Mum?"

His face tightens. He throws his napkin on the table. "There's no need to be sarcastic. You know very well what I meant. Isn't it convenient that the last time you showed any interest at all in your mother was around the time you started seeing Mikey? And we both know how well that turned out."

My pulse rings in my ears. I stare at Dad, unable to believe what I've just heard.

"What? What do you mean?"

"You know what I mean," he mutters.

Tears fill my eyes and my heart pounds. He knew? He knew all this time and he never said anything? I shake my head. I can't believe this. I just assumed from the way Dad keeps to himself that he hadn't heard.

"Why didn't you say anything?" I whisper. "I went through hell last year. I didn't think you… you…"

This changes everything. The fact that he's never bothered to ask me means he believed Mikey's lies just like everyone else.

"You never even liked him," I hiss. "But you still believed his lies. Why didn't you ask me for my side?" I shove my chair back, not caring that it scrapes against the tiles and makes a horrible scratching sound.

"Ellie, sit down. It wasn't like that. It—"

"It's fine," I say through bitter tears. "Next time he'll kill me, but that'll be a relief to you, won't it?"

"What are you talking about, Ellie? Sit down, would you?"

"No," I snap. "No, I won't. I'm sick of this horrible town and everyone in it." I turn and bolt towards the door. I can't be around him anymore. I'm not sure I can ever look at him again after what he's just admitted.

As I move past the kitchen counter, something shiny catches my eye. Even though I'm more upset with him than I've ever been before, I can't help but stop. The warm glittering gold is so out of place here in this horrid cold house.

I bend down and pick it up. It's a gold bracelet. I don't know much about jewellery but it looks old. Antique. It's elegant and pretty. I turn back around to him slowly, not understanding. Dad's never mentioned a girlfriend and there's no other trace of her here. Should I be surprised he hasn't said? Probably not after today's revelation. I knew we weren't close, but even I'm surprised by the distance between us.

"Does your girlfriend know you're the type of man who assumes the worst about his own daughter?" A horrible thought flashes through my head. I forget my hurt for a moment and take a step closer to him. I already know the answer to the question in my mind, but I can't stop myself from saying it. "Does she even know you have a daughter?"

"Give that here," he snaps, tearing it from my hand. "You're jumping to conclusions. The real estate agent must have dropped it."

"You're selling?"

"Thinking about it."

I grit my teeth. "You never said."

"It never came up," he says, not meeting my eyes. "I haven't made up my mind yet. I'd have told you if I'd made a decision and things were further along."

I shake my head. The shock has gone, leaving only emptiness behind it. Of course he didn't tell me. When's the last time we had an actual conversation about anything? All we ever do is make small talk.

"I'll see you next week," he calls after me as I hurry to the door.

"I have a better idea," I say without looking back. "Why don't you invite Mikey instead?"

I know it's childish, but I couldn't help it. It hurts so much that he never came to me. I'm sure nobody wants to confront their child about something like that, but isn't the alternative worse? Just accepting it? I slam the door behind me.

Why didn't he just ask?

CHAPTER 5
JOHN

ohn Cartwright wasn't sure what time it was, but he did know hours had passed since his blowup with Ellie: it had grown dark outside now.

He sighed and stared at the bracelet on the coffee table in front of him. He couldn't believe he'd been so careless. Why hadn't he cleaned the place up before Ellie came? He'd had a lot going on, but that was no excuse.

He reached for his glass and took another long draught of whisky. He wasn't a big drinker, but even he could appreciate the honeyed flavour of it as it burned its way down his throat. It had been sitting in the cabinet in the dining room for years, probably, a gift from a supplier.

He put down his glass and shook his head. *Look at me*, he thought. *Drinking alone on a Sunday evening*. Tea wouldn't have cut it after the conversation he'd had with Ellie.

The bracelet caught his eye again and he cursed it. As if things weren't bad enough. He got up and grabbed it, shoving it in his pocket. He could only imagine the conclusions she'd jumped to. He hadn't been able to think of an excuse quickly enough.

He sighed and looked around. The place was quiet, but it wasn't relaxing—well, it may have been for someone else. John couldn't relax. Not now. Not after what had happened with Ellie. Not since the letter. It had been waiting for him on the doormat when he came home from work last Tuesday. The familiar messy handwriting. The postmark blurred, but still legible, those few words instantly recognisable and dreadful.

The barely-veiled threat inside.

How the hell had he found John? He'd covered his tracks so well—or so he'd thought.

It felt like everything was falling apart. It was all going so well a year ago, but then things began to crumble one by one. And now this.

He was tired of the lies. He couldn't even keep track of them anymore. They'd come so easily when Ellie was questioning him earlier. But he wasn't a natural liar—nor a skilled one. The only factor in his favour was that Ellie wasn't naturally inquisitive.

He frowned. Today had been a different story. And she hadn't let up when he asked her to. What did that mean?

It was down to that lad. He just knew it. It didn't make sense otherwise. He took another drink, wincing as the amber liquid burned his throat. Was this something to be worried about?

He slammed his tumbler back down on the table with such force that the glass surface juddered in its housing.

He didn't know anymore. He was sick of the lies. He shouldn't have said what he did, but he'd been worried. He was just trying to look out for her. Seeing her with that lad had been a shock to the system. What was he sniffing around for?

A sharp knock at the door jolted him out of his thoughts.

Ellie? he thought, feeling a momentary burst of hope before he realised that it couldn't be her: she always rang the doorbell. But aside from that, it couldn't be her because he knew she wouldn't be back. Not after what had been said earlier.

Who the hell is there if it's not Ellie?

He didn't have a lot of visitors and those he did have

never showed up unannounced. Who knocked on some-body's door this late on a Sunday? Then it hit him.

No.

No, it couldn't be. But it made sense, didn't it? First the letter and now this.

There was another knock, more insistent this time. John got up. He cursed the whisky now. It had calmed him, but it had also clouded his mind.

He knew as soon as he got to the kitchen doorway. The figure visible through the glass in the front door was too big and broad to be female. It could have been any tall, broad man, of course, but John suspected that it was one man in particular.

I should have planned for this. I should have run when I had the chance.

This was the last thing he needed. The timing couldn't possibly be any worse.

He pulled open the door and shook his head when he saw Tony standing in the porch, his lips twisted into that familiar smirk.

"Hello, John."

John's heart hammered uncomfortably against his ribs. What was it, twenty years since he'd seen Tony? His hatred hadn't changed, but time had made him forget just how repulsive and frightening the other man really was. "What are you doing here? How the hell did you find me?"

"I'm here to see you. Do you always speak to your guests like that?" Tony laughed. "Not that you have many of those."

John's blood froze in his veins. It didn't take a genius to read between the lines. He was being watched and he hadn't even noticed.

He thought back over the last several months. He'd gotten complacent. How could he have been such a fool?

"So you've been watching me. Good for you. I thought you'd remember that I lead a very dull existence." John's heart thumped. That wasn't exactly true though, was it? He wondered just how diligent Tony's surveillance had been. John had been careful—but had he been careful enough?

"That depends on who you ask, doesn't it? Did you enjoy the market?"

John's heart sank. He should have known. Damn it, why hadn't he taken the letter seriously? He should have gone into lockdown as soon as he'd seen it. He'd seriously underestimated Tony—he just hoped he wouldn't have to pay the price for that. "What do you want?"

John's throat ached from the knot that had formed there. He had to face the possibility that Tony might ruin everything. He craned his neck to see the houses across the street. Passersby couldn't see in from the footpath, but if any of the neighbours were upstairs looking out their windows…

But what else could he do? He wouldn't invite this cretin into his home.

"Worried about what the neighbours might think, John?"

He shook his head, not trusting himself to speak.

"Imagine how they'd react if they knew what you'd done?"

John's blood ran cold. "What could you possibly gain…"

But Tony just smiled. "I'll go to the police if you won't help me."

He's bluffing, John told himself. People like Tony didn't go to the police. Even so, he couldn't stop shaking. "I can't help you."

He started to close the door. Tony shoved his foot in the way.

"Don't close the door on me! You owe me!"

John was too surprised not to react. "Owe you?" he snorted. "You ruined my life."

"You're fucking kidding me," the other man spat. "I spent the last twenty years locked away but *you* want to act the victim?"

You deserved every minute and more, John thought, but he said nothing. No good was going to come from antagonising Tony. He had to be clever about this. But what could he do?

Things were complicated now. He couldn't just pay Tony off —as much as he'd like to get rid of him.

"Look, it's not a good time—"

"Bullshit. I've waited long enough."

John sighed. He knew that look. He'd seen it often enough before. Tony wasn't going to give in. But neither could he—not on this. "No. No way."

Anger flashed in Tony's eyes. "You owe me."

John shook his head. "It's just not possible right now."

Tony took a step closer—close enough that John could smell the smoke and stale booze on his breath.

"I didn't come here to listen to excuses. I know what you did, John. Don't test me."

There was no point in denying it, was there? "You'd have done the same thing, Tony. Don't try to deny it." He looked around. He had to be careful. This was something the neighbours could never know about. That *no-one* could know about. "Think about it. You would."

Tony's lip curled into a snarl. "That's where you're wrong. I'd never have betrayed you like that." He took a step closer and jabbed John in the chest. "You're going to get what's coming to you."

CHAPTER 6
JOY
24 YEARS AGO

A sense of dread comes over me as I walk up the path to the house. It's sunny and light out on the street, but never in here. The light is always blocked by either the house or the trees that border the footpath. John loves the privacy of it, but if I'm honest I can't stand the place. Why do the trees have to be so high? It's not like we have anything to hide.

A lump forms in my throat.

I don't, but John does.

I clear my throat and try to talk some sense into myself. It's important that I keep my true feelings hidden. I'd rather be anywhere else in the world but here but he can't know that. He can't.

I stop and force a smile. It takes me a few goes. I have no choice: I'm terrified he'll see the truth in my eyes.

When did it get this bad? When did I start dreading the sight of him? Things used to be so good. I'm more certain than ever that this house has turned everything rotten.

I rummage in my handbag for my keys, resisting the urge to turn and walk away. Because I could. I could get on a bus to Leeds or even London. I could start again. I'd be starting with nothing, but anything would be better than this.

My hand is shaking so badly it takes me a few tries to get my key in the lock.

I take a deep breath as I push the door open.

He's waiting for me in the hall.

Damn.

I should have prepared for this.

"Joy."

I smile. And then I laugh because it's so ridiculous. Even after everything that's happened, I love him with all of my heart. "John."

"What's so funny?" he snaps. "What are you doing here? Why aren't you at work?"

Work, I think. If he only knew the truth. He can't know. Which can only mean he's picking a fight.

My hand instinctively flies to my stomach, before I catch myself and move it away. I'm not showing yet, but he's smart. I mustn't underestimate him.

This is the moment I should tell him. I know that.

But I can't.

"I took the afternoon off. To run some errands."

"Oh?"

Tell him, a voice inside me screams.

But I can't. Every time I open my mouth to tell him, the words get stuck in my throat. I'm frightened about how he'll react. That's the horrible reality I've been trying to ignore ever since the doctor confirmed I was pregnant.

"Yeah. Just some things I had to pick up around town."

I stare at him. Now's not the right time; not when he's in this kind of mood. Maybe it'll be different tomorrow.

"You could have told me. I'd have gone."

"No," I mutter, heart pounding. "Women's stuff. Tampons. That sort of thing. Do you want a cuppa?" I hurry past him to the kitchen, relieved to have an excuse to escape his scrutiny.

He follows me. "You look different."

It feels like my heart has stopped. All the warmth leaves my face and I resist the urge to turn and check his expression.

Does he know? But how can he possibly know? I've only just had it confirmed myself.

I clear my throat. "I got my hair cut this morning. Maybe that's it. Do you like it?" I turn and fluff up the ends, making the movements dramatic so I have something to do with my hands.

He shrugs. "It's nice." He turns away. "Did you remember to pick up biscuits?"

I grit my teeth. Of course I didn't. I had bigger things on my mind: not that I can tell him that. "I forgot. But I'll pop out now and get some."

I hurry out before he can stop me. It's good to have an excuse to get away. It feels like the walls are closing in on me.

I close the door behind me and hurry up the path. A horrible thought is playing on my mind: I can escape now, but soon it won't be so easy. What am I going to do then?

CHAPTER 7
JOHN

John ground his teeth and tried to keep his frustration out of his voice. "You don't get it," he said as calmly as he could. "I'm in trouble here."

"I'm not sure what you want me to do."

The voice at the other end of the phone sounded calm, and John knew it was genuine. He should have been reassured by that, but he wasn't. This was too serious. He'd been around the block enough times to know that there was no easy solution to this. Nobody was going to ride in on a white horse and save him from the consequences of his own actions.

John sighed. He didn't know what to do either.

"Look, you're a smart man. Tony might be dangerous, but he's a convicted murderer. Who do you think the police are going to believe?"

Disappointment shot through him at the realisation that the other man didn't understand the danger. "It's not as simple as that. It's not just his word against mine, is it?"

"He's probably bluffing."

"I'm not sure we can take that for granted." John clamped the phone between his ear and shoulder so he could massage his temples. Not that it did much good. No amount of poking and prodding was going to magically ease the tension in his brain.

There was a heavy sigh on the other end of the line. "Do you really think he'll stir things up?"

"Yes," John said without hesitation. Because he did. Tony wasn't bluffing.

"Well then."

John swallowed; resisted the urge to fill the silence. He'd used this tactic before. It was amazing what people came up with when they were faced with a yawning silence. It was human nature to try and fill it with words.

He waited, thinking. It seemed weak to wait for someone else to give him an answer to this problem, but he was stumped. Tony's return couldn't have come at a worse time for him and he was all too aware of the man's impatient nature. Stalling him wasn't an option.

"Have you thought," the other man said at last; slowly, like he was reluctant to even suggest such a thing on the phone, "about taking him for a drive? That would shut him up for good."

John winced as he realised what was being suggested. He hadn't expected that. "No. Jesus, no. We can't have anyone else knowing—"

"He wouldn't be able to tell anyone, would he?" There was a bark of cold laughter at the other end of the line.

"No," John whispered. He didn't want to go there. Not again. It was a nasty business and it had taken him a long time to get over it last time. He had a heart—despite what a lot of people seemed to believe.

"Well I can't think of anything else that'll do it," the other man said breezily, which reminded John that this new complication was his problem, and his alone.

He sighed. There was no point in labouring the point. He'd got his answer. He'd have to decide whether to go through with it, even though the thought pained him. This double life was exhausting. All the lies; the secrets. He wondered when it would end—or would it? Things had been quiet for a while and then Tony's arrival had thrown it all into chaos. He didn't know what else he could do, though. He had to protect himself.

"Right, well… Keep me posted, will you?"

"Wait," John said quickly, remembering the other reason he'd made the call. "That's not all."

Silence.

John's heart pounded. He wasn't sure it was a good idea to even mention this. What if… But he had to. Much like the Tony problem, he didn't know what to do about Ellie's sudden interest in her mother. "It's Ellie. She's been asking questions."

"Jesus Christ, John. And you didn't think to mention that until now? What sort of questions?"

"I'm sure you can guess," he said flatly. "I suppose I should count myself lucky that she's never noticed the inconsistencies in the stories I've told her about her mother."

There was a sharp intake of breath on the other end of the line. "Does she suspect?"

John's stomach flipped and for a moment he feared he was about to be sick. "No. No, of course not. But I'm worried she might if she starts digging."

"So what are you going to do to make sure she doesn't? This could ruin everything for both of us."

"I don't bloody know," John hissed.

"Well you'd better figure it out soon," the other man said coldly. "Get her off the scent before she finds out something she shouldn't." He hung up before John could reply.

John put his phone back in his pocket and stumbled to the couch. His palms were sweating and his heart was still pounding. It felt like things were coming to a head and he was powerless to control the outcome.

CHAPTER 8
ELLIE
MONDAY

The sound of my phone vibrating against the bedside table worms its way into my consciousness. I open my eyes and blink, still not sure what's real and what was part of my dreams. As soon as I sit up, the dreams fade away quickly and I'm left with nothing more than a vague sense of Mikey. I shiver.

I reach for my phone and smile when I see I've got two messages from Nathan. One was sent at six this morning.

How was lunch at your Dad's?

The other must have been what woke me up—it was sent just a few minutes ago.

Would you like to go for a drink some night this week?

A smile plays on my lips as I close the message for now while I think about what I'm going to say. It's then I see that I got a message from Steph around the same time.

How was your date? You've been quiet. Good/bad? Coffee later?

My smile widens. Having my friend quiz me about how my date went feels so *normal*. Not to mention the nerves and excitement fizzing in the pit of my stomach at the thought of seeing Nathan again.

I should be cautious. I need to remember that there are people in this town who don't want me to be happy.

I reopen Nathan's message and stare at it, drinking in the words as if they might disappear.

Sounds good. I'm free Wednesday if that works for you?

I'm free every night but I don't say that to him. I want this to work. I want him to think I'm just a normal carefree single girl in her twenties. I'm about to respond to Steph when it all comes back to me. Yesterday. Dad's house. Finding out he heard Mikey's lies ages ago and never said anything.

A lump forms in my throat as I force myself to get up and go to the bathroom. I've woken up early, which is great—I can take my time and still get to work early. I splash cold water on my face to try and reset my brain. It's frozen on an image of Dad's face—the look in his eyes when he realised he'd slipped and I knew that he knew. Or *thought* he knew.

I turn off the tap and look in the mirror. Even though my head feels reasonably fresh, my face is a mess. Puffy blood-shot eyes. Greyish skin. I'm not hungover but I sure as hell look it. I bend down to look in the cupboard under the sink. I need a face mask.

When I don't find one, I go back to my room to set a reminder to pick one up on my way home from work. It's tempting to go all out—to get a facial and a manicure—but I can't afford that. Every spare penny I earn has to go into my escape fund—Nathan or no Nathan.

I smile when I see he's messaged me back already.

What about tonight? Wednesday feels like ages away.

My heart skips a beat. Is he for real?

That could work. I finish work at 6.

My phone vibrates with another message from him.

Can you get off any earlier? Great cafe I'd like to show you but they close at 4.

I bite my lip. I really can't. I should be putting in as many hours as I can on top of my shifts and not taking off early. Resentment surges through me. I've been doing that for months on end and I'm barely saving anything. It's just one day.

But it will be at least nine by the time I get to the office this morning because I still need to shower and get dressed.

Can we go tomorrow instead? I can go in early then and still work a full day.

I frown as I try to figure that out. The earliest we can start is eight because the call volume before then is a lot lighter and management prefers to let people with kids take the very early time slots. But I suppose I can stay later the other evenings this week. It's not like I have anything else to do and it'll be worth it.

I'm buzzing with excitement as I make my way back to the bathroom. I step into the shower and turn on the water, humming to myself as I wait for it to heat up.

I grab my phone off the bed before I've even dried myself off. My heart leaps when I see the WhatsApp icon at the top of the screen. I almost drop my phone in my haste to unlock it and see what he's said about tomorrow.

I can't help but be disappointed when I realise the message isn't from Nathan. It's from Steph.

Well? I know you've seen my message.

My thumbs hover over the on-screen keyboard as I try to compose a reply, but I can't. I'm too agitated. I want to know what the plan is with Nathan before I meet up with Steph.

I open up the conversation with Nathan and frown when I see the two blue ticks beside my last message. He's seen it. And the status bar at the top of the screen tells me he's online now.

So why hasn't he replied?

I stare at it for a few moments. Nothing happens. It's only the empty feeling in my stomach that makes me put the phone down and go to the kitchen in search of something to eat.

There's not a lot to choose from. I haven't been to the supermarket since the time I met Nathan. There's half a box of Weetabix left so I settle for two pieces with the last of the milk and remind myself to go to the supermarket later. I really need to stop buying groceries from the corner shop where they're far more expensive.

There's still no message from Nathan when I return to my bedroom to throw on a pair of trousers and a plain black shirt—my unofficial work uniform.

I open our message chain and reread the messages. I really want to see him—now that I've had a taste of what it's like to have a social life again, I can't bear to spend the night on the couch watching telly when I could just stop being stubborn and go with his plan. I can make up the hours later in the week.

Tonight works too, I can try and finish at 3.

Except, I think as I catch sight of myself in the mirror, it doesn't. My shirt is loose and unflattering; my trousers cheap and shiny. I quickly change into a dress and tights. I check my reflection.

It's better, but still not great. I check the time. It's almost a quarter to. I need to leave. I grab my makeup bag from the bathroom on the way out. I'll have to do what I can in the bathroom at work.

My phone buzzes in my handbag just as I'm about to open the front door. It's Nathan.

Great, I'll meet you outside at 3. You'll love this place.

I run my fingers through my hair, frazzled. I meant I could leave my desk at three, not meet him at three. I'll have to leave even earlier now. I hurry out the door, trying to figure out what to say to my manager. I've done nothing wrong but I'm also trying to keep my head down and not draw attention to myself.

My phone buzzes again and I groan when I see it's from Steph asking if I want to meet her later.

I stop and message her back to see if we can meet for a late lunch instead.

Damn it: at this rate, I'll be catching up on work for the next month.

CHAPTER 9
ELLIE

"T his isn't a holiday camp, you know," Jason says, staring through me.

"I know that," I say, alarmed at how strained my voice has gotten. I know I'm not being unreasonable, but tell that to my pounding heart and sweating palms. I hate that what happened last year and the isolation that came afterwards has turned me into such an awkward nervous wreck. I clear my throat. "It's just that something's come up. I'll make up the hours later in the week."

He purses his lips. I look away, telling myself to stay calm and not allow myself to be rattled. I've done nothing wrong and I'm not being unreasonable. The crazy thing is Jason's usually alright: he's not overly aggressive or demanding. I begin to doubt myself: maybe I *am* taking the piss here?

"That's not the point, Ellie. You can't pick and choose your hours. The expectation is you'll be here ten to six, perhaps picking up some overtime as you need. That's the agreement we have with you. And that doesn't involve swanning in at nine and leaving at two."

"I'll work through lunch," I say. "It's just this once. I wasn't thinking when I agreed to the appointment time." I smile sheepishly but he doesn't smile back.

For a moment I think about cancelling on Nathan, but I can't. I will have to cancel on Steph, but she'll understand.

"Look," I say hurriedly. "I'll cancel the hygienist part of my appointment and rebook it. Then I can stay another hour."

"Can't you move the whole appointment?" He glares at me and for a moment I think he's seen through my lies and knows exactly what I'm doing.

What am I doing? Why am I risking my job for this? I know deep down that I'm being a fool over a guy I hardly know, but I can't help it. I feel like I've won the lotto meeting Nathan. He hasn't admitted it, but he was obviously a little bit quiet and nerdy when he was here during the school holidays as a teenager. I've met the only guy in town who's not connected into the tight gossip network that comes with living in a town this small.

I shake my head and tell myself to get a grip. "No, I've been putting it off but I've got a toothache. Best to get it seen to. I don't want to have to take more time off in the future."

Jason rolls his chair forward and plants his elbows on the desk, clasping his hands in front of him. "Is there something going on I need to know about?"

I shake my head. "No. Why would there be?"

"Your metrics have been off lately."

"I don't know," I say, forcing back the lump in my throat. It's kind of true: between daydreaming about Nathan and searching for more details about my mother, I haven't exactly been focused on work today. But that's just one day! I want to tell him how unfair it is when I usually work my arse off, but I don't. Lots of people may see my job as a crappy one, but for a long time it was one of the only things in my life and I'm actually more dedicated to it than I realise. "Maybe I've had off days or something." I swallow, determined not to cry in front of him.

"Just try not to let your work slide any further, alright? Because it reflects badly on me and I won't have that."

He turns his attention back to his computer and I walk out of his office with my ears burning.

I need this job, but am I really willing to sacrifice my only chance at happiness for bureaucracy?

———

I look around what used to be a petrol station and try my best to look impressed. What I'm really thinking is *I risked my job for this?* Why the hell did Nathan insist on bringing me here? It's a new cafe in a grubby old building. Yes, the sign on the door says it closes at 4, but I can't see why we couldn't have met later and gone to anywhere else in town.

"What do you think?"

My stomach flips when I turn to Nathan and see the expectant look on his face. He cares about my opinion. Any resentment I felt about being dragged here melts away. "It's great," I say.

"Really?"

I force a smile. "Really. It's great. It's so…"

I guess the good thing about being so underwhelmed by a place is that thinking up a lie to describe how much I love it is pushing other more destructive thoughts out of my mind. Dad hasn't been in touch since I left his house yesterday. I make a decision to throw myself into this thing with Nathan —as if I needed an excuse to do that. Moving away is so far in the future. I need something positive right now.

"So…" a smile tugs at his lips.

"So… hipster. With the…" I wave my hand around, desperately looking for something to compliment. It's all old school tables and cans of beans repurposed as vases containing scrappy bunches of what look like weeds. Not my style at all. "The decor. Industrial. How did you find it?"

"It's on my way to work," he says proudly. "I wanted to check it out."

I smile as brightly as I can as he hands me a grotty clipboard with a coffee-stained menu attached. Inside, doubts niggle at me. He's gorgeous, funny, clever. But why the big deal about dragging me here? Why was it so important that I leave work early? I try to shut that voice up, but I can't.

I steal a glance at him as he studies his menu. Even as my heart flips, something else tells me I need to keep my guard up and not let him get too close too soon.

———

"Another drink?" Nathan's face blurs in and out of focus.

I shake my head. "I can't. I have work tomorrow."

"So?" He pokes out his tongue and I swear it's the sexiest gesture I've ever seen. "It's only ten o'clock."

I check the time on my phone, convinced he's wrong. The digits blur. How much have I had to drink? I've lost count. It may only be ten o'clock, but we've been drinking since shortly after three. It turns out the cafe in the old petrol station serves amazing margaritas and homemade tacos. It's a pity that we didn't think to try those tacos before we moved to the pub because I'm starving now.

So much for keeping my guard up.

My stomach rumbles so hard it's almost painful. "We should get something to eat," I say, slurring my words so badly that even I notice it. I should really go home, but there's no food there.

"Just one more?" he says with a smile I find hard to resist.

CHAPTER 10
JOHN

The landline on John Cartwright's desk buzzed. He glanced up and saw *Reception* flashing on the display. Reception. What did they want? He didn't have any meetings planned for today.

He sighed. He had too much on. He always thought he'd be long retired by this stage of his life.

Now everything had changed.

"Hello Hannah," he said with a sigh. "What is it?"

"You have a visitor, sir."

"A visitor?" he checked the calendar on his desk. He much preferred it to using a virtual one—he liked being able to see his day at a glance every morning when he sat down at his desk. "I'm not expecting anyone."

She exhaled loudly and John's ears pricked. There was something in her voice. "Yes. There's a man here to see you."

It didn't take John long to figure out who his visitor was. This was a complication he didn't need—especially not now. "I'll be out in a moment."

He hung up and rubbed his face with clammy palms. What was Tony doing here? The bloody idiot. Twenty years in prison and he couldn't find something more interesting to do with his time than follow John around and make life difficult for him? He never did have much of an imagination.

John shook his head. He knew what to do. He'd been told what to do. He just didn't have the heart to do it—not even to Tony.

———

Tony leapt to his feet as soon as John walked through the double doors into the reception area. "I thought you'd have retired by now."

John forced a smile for the sake of appearances. "Tony," he said, holding his hand out as he approached the man who'd been a scourge on his life for the last twenty years. "I wasn't expecting you."

Tony took his hand and matched his firm grip, squeezing so hard that it was an effort for John not to break contact first.

Anger and frustration bubbled up inside him. It was Tony's fault that he was in this position. His life might have turned out very differently if it hadn't been for Tony. His last bit of resistance to the plan fell away. There was only one way to get Tony off his back for good. He didn't like it, but it was starting to look a lot more appealing. The man was a weasel; a blight. He deserved everything that was coming his way.

"I'm afraid you'll have to walk with me if you want to talk," he said breezily.

"What?"

"I have a client meeting," John said. "I'm already late." He strode off towards the lifts, resisting the temptation to look back and see if Tony was following.

He desperately needed to get Tony into his car before this thing escalated even further out of his control. But would the man take the bait?

There was a loud chime and the doors of the nearest lift slid open. John stepped inside without looking back. He turned around slowly and his heart leapt when he saw that Tony had followed him across reception and into the lift.

"Don't forget, John," Tony said, as soon as the doors had closed. "I have something on you."

John grimaced. There were cameras in the lift and the bloody fool hadn't even thought to check for them. "Cameras, you idiot," he hissed.

"Cameras are the least of your worries," Tony said with a smirk.

John turned to him. "Enough, alright? I know somewhere private we can talk. For God's sake can you just wait until we get there?"

Tony grinned and John tried not to do the same. He had Tony right where he wanted him.

CHAPTER 11
ELLIE
TUESDAY

wake up with a pounding headache. My mouth is so dry I can't even swallow. I sit up too quickly to check the time and that's enough to send waves of nausea shooting up my throat. I lie back and breathe shallowly for a few moments and it helps a bit. When I risk moving again, I'm relieved to see it's only ten to seven.

So much for a rejuvenated liver, I think before being plunged into a pit of shame. It's partly to do with the hangover, I know, but not fully. I swore I'd never drink again after what happened last year and now look at me. When I try to play back the last few hours of last night, it's fuzzy in parts and completely missing in others.

I squeeze my eyes shut as the nausea returns. I can't afford to lose control like this. I have a vague memory of kissing Nathan in a taxi outside and then fumbling for my keys, but knowing how I got home doesn't set my mind at rest.

I ease my way out of bed to fetch a glass of water. As I walk through to the kitchen, a strange memory floats back to me. Jason. Laughing.

My stomach rolls with dread and then confusions takes over. If we met Jason, he wouldn't have been laughing, would he? Not when I lied about going to the dentist. I pour a large glass of water from the tap and lean against the counter. The only explanation is that I came up with a good excuse and he believed it.

I pick up my phone and start to type a message to Nathan, but then delete it. I don't want him to know my memory of last night is patchy.

I'm about to go back to bed when I remember I agreed to meet Steph for breakfast.

———

Steph is waiting for me by the time I hurry into the cafe.

"Sorry I'm late."

She shrugs as I sit down. "Don't be, I just got here. Things must be going well if you cancelled on me to meet him again before we've even had a chance to talk about your first date."

I start to apologise and then stop myself. I'm just going to have to wear the shame because I can't tell her how important it is to me that things develop with Nathan.

Steph catches the attention of a passing waitress and orders a muesli bowl. I go for the full breakfast with the biggest coffee they have.

Steph leans forward and wrinkles her nose. "How late did you stay out last night?"

I wince. "How did you know?"

"Partly the big greasy fry you just ordered." She grins. "You also smell like a brewery."

"Shit," I hiss. "Shit shit shit."

"What's the matter? You're not late for work, are you?"

I shake my head. "No. It's just that I said I had a dentist appointment. I don't want to turn up there reeking of alcohol and making it really obvious. Though I did meet my boss in the pub last night."

"Well then," she says, rummaging in her handbag and pulling out a pack of mints. "He's not going to be in any position to judge you, is he?"

"No," I mutter.

A waitress bustles over with our food and we stop talking for a while. It's only now I have food that I realise how hungry I was.

"So how was it?" Steph asked when we've finished.

Now that I've started thinking about it, I can't wipe the smile off my face. "It was great. He's great. Funny and sweet and just a good guy."

She grins. "That's brilliant. So you'll see him again?"

I nod enthusiastically. Of course I will. It feels like we have a lot in common and I really like him. A cloud comes over me then. Is it wise for me to talk about him in public like this? I glance around the busy cafe. There's nobody here that I recognise so that makes me relax a little.

"What's wrong?" Steph asks.

"Nothing. Just antsy."

"That'll be the hangover," she says, sipping on her coffee.

I smile wistfully. If only the nervous feeling in my bones was purely hangover-related, but it's not: I've felt it on and off for the past year and I haven't even been drinking for most of that time.

"What about you?" I ask to change the subject. "Have you met anyone since you moved here?" I feel a bit more comfortable asking about her love life now that I've been out with Nathan. In a way it feels like I'm a step removed from Mikey.

Steph makes a face. "This is a small town. It seems like everybody our age is coupled up."

I roll my eyes, well aware of that. "What made you move here?" I ask before I can stop myself. It's something I've often wondered. It's silly really: anytime I've thought that when I've been with her I've stopped myself saying it, just in case she realises what a shit town this place is. I don't want her to see that and move away.

Her expression darkens. "Come on," she says, reaching for her coat. "I'd best get to work."

———

All the way to her office, I try to think of a subtle way to ask her about her odd reaction to my question. I can't think of one. Maybe that's down to the fuzzy feeling in my head.

I can't wait for this day to be over: it hasn't even started and I'm completely exhausted.

When we reach Steph's office, I turn to say goodbye to her and I'm almost bowled off the footpath. I jerk away in a panic from the unexpected physical contact and see it was a girl our age who shoved past me. She's now stopped to talk to Steph.

My cheeks burn. I recognise her from somewhere but I can't think where. "You might want to watch where you're going," I snap. "I could have sprained my ankle if I'd fallen off the kerb just now."

"It was an accident."

Steph holds her hands up. "Trish this is my friend Ellie." She turns to me. "Trish is our receptionist."

I glare at the girl. Her sharp features are set in a way that doesn't even try to hide the fact that she doesn't like me. Her lips twitch as though she's dying to say something. "I'd best get into work," she snaps.

"Wow," I say to Steph when the girl has gone inside. "She's pretty rude. She almost knocked me over just now."

Steph smiles. "She's a bit intense. I'd better get inside: busy day. I'll call you later."

I watch her walk through the automatic door and turn in the same direction as that girl Trish. I clench my fists and force myself to walk away. How long until Trish tells Steph what she's heard? I thought I was prepared for the day that Steph heard the rumours. Am I, though?

I turn towards my office and almost collide with a woman in a gorgeous red coat.

"Sorry," I mutter automatically as I step out of the way.

It's only when the words are out of my mouth that my brain makes the connection. I know that coat. I helped her pick it. Katie. My former best friend.

I stare at her as she breezes past me, not stopping or even

acknowledging my existence. I want to shout after her, to take back my apology because she of all people certainly doesn't deserve it.

I say nothing—what good would it do?

CHAPTER 12
MIKEY

Mikey's phone buzzed in his locker. He dropped the towel he'd been using to dry himself and reached for it. He frowned when he saw it was a private number. Probably a journalist or PR. His finger hovered over the reject button for a few seconds, before he remembered the talk he'd had with management earlier in the week.

Things were different now; his career was different. He'd been shooting for the top before—and it looked like he was going to make it. Then there'd been that big fuck-up and he'd had to go away for a while and keep a low profile until it all blew over.

The message from the higher-ups had been very clear: suck up to the journalists and PRs. Build his profile by going out of his way to give soundbites or whatever they wanted. The unspoken implication was that the big clubs would be wary of him now. Word travelled fast and the last thing he wanted was to to be labelled as trouble.

He sighed. He resented that. What happened wasn't even his fault. But he wasn't going to disobey a direct order. He was even more determined now to get where he wanted to be —and nobody was going to stop him from achieving that.

Besides, who knew—maybe someone would offer him a

sponsored holiday flying first class to the Maldives. It might be worth it in the long run.

He grabbed a towel and hurried out of the changing room into the corridor. He didn't want the other lads to hear this conversation.

He cleared his throat and hit the answer button, remembering what Graham had said. *Squeaky clean, alright? That's the image I want you to put across. Help old ladies cross the road. I don't care, Mikey. I won't cover for you again.*

He hit the answer button. "Mikey speaking."

"Mikey." The voice was female and she sounded rushed.

He frowned. "Yes. Who's this?"

He became aware of the cold for the first time. He'd rushed out wearing nothing at all. He held the phone between his shoulder and ear as he wrapped his towel around his waist.

"Look, you don't know me."

His frown deepened. "Should I know you? Where are you calling from?"

"Um…" she cleared her throat and paused, like she was unsure whether to answer. "My office."

Mikey rolled his eyes. Was this a prank? Had Graham put one of the girls from the office up to this, knowing that Mikey would feel obliged to stick it out in order to get back his good name at the club after so long away?

But no. He didn't think so. Not after the way Graham had looked at him in that strategy meeting.

He shivered. It was freezing out there with the draughts blowing through—somebody always forgot to close the doors after them. "Is this some sort of prank? Because I'm busy."

She sighed. "No. No, it's not. I know this seems weird— and I've spent the whole day going back and forth about whether to tell you this—but I think you should know." She paused. "It's about Ellie."

He didn't have to ask what Ellie. He knew. There was only one Ellie as far as he was concerned. His pulse quickened. Hearing her name always had that effect on him. Her face flashed into his mind, a vision of laughter and loveliness before it morphed into something far darker. Ellie. He'd loved her so much, but she'd caused him so much trouble and almost cost him his career. He'd had a lot of time to think about her over the past few months and he still wasn't sure how he felt about her now. Some days he cursed her name and everything she'd cost him. Other times he couldn't stop thinking about her. Part of him thought he still loved her, though he'd never admit that to anyone.

"What about her?" he snapped.

What had she done now? He'd been away for months waiting for this thing to blow over. That should have been the end of it. He'd been back less than a week.

"I saw her today. She was really aggressive."

Mikey massaged his forehead with his free hand. "Aggressive? What do you mean by that?" He sighed. "Who is this?"

"That doesn't matter," she muttered. "I don't want to make a big thing of this but I thought she was going to hit me. I was actually—"

"What the hell do you want me to do about it?" he snapped. This wasn't a journalist—it was a local crackpot. The only reason he hadn't hung up yet was that something was niggling at him: what did she want? "And how did you even get this number?"

"We have friends in common," she said carefully. "And I'm just trying to help."

"Help? Ellie and I aren't together anymore."

"Oh, I *know* that." She said it with such certainty that it shocked him.

"Who the hell are you?"

"It doesn't matter. Like I said, we have friends in common and I know you're a good guy. I just—"

He ended the call. What was her game? There was no point in asking because she'd never have admitted it. Was she just one of those rugby groupies who hung around the lads on nights out? Or was there more to it?

He gritted his teeth. He'd been away for months and

people were *still* associating them? What did he need to do to get a clean slate?

Ellie was going to ruin everything for him.

Someone cleared their throat nearby. Mikey spun around. Graham, his coach, was standing a few feet away.

"You shouldn't creep up on people like that," he snapped, wondering how someone of Graham's size could move around so quietly. He was shorter than Mikey, but only by a few inches. He was built like a tank, though the muscle had long ago turned to fat. He was glaring at Mikey with those sharp blue eyes that never missed a trick.

"She still giving you bother?" Graham never danced around a subject—no matter how difficult. It was one of the things Mikey liked about him.

Usually.

Now it was a pain. He didn't want to talk about this. Not now, not ever. They'd done enough talking.

"Who?"

"You know who."

"Jesus Christ, why are people so bloody obsessed?"

"So it was her?"

"No," Mikey grunted. "It was about something else."

"Yeah?" Graham's tone made it clear he wasn't convinced.

"Yeah. Something about an interview with one of the local papers."

"Bullshit," Graham snapped. "Do you think I'm a *complete* fool? As good as it is to have you back, this is worrying. You're straight back into old habits."

"I'm not! I haven't—"

"You don't need to waste your time on that little bitch. Do I have to remind you that she nearly destroyed you? Do you have any idea of the trouble I had trying to fix that mess?"

Mikey gritted his teeth. He had to be careful here. There was a lot Graham didn't know about what had happened and he needed to keep it that way. Graham was on his side—he couldn't afford to lose the support of a man with a lot of influence both in the town and in rugby.

"I know, Graham, but you've got it wrong. That call just now wasn't anything to do with her."

"Wasn't it? You're forgetting how well I know you, lad."

"And you're assuming I can't take care of myself," Mikey spat. "I don't need looking after."

"Don't you? From where I'm standing you have a blind spot when it comes to that girl. It'll cost you."

Mikey shook his head. That wasn't true. Graham had no idea. "Just leave it. It wasn't her." He cursed that girl for calling him. The bloody busybody.

"Who was it then?"

"I didn't catch her name. From the local paper."

Graham shook his head slowly. "It's not like you to miss a name when it might benefit your career." He pursed his lips. "Look, I'm not blaming you. That's not what this is about. But something needs to be done all the same. This isn't just your career anymore. Think about all the hard work I've put in; that the other lads have put in."

Mikey shook his head. "You're worrying about nothing, Graham. If she causes trouble again I'll handle it, alright?"

Graham rolled his eyes and walked away, leaving Mikey staring after him, confused.

CHAPTER 13
ELLIE

"Ellie!"

I almost jump out of my skin when a hand appears in front of my face and the fingers click inches from my nose. I tear my headset from my head as I spin around on my chair. "What the hell? You scared the life out of me." I falter. Jason is standing over me with a thunderous expression on his face. "What is it?"

"Come with me."

I follow him to his office, keeping my head down the whole way. I don't want to see my colleagues poking their heads out of their cubicles like meerkats.

"I said I'd make up time and I meant it," I say as soon as I've closed the door behind me. "I'll stay until eight tonight and eight tomorrow and make up the time before the week is—"

"That's not the point. You've just been sitting there staring into space. You weren't on a call." His eyes narrow. "Are you drunk?"

I recoil. "What? No."

He shakes his head. "Maybe you shouldn't go out drinking on Monday nights if it affects your performance at work."

"But it's not affecting—"

"Trust me," he snaps, gesturing to his screen. 'It's affecting your performance."

A cold sweat breaks out across my skin. I open my mouth to apologise but something snaps inside me. "So it's alright for you to go out on a Monday, but not anyone else? Is that it?"

His face turns red. "Excuse me?"

All I want to do is back down and go back to my desk, but I can't—not with the way he's looking at me. Besides, it's not fair, is it? It's alright for him sitting in his office where he can do what he wants. The open packet of crisps lying on his desk beside his mouse only highlights that. "I saw you out. I'm just saying: It's hardly fair if there's one rule for you and one for the rest of us."

He leans closer, scrutinising my face. "Where did you meet me, Ellie? Fifty pounds says you don't even remember."

I shrink back, feeling more ashamed of myself than I've felt in a long time. It wasn't in the first pub we went to—I know that for sure—but I can't really remember where we went to after that.

He shakes his head. "You see? That's the difference. I never said there was anything wrong with going out on a weeknight and having a couple of pints. But going out and getting bladdered? That's another thing."

I close my eyes and recall the look on his face. My memory is faint, but I realise now that he might not have been laughing at all, but angry.

Oh shit. Why did I throw it in his face like that? I should have kept my head down and taken the bollocking.

"Go on," he says. His voice is full of disgust. "Get back to work."

I hurry out of his office as fast as I can. It feels like everyone is looking at me as I make my way back to my desk. I've got to get my head down and get my call stats back to where they were.

———

My phone buzzes in my pocket and I make myself ignore it. When it goes off again ten minutes later, I'm suddenly on edge. I risk a glance in the direction of Jason's office. There are a few people in there with him so he's distracted for the moment. There's no rule to say we can't look at our phones in work, but I don't want to give him any excuse to think badly of me.

I pull my phone out.

Do you want to meet tonight?

The second message makes my stomach plummet.

It's okay if you don't. You can just say.

I quickly tap out a reply.

> **Sorry, I wasn't ignoring you. I'm at work. Tonight sounds
> good.**

I could have used a night in to do laundry and stuff but I didn't want to risk postponing.

Great, meet you outside your office at 5?

I shake my head. I should have mentioned what time I get off work. I click my tongue. As much as I want to see him, I can't leave early after the conversation I just had with Jason.

> **I've got to work until at least 8. Can we meet around 8.15?**

Two blue ticks appear beside my message almost immediately, but Nathan doesn't respond. After a couple of minutes, jittery with nerves, I put my phone away and tell myself to focus on work.

———

My phone vibrates at a few minutes past five when I'm on a call. At first I think it's a text and it takes all my self-control not to check it. The vibrating continues and I realise it's an incoming call, not a text.

I fish my phone out of my pocket and glance at the screen. It's Nathan.

My pulse skyrockets. I have no choice but to cancel his call because I'm in the middle of a customer call.

"Hello, are you still there?" says the voice in my headset.

"Yes, I'm here," I say with forced cheeriness. I try to refocus on the conversation I've just been having with this customer. "I've just been double-checking your file. I can't see any record in the system of you requesting a service call-out."

"But there must be," she says sternly.

I need to get my head in this call, but I can't. Something is niggling at the back of my mind. I realise I'm waiting for my phone to buzz with a text message or to start vibrating again, but it doesn't.

"There isn't, I'm afraid." I have to form the words deliberately because I'm afraid if I don't I'll blurt out something about Nathan.

Why did he call? Was it to cancel? Or was he calling because he was outside? Didn't he get my message? But I know he's seen it.

"What do you mean, there isn't? There must be."

I sigh as quietly as I can. How many different ways can I tell her the same thing? "There's no note on your file to say you requested a call-out from a technician. I can't say why that is. Perhaps it was never added or maybe there was a note and somebody deleted it."

"Well, can't you see which it is? Isn't there a log of changes made to my account and a record of the member of your staff who was responsible for those changes?"

"I'm afraid not, madam," I say as sympathetically as I can. "What I can do is put in a request for you now. I'll just need to take a few details."

"What's the point? Who's to say that request won't disappear too?"

I shake my head. I don't have the brainpower to deal with where this conversation is going. Plus there's the fact that if this call goes on for much longer, it'll affect my stats for the day and I've been working my arse off to get them up after that telling-off from Jason earlier. "Look, that's all I can do. I don't know what happened before."

"There's no need to take that tone," she chides, before hanging up on me.

I stare at my screen with a growing sense of terror. I should be glad to finally have her off the phone, but I'm not. She's the type who'll call back to complain and I can't afford to have that happen.

I bury my face in my hands. This is all too much. I feel like I'm on a knife-edge. It's not just the angry caller—my phone hasn't vibrated again since I cancelled the call from Nathan. Why do I even care so much? I hardly know him.

When I look around, Jason is standing at the door watching me with a frown on his face. I look away, heart pounding.

I'm a nervous wreck. I haven't been to the toilet in hours and my bladder is full to bursting. I haven't wanted to run the risk of walking past Jason. Why the hell did I admit that I couldn't remember where I saw him last night? I should have tried to bluff him: anything would be better than admitting to my boss that I got blackout drunk last night.

I take another call and try to immerse myself in helping the caller, but it's impossible. When I'm not fretting about losing my job, I'm worrying that Nathan has given up on me. The thoughts are swirling around in my head and I don't know how to free myself.

———

By the time eight finally ticks around, I've calmed down a little about work. Jason works nine to half five, so I've been able to relax a bit without him breathing down my neck. I've had a few good calls that I was able to resolve quickly and even been praised by a couple of the callers. It's not all doom and gloom: I'm good at my job and I'll get my numbers back up soon.

I'm not completely relaxed, though, because I haven't heard from Nathan. I've messaged him a couple of times but heard nothing back.

I log off and remove my headset, reaching up and stretching to ease the stiffness in my neck from sitting in the same position all day. The hangover has eased, but my stomach feels horribly empty like I'll never be full again. I need to get something to eat—fast.

I try to call Nathan but it goes straight to voicemail. It's not even his voice I hear, but an automated voice from the phone company telling me to leave a message.

I hang up and hurry out of the building. It's dark now and deserted. There's supposed to be a security guard at the desk downstairs, but he's nowhere to be seen. I linger in the lobby for a few moments, looking out at the dark deserted streets beyond and a weird feeling comes over me.

There's a man across the road, just standing there. I take a few steps back towards the lifts to make it harder for him to see me.

Is it my eyes playing tricks as they adjust to the darkness?

I blink a few times. No, he's still out there. What's he doing? There's no bus stop over there; no businesses on that stretch of the street.

I look around. There's only one way out of this building and that's through the front doors directly opposite him. I swallow back my fear and dash out, telling myself it's probably just exhaustion and there's a perfectly good explanation for this.

CHAPTER 14
ELLIE

've just about managed to calm myself by the time I get off the bus down the road from my flat. If there's one thing I like about working late it's that the buses are empty by eight and I don't have to squish in next to somebody.

I jump off and hesitate when I see the lights from the corner shop up ahead. Should I get a bottle of wine?

No, I tell myself. No, that's the remnants of the hangover talking. I can tell because the thought of a cold soft drink can is enough to make my mouth water.

Then I remember there's no food in the house so I have to go there anyway.

The guy behind the counter mutters hello and immediately turns his attention away. I can't see whether he's got a phone or a TV back there. It doesn't matter. I've been in here at least once every week for the last several years, but we still don't make small talk—let alone have actual conversations. I don't know if that's just me or if he's like that with everyone else too. I try to remember if Mikey ever chatted to the staff here when we were together and we'd pop down to get a carton of milk.

I wince. Sometimes it's still too raw, especially when I remember the normal times when it seemed like we were just one more happy couple in a whole sea of other couples like us. I loved him so much. No, I wasn't perfect, but I didn't deserve to be treated the way he treated me: he's turned me into a pariah in my own town. I look up and see the owner staring at me. I hurry to the back and stare at the uninspiring selection in the freezer cabinet. It's either this or canned food. I choose a frozen lasagne. Judging by the battered corners of the box it's been there a while, but it's still in date. It'll have to do.

I pay and walk out, surprised by how cold it's gotten in the few minutes since I entered the shop. I pull the collar of my coat tighter around my neck and walk as quickly as I can. My flat isn't far away: just ten houses down. Traffic is so light now it may as well be the middle of the night.

My hand feels like it's going to stick to the frozen box so I shove the box under my arm. I don't need to worry about it defrosting because it's going straight into the microwave as soon as I've…

I reach the front door and stumble backwards. The lasagne falls to the ground.

The door.

I stare at it, desperately trying to remember leaving the house this morning.

Did I leave it open?

I'm always so paranoid about leaving it open. Sometimes I run back to check it. But I can't remember doing that this morning…

I take a step closer, holding out my hand to push it open, as though I need physical proof of what I'm seeing with my own eyes. The door is definitely ajar. I can see two or three inches of the hideous wallpaper that lines the hallway.

I blink. My palms are clammy despite the cold night and I tell myself to keep it together. This would be the worst possible time to panic when there's nobody around to help me.

I look around behind me. There's nobody there that I can see but what if somebody's lurking out here?

I turn back to the door and take a deep breath. There's nobody out there. I was hungover this morning and in a hurry to meet Steph, that's all. I was distracted and forgot to check I'd pulled the door behind me.

Still, it takes a while to work up the courage to walk inside.

I lose my nerve and rush outside again. I think about calling Dad, but I can't bring myself to do that after how we left things on Sunday. I try Nathan, but the call rings out. Biting my lip, I call the only other person I *can* call. Luckily she answers immediately.

"Ellie. Is everything okay? I'm still at work."

"No," I hiss through clenched teeth. "I just came home and the door was open."

"Oh no," she gasps. "Have you called the police?"

"No. Look, I'm pretty sure it's nothing. I was distracted this morning and I forgot to close it after me." I hesitate. "Can you come over and come inside with me? I know it's silly, but—"

"Of course, Ellie, no problem. I'll be there in five. Is there a neighbour you can sit with before I can get there?"

"Thanks, Steph." I look around. I could go knock on one of the doors across the street, but I don't want to pester people. They could be putting their kids to bed or having an early night themselves. I'm just being paranoid. Nobody else needs to know about this.

I linger on the footpath as I wait for Steph, praying she'll be as punctual as usual. It's cold out here but I don't want to go in there alone. I try not to think about who's out here. I'm safer out here until we can check the flat and make sure there's nobody inside.

After a few minutes, a car pulls up on the other side of the road. It's too dark to see who's inside. I watch, holding my breath. Please let it be Steph.

I'm almost giddy with relief when I see that it's her.

"Thanks for coming. I appreciate it. I'm probably just

being a big baby," I say. A bolt of fear hits me then. What if I'm not? What if someone *has* broken in?

"Come on," she takes my arm. "Let's go check it out."

The house is quiet. I hold my breath as we flick on the light in the hallway, but there's nothing out of the ordinary there. We'll only know for sure when we get into the flat itself because there's nothing in here—it's just a long hallway that runs past the boarded-up shop at the front to my flat at the back. The shop has been empty for as long as I've lived here. It's all boarded up with no access from my place. I always liked the peace of not being surrounded by neighbours, but now I wonder if it might feel safer to have neighbours close at hand because the houses on either side are empty too.

I tiptoe towards the door that leads to the kitchen and living room. This hallway has never seemed so long. I hold my breath as I reach for the door handle. I twist it and shove the door with as much force as I can.

Dread fills me in the few seconds it takes to look around.

"Shit," Steph hisses. "Stop. We should get out and call the police. This is crazy."

"No. We can't."

"What do you mean, we can't? That's what they're there for."

Oh God, I shouldn't have called her. She's not going to let this go.

I run on ahead, quickly checking the bathroom—it's a mess, but it's my mess. Nothing looks out of place in the living room, so I'm starting to relax by the time I walk into my bedroom.

I scream.

The boxes of paperwork and memories that I keep on the top shelf of my wardrobe are lying on the floor. Someone's been in here and tipped them out. There are bits of paper all over the floor.

"What? What is it?" Steph hurries over to me.

I quickly shut the door so she can't see. My heart is pounding. What were they looking for?

"Ellie, what happened? What's in there?"

"Nothing," I lie. "Nothing. It's just… I feel like such a fool, Steph. I'm so frustrated at myself."

I do feel like a fool—for calling her. Someone's just broken into my house and calling Steph was a mistake because she'll insist on getting the police involved. And even if I can convince her not to, she's going to wonder why I'm being so cagey.

As much as I want to tell her everything and lean on her for support, I can't. I can't risk losing her as a friend.

"I'm so sorry," I whisper. "What an idiot. It's because I'm hungover."

"It's alright, Ellie." She pulls me into a hug.

I get no comfort from it. My mind is racing, wondering what anyone could have wanted in those boxes. It's just paperwork, mostly, and a few souvenirs.

Was Mikey behind this?

I need to get Steph out of here so I can take stock and try to figure out what's missing.

"I feel like such a moron," I wail, before making a big show of yawning.

Steph picks up on it straight away. "Oh you poor thing, you're exhausted."

I sigh, feeling like such a bad person for lying to her. What's the alternative? Tell her everything? There's no way I'm doing that.

She pulls away from me and puts her hands on my shoulders, staring into my eyes. "Look, are you sure this was just a mistake? You're certain there's nothing out of place?"

I make myself nod and hope she can't see the fear in my eyes. "I'm sure. I was rushing this morning."

She seems satisfied with that. I walk her to the door, discreetly scanning for signs of other damage as we pass. The good thing about it being such a small flat is there are very few hiding spaces and we've already checked them all.

The bad news is that's not going to help me sleep—not

when I know somebody was in my flat earlier today, poking through my things.

I wave Steph off and once her back is turned I check the lock. There's no sign that it's been forced. I test my key in it and it works just as smoothly as before.

What does that mean, exactly? Was the person who broke in here an accomplished burglar or did they have a key?

I bury my face in my hands. Neither option puts me at ease.

But I still haven't been able to answer the more important question: what were they looking for?

Perhaps they thought I had jewellery hidden in those boxes? I don't know. This doesn't make sense to me. Anyone with half a brain could tell from the clothes in my wardrobe that I'm not the sort of person who has valuable jewellery hidden away.

An hour later I'm still none the wiser. I've been slowly working through the piles, forcing myself to confront once-happy memories that are now so painful to look back on. I've got to if I have any hope of finding out what they were looking for or what they took.

I take another sip of wine and I'm filled with self-loathing for having run to the corner shop to buy two bottles to help me through this.

I needed the crutch.

I can't describe what it's like to look through smiling pictures of my former best friend and know that she turned her back on me when I needed her most. I can't help but feel bitter every time I find a ticket stub to a concert we all went to together. Those pictures of me and Mikey and Katie where it looks like we were having the time of our lives—and we were. How will I ever be able to look at them again without feeling bitter about what happened next? Katie used to be my best friend and now she acts as though I'm invisible when I pass her on the street. How can I keep those pictures? It's not like I'll ever want to flick through them again now that they cause more pain than happiness.

I reach into a pile and pull out another photo. This one is older, faded.

Mum, I think, looking at it with a rush of relief. The one person in my life who didn't deliberately let me down. I clutch the shiny paper to my chest and feel a stab of guilt. Dad said a lot of hurtful things the other day, but he was right about one thing: I've never shown much interest in finding out about her.

It doesn't seem fair. He can remember her but he chooses not to. I don't remember her at all, but then I haven't even tried. And there are other things I can do. I can find out more about her; I can make sure the memory of her lives on.

I stare at the picture and trace the outline of her face with my fingertips. I feel a sudden surge of love for the girl who can't be more than seventeen in the picture. Who was she, really? What did she like? What drove her crazy? She looks so carefree. She's leaning against a car in front of an old stone wall with a forest in the background. There's no indication of where it is—no signs in the photo or writing on the back.

I dig into the pile with a renewed sense of purpose. I have other photos of her, two of them I think. Perhaps there's somebody in the background, a friend or distant relative I can trace.

It doesn't take me long to find them, but my hopes are dashed. In one of the others, she's all dressed up standing beside Dad, who's in a suit. Perhaps it's a wedding, but there's nobody else in the picture and no date on the back. The other one is a close up of her laughing—I can't even see what she's wearing in it, let alone where the photo was taken.

I look through the three pictures again before putting them in their own separate pile on my bed. For the first time I wonder why there are no pictures of the two of us together. Didn't either of them want a photo of us as a family?

I squeeze my eyes closed and concentrate on my breathing. *In in in* hold *out out out* hold. This is no time to start feeling sorry for myself.

I refill my glass and get back to sorting through the mess of papers on the floor. I move quicker this time, forcing myself to stay detached from what I'm seeing. I have to stop when I find some old valentines cards from Mikey as well as a birthday card from Katie, the whole inside of which is crammed with impossibly tiny writing.

I don't read any of them. What would be the point? I throw them on top of the burn pile and move on.

It takes at least another hour to go through everything. When I'm finished, I'm left with three piles: paperwork, painful memories I have no intention of keeping, and the photos of my mum.

As far as I can tell, there's nothing missing and I still have no idea why he'd do this. The only thing that's changed lately has been me seeing Nathan. Is that it? Is that the reason Mikey's come back to mess with me?

CHAPTER 15
ELLIE
WEDNESDAY

step into the shower feeling groggy and lethargic. My head aches behind my eyes, which are almost swollen shut. I barely slept last night, despite the wine. Even the slightest noises had me leaping out of bed. I even fetched a knife from the kitchen and put it under my pillow—not that it made me feel any safer.

Steph's words have been rolling around in my mind ever since she left last night. Should I have called the police?

I don't have to think about that for very long. The answer is no—they wouldn't help me before and the situation was definitely worse then. They're not going to help me now. I have no proof that it was Mikey.

I lean against the plastic shower wall and try to think clearly. Who else could it be? It has to be him.

I turn off the water and reach out to grab my towel from the hook. My thigh skims the shower curtain and its horrid mouldy dampness clings to my leg like a second skin. I kick it away. Nausea rises in my throat and I breathe shallowly to try and quell it.

———

I check my phone and there's still nothing from Nathan. Maybe it wasn't Steph I needed to worry about—what if Nathan has heard about me and chosen to believe the lies? I can picture it now: all he had to do was ask a mate or colleague if they knew Ellie Cartwright.

I stare at my phone, deciding what to do. Should I cut my losses now and concentrate on saving to get out of here? Or should I give him the benefit of the doubt—maybe he's been busy at work and he's not had a chance to message me since I missed his call.

It's too early to call so I send him a message.

I tried calling you back after I missed your call. Had to work until 8. How about a drink later in the week after 8 or at the weekend?

Pressing send doesn't make me feel any better. Deep down I know that I shouldn't be chasing after him like this; that I must seem desperate.

This is the last time.

Except I'm not sure I'm ready to stand by that if it comes to it.

I force down a dry Weetabix for breakfast, taking large sips of water between bites. I really need to go to the super-market later.

The three piles of papers catch my eye when I go to my bedroom to get dressed. I haven't thrown anything out yet. I tell myself to scoop up the pile of photos and tickets and chuck them in the bin but I can't. It feels like too big a step.

I dress quickly: black shirt and trousers as usual. I consider wearing a dress in case Nathan gets in touch with me, but even thinking that makes me feel wretched: I've got to stop planning my life around a man I barely know.

The first thing I register when I step outside the front door is the miserable weather. It's raining: the kind that lingers in the air and makes your hair frizz up. I reach back to grab my umbrella. It's when I turn back to walk out the door that I see him.

He's near the bus stop across the road, but he's not waiting for a bus. I know that because one's just taken off and they're not busy in that direction at this time in the morning. He's also staring straight at me.

My heart starts pounding. Instinct tells me to go back into the flat and lock the door behind me, but I can't do that. I've got to get to work.

The man turns and hurries away with his head down, going away from town. I stand and watch him for a couple of seconds, absolutely horrified. Was I wrong? Was the bus full? It can't have been. It never is.

I close the door and check it carefully to make sure it's locked. I can't afford it, but I'm going to have to look into security measures. Maybe I can convince Dad to help me pay for a CCTV camera. He'll have to make an exception for that, won't he?

I look around. The man is long gone now, but my pulse still hasn't returned to normal. I walk as fast as I can and that quickly turns into a run because I've got to put as much distance between me and him as possible.

As I run, I try to remember anything distinctive about him, but my mind is a blank. He was all bundled up with his hood up and a scarf over the bottom part of his face. He's older; older than Mikey and me. A friend of Graham's? That guy never liked me. He was always in Mikey's ear to get rid of me. But it's hopeless: it could be anyone. Mikey was always persuasive. People fall over themselves to do what he wants.

———

My lungs are screaming by the time I turn onto High Street. I walk a lot but I don't much like running and I like it even less now. My feet feel raw in shoes that weren't made for exercise.

I allow myself to slow down: there are a lot of people around now and there's no sign of him behind me.

My office is in sight now and I need to get to the bathroom before anyone sees me. I haven't seen my reflection, but I don't need to see it to know that I'm a mess. Sweat is rolling down my back and my hair is all over the place. Thankfully the hallways are quiet and I don't meet anyone on my way to the bathroom. Even better, my makeup bag is still in my handbag where I put it the other day before my date with Nathan.

I reach for my phone automatically, but there's no reply from him yet. I grimace at my reflection in the mirror. Why does it matter that he hasn't replied? I shouldn't even be thinking about him right now with everything else that's going on.

Who was that man waiting for me on my street?

I close my eyes and breathe, trying to recall every detail that I saw. I don't have much to go on. No amount of concentration is going to change the fact that I couldn't see his face. Besides, who am I going to tell? The police?

I shake my head.

I can't.

Not after last time. It feels like a lifetime ago that I walked into that police station, determined to do the right thing and tell them the truth. It annoyed me that they were too busy to come and see me in the hospital, but I swallowed that annoyance and went to them. It wasn't just for myself but for any other girl who might get sucked in by Mikey's good looks and charm. Because by that stage we were done—no question. I didn't much like thinking about how long it would take him to find somebody new.

I don't know; I just wanted justice.

I expected a bit of resistance because of how popular he was in town, but nothing could have prepared me for the reaction I got. They wouldn't even take my statement, it was that bad. I can still picture the face of the Detective Sergeant I spoke to. He looked at me with such disgust that it makes me shudder to even think about it. I got up and walked out when he said I was the one he'd have charged if he could find the proof. I tried to tell him there was no proof of Mikey's lies because that's what they were—lies, but I couldn't even get the words out I was crying so hard.

I stare at myself in the mirror, blinking to stop the tears from coming again. Almost a year has gone by but it still hurts to remember. He didn't just hurt me physically, he manipulated everyone around me into believing I was the bad one. I don't know how he managed it—by the time I got out of hospital none of my friends would talk to me anymore.

But I expected better from the police. I still don't know why they wouldn't at least listen to what I had to say.

I sigh and wipe my eyes before I dab powder foundation on my nose to try and take down the redness. There's nothing I can do about my puffy red eyes. If anyone asks—which they probably won't—I'll tell them it's allergies.

I've got to stay focused and stop the past from dragging me back into those old emotions. I already know why he's doing this. The only thing that's changed in my life lately is the fact that I've started seeing Nathan.

I zip up my makeup bag and put it back in my handbag. This is exhausting and I'm going round in circles. I check my phone one last time before I leave the bathroom. There's still nothing from Nathan even though he's read my last message.

The morning drags. I start writing a message to Steph to see if she wants to meet for lunch, but I'm too worked up about the man following me and I'm afraid I'll just blurt it out if I see her. I wish I'd thought to get a picture of the man, but he was gone before I realised what was happening. It's probably a good thing: who knows how he would have reacted? Besides, who would I have shown it to? I put my phone away and try to focus on updating the record of my last call.

"Got a minute, Ellie?"

I turn around. Jason is standing there with a weird look on his face. I resist the urge to swear under my breath—this is the last thing I need.

I get up and follow him to his office.

"Big night last night?" he asks when I've closed the door.

I shake my head wearily. "It wasn't, actually. If I look like shit it's because I've been dealing with some personal stuff."

"Personal stuff?" he asks, looking sceptical.

I must be desperate because the possibility of telling Jason everything and crying on his shoulder seems appealing for a few seconds. But then I put that thought right out of my head. He's my boss and he already thinks I'm crazy.

I wave my hand dismissively. "It's nothing. I wasn't out last night, that's all."

He watches me closely. "Are you sure there's not something you want to tell me?"

My exhausted brain can't handle this right now. Should I tell him everything? Will that get him on my side and less likely to fire me? Or will it make him think I'm a loose cannon?

Get a grip, Ellie, I think. He can't fire you without following the process.

"No, there's nothing," I say tightly. "What did you want to speak to me about?"

He sighs. "Consider this a first verbal warning, Ellie. I hate that it's come to this, but look at this." He picks up a printed sheet of paper and shoves it in my face. "You've been slacking off all week. You're not meeting expectations here."

"All week?" I repeat hoarsely. "It's only Wednesday! That's three days. I've been working my arse off here for years."

"I wouldn't exactly put it like that," he says drily. "Don't act like you've done us all a favour or anything."

"I wasn't, I—"

"This is a call centre, Ellie. It might be only three days in your eyes, but that's three days below target and my boss is going to come to me to ask why my team's numbers are off."

My eyes widen. He can't mean that my performance has impacted the entire team, can he?

He raises an eyebrow. "Yes, it's that bad. Now get to work, please. I'd hate to have to let you go, but I need to do what's best for the team."

———

When I get back to my desk, a light on my phone is flashing. I unlock it and my heart leaps. It's a message from Nathan. I'm immediately on edge. I hope he's suggested a time that won't interfere with my work hours because I can't take liberties anymore.

I read the message and my heart sinks. I shouldn't have been so presumptuous. He's not asking me out on a date.

Sorry Ellie. I think it's best if we just leave things.

Tears well up in my eyes and I realise I've been lying to myself about just how much I'm depending on a future with him.

What's happened to make him lose interest all of a sudden?

I text him back before I can stop myself.

What? Why?

A new message appears and I'm reading it before my phone has even had a chance to vibrate.

It seems like you've got a lot on your mind. Maybe you're not ready for something new.

I shake my head.

No. That's not true.

I wait, staring at my phone. He sees the message but doesn't respond.

CHAPTER 16
ELLIE

When I get outside, it's dark and deserted. I go back into the lobby and call a taxi. It feels extravagant, especially now that Mikey has no reason to bother me anymore, but it's going to take time for word to get back to him that Nathan and I aren't a thing anymore.

I try not to look outside, but I can't help it. There are dark shadows everywhere—places to hide and watch and remain unseen. I shiver.

It's over now, I tell myself.

But there's no relief even though this might stop Mikey's harassment campaign. The likelihood of meeting one guy was low. The chance of meeting someone else? I have a better chance of winning the lotto.

I manage to hold it together until the taxi pulls up across the road from my house. I jump out, muttering a strangled *thank you* and bolt across the road. The same sense of unease comes over me again. Anyone could be out there in the darkness.

I realise the taxi is still there, waiting until I get inside safely. I wave, feeling grateful. It's a nice gesture.

I shove my key in the door and bolt inside as quickly as I can. I collapse against the wall as soon as I've flicked on the lights.

I'm tired. So tired.

I fumble for my phone and look at Nathan's messages again. I shake my head. Did I really give him the impression that I wasn't ready for a relationship? He's wrong. I'm ready.

Should I have told him the truth? Should I have explained why I've been on edge?

I chew on my thumbnail and think about it. For a moment I think I should just call him and explain now, but I know it's gone beyond that. It's too late. Maybe he's heard the rumours and that's why he wants to stop seeing me.

I sigh.

Whatever it is, it's over now and I'm just going to have to accept that I'm on my own until I can save enough money to get out of here. Nathan was my one chance to meet somebody and be happy.

And I ruined it.

I zone out for a while, staring down the hall. That saying goes around and around in my head: it's better to have loved and lost… it's not like I was in love with Nathan, but still. I'm not sure it's true. It wasn't so bad before—I'd gotten used to being on my own. Now? It's different. He gave me hope again. I don't know how I'm going to deal with the long evenings with nothing to do.

Tears well up in my eyes. I know I'm letting Mikey win, but I can't help it. I liked Nathan. I'm so disappointed by the thought that this thing between us is over.

I've still got Steph, but that's not the same.

I shake my head. Thinking like that won't do me any favours. Only a few months ago I couldn't believe my luck that she wanted to be my friend. I was standoffish at first, thinking she'd soon realise her mistake, but she kept inviting me for coffees and soon I couldn't think of any more excuses.

I send her a message and briefly explain what's happened. Then instead of wallowing in the past, I decide I'm going to figure out once and for all what happened to my mother. It's been playing on my mind and the only way I'm going to find out more is by doing my own research: Dad's not going to help me. I've done a bit of searching at work, but I've been conscious of my off-call time this week so I haven't really been able to focus on it properly.

Joy Cartwright Accident

None of the results relate to her.

I frown. I've searched this before. This time, I look past the first few pages, convinced there must be something. I open another tab and bring up the local paper's website. Within seconds I've confirmed what I already suspected: they've digitised their archive as far back as the 1960s. So why wouldn't they report on the death of a local personality?

I try to narrow it down.

Joy Cartwright Actress Accident

Nothing.

I scramble to my feet and move to the living room. What started as an excuse to distract myself has me puzzled now—and ashamed. Why have I not looked into this before? I've asked Dad in the past, but I've never even searched her name.

I find a pen and paper and sit on the couch. I stare at my screen. There is so much information online about absolutely everything, so why can't I find anything about Mum?

Joy Cartwright Disappearance

There are almost as many results as before, but nothing relevant. As I think of search terms and they come up with nothing, I jot them down on my notepad so I'm not repeating myself.

I sigh. The poor sleep I had last night is starting to make itself felt.

I try every different combination of her name, Dad's name, the street he lives on, but there's nothing. Finally, I type in the thing that's been bubbling away at the back of my mind.

Joy Cartwright Murder

I hesitate. What if I don't like what I see? What if this is the reason Dad won't tell me anything about what happened?

I hit the search button and hold my breath.

When the results come up, I don't give up after the fourth or fifth page like I did before. I keep going until the results stop pointing to legitimate sites and direct to pages where the summaries are just a collection of words that don't mean anything.

I clench and release my fists. What the hell happened to her? People don't just disappear, but I'm running out of words to search. Why is there no record of her accident?

My phone starts to ring, which makes me jump. It's Steph.

"Ellie?" she says. "Where are you? Are you okay?"

"I'm at home. I'm fine." I pause. The truth is, this search has taken my mind off Nathan. Now, though, the pain comes flooding back.

"Are you sure? I can come over for a cuppa and a chat if you like?"

I glance at my notebook. As distracting as this is, it's pretty dark. "That would be great," I say, trying not to let my relief come across in my voice.

"I'll be there in about fifteen minutes."

———

I jolt when there's a loud knock at the door. It's only when I become aware of the drool on my chin that I realise I dozed off after talking to Steph.

I jump to my feet and hurry to the door.

"Steph!"

She pulls me into a tight hug and I feel myself relax for the first time all day.

"You poor thing," she whispers. "What happened?"

I lead the way back into the flat and gesture towards the couch. Steph picks up my notebook and frowns when she starts to read. She turns back to me. "What's this?"

I flush as I hurry over to take it from her. "Nothing. I was just trying to see what information was online about my mother."

She sighs sympathetically. "Darling, you shouldn't dwell on the past. It won't do you any good."

"I know, but I haven't dwelt on it, that's the problem. I feel like I know nothing about her. What kind of daughter does that make me?"

"How'd you mean?"

"I never asked questions about what happened to her. My dad doesn't really like talking about her and I just accepted that."

"And now you want to know more."

I shrug. "Yeah. She was my mother. I feel like I should know more about her."

She unfurls her scarf and starts to unbutton her coat, but then hesitates and buttons it back up again. "Why now? What's brought this on?"

I flush as I recall how willing I was to change everything at the drop of a hat for Nathan, including my behaviour. Dad's words come back to me. Was he right? Do I just change as soon as a lad I fancy shows the slightest interest in me? "Something Nathan said got me thinking." I turn away because I don't want to see the look on her face. Of course she's judging: I probably would too if the situation was reversed. "Do you want tea?"

"Yes please. Do you mind turning the heating on too? It's bloody freezing in here."

I stop and fiddle with the thermostat. I hadn't noticed the cold but then I'm used to it. Steph's building is much newer and fancier so I expect she doesn't have the same problem as I do. "There," I say without a lot of confidence. "I've changed the settings anyway." I feel a tug of sympathy for the way she's standing there shivering. It's my fault for dragging her here. "Do you want a blanket or something?"

She shakes her head. "No, that's fine. But I'll leave my coat on for a while if you don't mind."

"Not at all," I say, moving into the kitchen and picking up the kettle. As I hold it under the tap and wait for it to fill, I'm aware of her watching me. "Would you like normal tea? Or chamomile?"

"Chamomile for me please."

I replace the kettle on its base and flick the switch. "Yes, it's a bit late for caffeine. Sorry for dragging you over here."

She smiles. "That's what friends are for, isn't it?" There's a sudden clattering noise and she looks startled.

"Don't worry, that's just the radiators."

"So what happened?" she says when I sit down beside her on the couch.

I shake my head. "Nothing. Pretty much what I told you. He said he doesn't want to keep seeing me."

"And what did you say?"

"Well, he said it seemed like I have a lot on my mind. So I messaged back to say—"

"Wait a sec. He *texted* you?"

I nod. I go back to the kitchen and get out two mugs. I pop a chamomile tea bag in each. My mind is racing fast enough as it is without adding caffeine to the mix. I think about taking the half-finished bottle of wine out of the fridge but I don't. Herbal tea will do. I wait for the kettle to click off, then I pour boiling water into the two cups.

"I can't believe he just texted you that. How was it the last time you saw him?" she asks as I put the cups on the table and sit down on the couch beside her.

"It was all going well," I say almost scalding my tongue on the hot tea. I put my cup down too quickly and tea sloshes out onto the table.

"Oh no," she says. She's on her feet before I realise what she's doing. "I'll get a cloth."

"Go on," she says, coming back and lifting my cup so she

can dry the table around it. "What happened? You said it was going well."

I sigh. "I really don't know. We went out on Saturday and then again on Monday. We had a lot of fun together. It was early days, but I thought it was going somewhere." I bow my head. This is getting to me and I don't want her to see that.

But she notices. She puts her arm around me. "I'm sorry."

"No, I'm being silly. It was only two dates, Steph."

"Yes, but you liked him. That's all that matters." She takes a sip of her tea. "Was he right? Do you have a lot on your mind?"

I think about it for a moment and then shrug. "Not really. I guess I was worried about what might happen when…" I stop and clear my throat, alarmed at how close I came to telling her how worried I was about Mikey's reaction. "Just work stuff. The usual."

She shakes her head. "It sounds like an excuse. I can't believe he did that."

I smile, but inside I'm wondering why I'm surprised. I shouldn't have gotten so caught up so quickly.

Steph waves her hand in front of her face. "It's boiling in here. I thought you said your heating was rubbish?"

"I did," I say, laughing. "I don't know what's going on. Maybe it's behaving because you're here." I roll my eyes when I realise she's still wearing her coat and scarf. "I know why you're boiling: you're still wearing that massive coat." I get up to turn the heating back a bit, aware that it'll probably drop to freezing again as soon as I touch it. When I turn around she's shrugging off her coat. I don't really pay attention. I'm too busy trying to find the words to explain how I feel about Nathan.

There's a loud clink and I look up to see what the noise was.

It's then that I see it. She's wearing a three-quarter sleeve blouse so there's nothing covering her forearms. There's a shiny gold bracelet on her left wrist. Not just any shiny gold bracelet either, but one that's identical to the one I found in my father's house. Shiny and gold, but with darker tarnished sections. It's the same bracelet. I'm sure of it.

"Sorry, I whacked my arm off the wall."

I force a smile and look away, conscious that I've just been staring at her wrist.

Why did he tell me it belonged to a real estate agent?

I knew deep down he was lying.

I should have trusted my instincts.

It was Steph's bracelet. But how? I didn't think they knew each other. What was she doing in his house?

I want to ask her about the bracelet, but I don't let myself. I have the strongest feeling that there's something else going on and it would be stupid to act too soon.

Am I being paranoid? Maybe. But I don't think so. That doesn't look like cheap high street jewellery.

It's a struggle to stop myself from confronting her, but I don't. I need to think about this.

I watch her while she's distracted with her phone. Does she know that I found that bracelet in Dad's house? What the hell is going on?

CHAPTER 17
JOY

"Whose is it, Joy?"

I hate it when he's like this. He's normally so calm and controlled, but now he's on the verge of losing it with me. I know I should keep my cool. I'd do anything to avoid fighting with him again. But how can I? How can he stand there and ask me this?

"It's yours. She's yours. Jesus Christ, how can you even ask me that?"

He takes a step closer to me and I can't help but flinch. I know what's to come. There's that look in his eyes, that coldness. Even if he doesn't lay a finger on me, he's still out for blood. He won't stop until I'm in tears on the couch—the only unknown is whether that'll be because of his words or his fists.

But I can't. I can't stand here and take it.

I splay my hands over my belly. I won't let him talk about you like that. This is your father. I shake my head. Looking at him now, I feel nothing but misery. How could I let you come into the world when it's nothing but hatred and ugliness?

He sees where my hands have gone and his face twists into a sneer. "You're starting to show now. What are you going to do then?"

I tell myself to let his words wash over me, but it's hard

when there's such spite in them. I shouldn't care, but I do. Sometimes his words are more hurtful than his blows, but I know now which punishment I want. There's no choice. His blows could hurt both of us—his words can only get to me.

Or do you know? Can you hear? Is all of this somehow making its way inside me?

"What are you crying for?" he spits. "Look at the bloody state of you."

I grit my teeth through my tears. It's true. I've been a mess lately. And what happens when I can't work? He promises to support me, but that's forgotten the moment he's had a bad day and feels like taking it out on somebody. Our cold, horrible house is not a place I want to raise a child. I hate it. I should never have gone back to him.

"I should go now. Get ready," I say calmly. I'm staying calm for me, not for him. I need this job. Not only does it help me scrape by, it also means I can spend hours away from him.

"Yeah, do it while you can."

I flinch. The sound of his fist hitting the table is so loud and unexpected that I can feel it in every bone in my body. I don't know what's set him off again. "Please. Calm down."

A sudden clarity comes over me. Things have got to change. I can't live like this. *We* can't live like this.

"Who is he?"

"What?" I take a small step backwards—it's as far as I can get without falling onto the couch and I don't want to sit down right now. My bump may not be big, but pregnancy is affecting me in other ways. I'm not as agile as usual and I'm clumsier, but it's better to stay standing. If I sat down I'd feel more vulnerable and he'd sense that.

"You heard me." He takes a step closer. "Who is he?"

My heart flutters in my chest. How do I wriggle my way out of this one? When he's like this, there's nothing I can say that he won't take offence to. If I deny it, he'll accuse me of treating him like a fool. I could smile and try to distract him, but the thought of having his hands on me right now makes me more nauseous than the morning sickness I've been suffering for weeks. I feel so trapped.

"Are you joking?" I mumble, trying to hide my fear and put on a carefree voice. "In my condition? Darling, if I even wanted another man—which I don't—can you look at the state of me for a moment?"

I watch as he processes this. Now I see something I missed earlier: his pupils are huge. He's taken something. Oh shit. I should have known. My smile freezes on my face.

He blocks my way.

"I've got to get ready now."

"You think that's funny? How do you think that makes me feel? I'm stuck with a woman no-one else wants to touch, is that it?"

"No, that's not what I meant."

He grips my wrist tighter and pain radiates up my arm. When we first met I liked his strength. He seemed so manly and powerful, but calm. He seemed unflappable. Compared to all the other hotheads I'd gone out with, he seemed like a sweet relief. That was before I really got to know him and realised that the good thing about hotheads is they're predictable; that their anger blows over quickly. "What did you mean then?"

Yes, I'd prefer if he was screaming at me. It'd be better than this; this cold, quiet menace.

"Nothing," I whisper, smiling up at him as my stomach churns and leaps.

I've made a huge mistake. I thought this baby would change things, but I was wrong. Nothing has changed except that I've brought a new life into the world that I'm not sure I can protect.

I've got to get out.

But where? My only friends are work friends and even though we have a laugh, I suspect none of them would go out of their way for me if it came down to it. I've run once and I didn't last very long.

I rub my belly with my free hand and that strange calm washes over me again.

Maybe I have no choice but to go it alone. It's better than being trapped like this; held hostage to someone else's moods.

But how can I? I don't know the first thing about babies.

"Nothing? That's all you've got to say? It's not nothing." He looks at his watch and my heart sinks. He'll know now that I'm not due in work for another two hours. He looks up at me again and there's a revulsion in his eyes I've seen a lot in the past couple of weeks.

Just as I brace myself for more, the phone rings in the kitchen. I scurry past him and close the bedroom door behind me, not wanting to dwell on how close I came to setting him off yet again.

I've got to find a way out.

CHAPTER 18
ELLIE
THURSDAY

I groan and roll over. It feels like I've been lying here for hours as a giant ball of negativity swirled around inside my mind. I've tried to fall asleep but it's just not happening.

Nathan and Steph were the two things in my life that gave me hope.

Now they're gone.

I didn't say anything to Steph last night. I didn't see the point when I've only known her for a few months. I waited for half an hour so she wouldn't suspect her bracelet was the reason I'd suddenly wanted her out. I tried to think of sneaky questions that might catch her out but I was so tired I couldn't trust myself to be clever enough that she wouldn't realise what I was doing.

I pull the duvet over my head. Am I just being paranoid? Should I have come straight out with it?

I can't see how. She could have just lied and then I'd never know. After all, I had no idea up to now that she was involved with Dad.

Is that the only reason she was friends with me?

My head is swirling and the lack of sleep doesn't help.

Did she target me? Is that what happened?

Tears swim in my eyes as I throw off the duvet and rush to the bathroom. First Nathan and now this. I'm alone again.

I turn the water as hot as it will go and wait for the room to steam up before I step into the shower. I wince from the heat of the water on my skin, but it does little to stop the thoughts that are racing through my mind.

Why did Dad never say anything? Did he know we were friends? I close my eyes and turn my face up towards the water. He said his real estate agent left that bracelet in his house.

Steph's not a real estate agent. She works in accounts for a finance company. And it's definitely the same bracelet.

Isn't it?

I spent ages on my phone last night trying to find a similar bracelet online. There's nothing like it in the shops right now.

How do I find out for sure without asking them—because I'm not sure I can rely on either of them to tell me the truth.

I gasp as an idea starts to form in my mind.

There *is* something I can do.

I turn off the water and jump out of the shower, shivering in the cold air as I reach for a towel to wrap around me.

I hurry back to my bedroom and get dressed quickly. I find the key to Dad's house easily enough: it's on top of one of the piles I made the other day that I still haven't thrown out. Getting rid of them is no longer the foremost thing on my mind.

I check the time. I don't have to be in work for hours yet: plenty of time to check Dad's place and see if that bracelet is still there. And I pray that it is: otherwise I have no idea what's going on around me.

I put on my coat and slide the keys into my handbag. Should I feel guilty for what I'm about to do? Because I don't. I'm sick of being lied to and lied about. I'm only doing this because it's impossible to get an honest answer out of anyone.

I see him as soon as I open my door. I don't know if it's the same man as yesterday—he's similarly bundled up in a cap and scarf and I can't see his face. Anger bubbles up inside me:

isn't it enough that Nathan's decided he doesn't want to see me anymore? What else do they want?

"What the hell do you want?" I scream, before I can stop myself. "Tell Mikey he's got what he wanted."

The man turns and hurries off without acknowledging me. I stand watching him, shaking as the adrenaline leaves my body.

What the hell have I just done?

I turn and walk in the direction of town, checking behind me every couple of steps. I shouldn't have lost my temper: I can't help thinking that he'll get me back for that.

I'm just so tired of being a punchbag for everyone in my life. When is it going to end?

It's no wonder Jason is pissed off at me. I've gone from model employee with no life outside of work to an emotional wreck who can't keep her mind on the job. Well, that stops today. I'm going to figure out what the hell is going on between Dad and Steph. Then I'm going to go to work and focus harder than I've ever focused.

I don't go straight to Dad's. Instead, I walk into town, to his office. He's usually at his desk by seven, but I can't rely on his routine anymore since it's possible I don't know him as well as I thought I did.

I check around to see if anyone is watching me before I walk down the ramp into the car park under Dad's building. It only takes me a few seconds to check he's in—his is one of the only cars there.

I hurry out of the car park and cross the road. I glance back up at the sign. *Cartwright Packaging*. A horrible sensation of sadness comes over me. I want to be wrong. I want so desperately to be wrong. I turn and walk in the direction of Dad's house.

———

I turn the key in the door and I'm struck by how weird it feels to let myself into this house. It's not my home anymore and I don't feel like it ever was.

It also strikes me that there's little need for Dad to still be working. He must own this place outright by now. His lifestyle is the opposite of extravagant. He must be loaded. I shake my head. I don't understand him. I never have and I probably never will. Now is not the time to start getting bitter at him for not helping me out when I needed his help the most. The important thing is that my key still works. I had my doubts. I could just imagine him calling the locksmiths the moment his irresponsible daughter moved out.

I look around the hall. It's different being here alone. I can't remember the last time I came here outside of one of our Sunday lunches. I didn't think this place could be any eerier, but it's downright creepy being here without Dad. I don't know how I ever managed to sleep here—not that I was ever in the house by myself. My school friends used to tease me about that. Their parents would go off for weekends away when we were teenagers and they'd have parties in their houses. Dad never went anywhere and somehow he always seemed to know when there was a party on, even if I tried to make up a lame excuse about going to a friend's house to study. I was never allowed to do anything.

My heart hammers as I walk along the hall to the kitchen, staying as quiet as I can just in case he comes back unexpectedly. Or—my blood boils—in case *she's* here. By now I'm desperately hoping that I find that bracelet; that I've misread things.

He left it on the kitchen counter. It's the first place I look, but it's not there. Of course it's not: he doesn't leave anything out. I start checking the drawers and cupboards. The good thing about his Spartan ways is there isn't a bunch of stuff to camouflage the bracelet.

It only takes me a few minutes to search the kitchen. There's no sign of it. I search the living room next, wondering if I'm looking in the wrong places. But he wouldn't have hidden it away—why would he? Not in his own house.

The dining room at the front of the house is hardly ever used but I check it too just in case. There's nothing there. The table is clean and free of dust and I start to wonder if that's because he's a clean freak or because he's got a whole other life I don't know about.

I grit my teeth as I walk up the stairs. I know I should give up and acknowledge that I won't find that bracelet, but I can't. Finding the truth is consuming me now. There has to be something here that explains it. That's the only way I'll find out.

It's not that I resent him for trying to find love. The age gap is a bit weird but I could have gotten over that. It's the deception I can't deal with. Why not just tell me the truth? Why didn't she just tell me? Why didn't he?

I turn the handle of Dad's bedroom door, trying my best to ignore the guilt that rises in me at the thought of snooping in his personal space. Guilt's not all I feel. I'm not sure what to expect as I push the door open and walk inside.

I look around. It's just as bare as the rest of the house. I check the bedside drawers first, just to get that over with. There's nothing in one of them. The other one holds some prescription bottles and some throat lozenges. I take out the prescription bottles. They're both in his name. I don't recognise the names of the drugs.

I move to the wardrobe, anxiety rising again as I wonder if I'll be faced with a rail full of familiar women's clothes. But I'm not. It's just suits and a selection of white and blue shirts. On the floor is a pair of brown leather shoes and a pair of trainers that don't look like they've been used very often. The shelves are stacked with neatly-folded jumpers and polo shirts.

I close the wardrobe doors and hurry out. I check the guest bedroom next. The drawers and wardrobe are empty and there's a faint mustiness to the room. I'd be surprised if he changed the bed linen frequently, though the headboard and bedside tables are just as clean and dust-free as elsewhere in the house.

A quick glance in the bathroom cabinet reveals only his toiletries. Either that or the woman of the house is incredibly low maintenance, which I know Steph is not.

I linger in the bathroom, looking around. What does she do? Bring a toiletry bag with her every time she comes here?

I shake my head. I don't want to think of them together, but the conclusion I'm coming to is that they spend most of their time in her flat. I'll have to find an excuse to snoop around it. Perhaps I'll try and invite myself round this evening: that's if she doesn't suspect I'm on her trail.

But I can't, can I? How can I look her in the eyes after this? She lied to me. They both did.

I come to the last room upstairs: the office. I check the time on my phone. I'm not sure whether to give up and go back to work or keep going. My heart skips a beat as I open the door. This isn't just about him and Steph, I realise, but about my mother. Is there something in here that can help me make sense of why he won't talk about her?

It's as neat and orderly in here as the rest of the house, just a black leather chair and a desk pushed against one of the walls. There's a computer monitor but no hard drive or laptop: he must take it to and from the office.

There are three drawers and I start with the first one, finding nothing but a few pens and pencils, paperclips, that sort of thing. The next one down has various business cards and more unused stationery.

The bottom drawer is more than double the size of the other two. And it's locked. That puts me off initially, but then I grip the bottom and pull. The drawer bucks against the flimsy lock and before I know what I'm doing, I've grabbed a metal ruler from one of the other drawers and used it to reach in. After a few tries, I manage to knock the lock bar out of the hook it locks into.

The drawer slides open and I realise that I've bent the lock enough that it won't slide back in. How the hell am I going to cover this up? He'll know it was me—who else would have broken into his office desk?

I stare into the drawer. This was a stupid idea. There's nothing in there except paperwork.

I start lifting out the papers, glancing over them and placing them upside down so I can put them back in the same order as I found them, though I'm impatient to get through them and get out of here.

It's all boring stuff like insurance documents, legal agreements and that sort of thing. My attention starts to drift. Why are there no newspaper clippings; no pictures of my mother?

I forget all that when I see what's next in the pile. I glance over it and think nothing of it at the start, it's something to do with the company.

Then I notice the name.

Her name.

Two months ago, Dad transferred all his shares in Cartwright Packaging to the Stephanie Price Trust.

I sit back heavily on the floor, devastated. He's given the company to Steph? This is so much worse than I thought.

He set up that company when I was little and he's built it into what it is today. It's his pride and joy.

No wonder they didn't tell me.

I shake my head. This is bad. This is so bad. Has he lost the plot? He didn't seem any different the last time I saw him, but then we never talk much beyond polite small talk on my Sunday visits.

Is it possible I've missed the warning signs?

Struggling to process what I've just seen, I forget my orderly investigation and tip everything from that drawer out on the floor. I scramble blindly through the bits of paper, desperate to find something that will help me make sense of this.

Why?

Why would he sign everything over to her? Is he ill? Has she tricked him? This is wrong.

I'm almost at the end of the pile and I'm about to give up.

It's all just old electrical warranties now and the TV down-stairs is at least ten years old so there's nothing recent here. The pile of documents left to go through is only a few sheets deep and I'm exhausted, even though it's still only half eight in the morning.

Then I see it.

The envelope.

It's white, which explains why it didn't stand out from the rest of the pile. I stare at it. It's discoloured from age, which means nothing of course, but there's something about it that makes me feel on edge. Nothing else I found this morning was in an envelope and there's no name written on the front.

The flap is open and there's no sign that it's ever been sealed shut even though the glue has turned yellow with age. I prise open the top and pull out the sheets of paper inside.

I place them side by side and stare at them. At first they make no sense to me. It's a death certificate for someone called Josephine Kent and a birth certificate for Eleanor Kent. Then my vision starts to swim and I scan through the tiny writing for dates.

I shake my head as panic washes over me.

Eleanor was born the same year as me. The same month too—just five days earlier. I pick up the page and hold it right up to my face. Is this me? My hands shake. It seems like too much of a coincidence, but why would it say my name is Kent?

Then my brain makes another connection and it's all I can do to keep breathing steadily. Josephine Kent is listed on the birth cert as Eleanor's mother. Josephine… Joy… could it be?

My mother's name was Joy. But she was Joy Cartwright, not Joy Kent.

What the hell is going on? If this is my birth certificate, then why does it say I was born in Hull? I've never been there. And why isn't Dad listed as my father? The section where his name should be is completely blank.

Dread consumes me as I drop the birth certificate and pick up the other document.

Josephine died when I was almost two. That's consistent with what Dad has told me, but that's the only thing that's consistent.

It's not just the name or the fact that her death was recorded in Hull. It's the cause of death. When I finally bring myself to read those words, I'm stunned and more confused than ever.

Because Josephine Kent was poisoned.

CHAPTER 19
ELLIE

walk back to town in a daze, barely aware of whether I've even closed the front door of Dad's house, never mind had the mental clarity to fix the lock on his desk drawer. Everything is a blur. Everything is a lie.

I'm not stupid.

The envelope feels heavy in my pocket. Perhaps I shouldn't have taken it, but I was worried Dad might destroy the documents and deny everything.

Dad…

Why isn't his name on my birth cert? If I'm not Eleanor and Josephine wasn't my mum, why would he have those documents?

Is he even my dad?

A horrible thought pops into my mind. Did he kill her?

My fists clench by my side. What am I supposed to do? I'd planned to go to work after this, but how can I go in and sit at my desk after what I've just found?

I want to walk right into his office and confront him, but how can I? My thoughts are all jumbled up. I don't even know what I'd say.

I can't keep running away, though, can I? I check the time and realise if I hurry I can swing by Dad's office and still get to work on time.

Tears well in my eyes and I bite my lip to try and stop them. As if this can be resolved in a quick visit to his office.

————

I turn onto the street where Dad's office is and change my mind again. I'm too worked up to see him. I need some time to process this first.

I keep walking along the other side of the street, but I can't take my eyes off the sign. Cartwright. Is that even my name? Why didn't she put his name on my birth certificate?

My stomach heaves. Were they ever together? Those photos he gave me—how do I even know that was her?

Somebody emerges from the building. At first I don't pay much heed: I'm too wrapped up in trying to make sense of the lies he told me. Slowly, though, I register the coat and realise it's not one of Dad's employees.

I look up, horrified. It's her, sauntering along the street in that gorgeous black wool coat with the sky blue lining that appears in flashes.

It's silk, she told me once, proudly stroking it and inviting me to feel how soft it was.

I watch her in disbelief as I see her enviable wardrobe in a new light. I was so grateful to have a friend that I never stopped to ask myself how someone working in accounts could afford clothes like that.

She didn't.

My dad did.

I did.

I grimace. I've never thought of his company as mine, but it's a slap in the face to know he's been spoiling her with luxuries and he wouldn't even give me a loan when I needed it.

I'm too far away to see the look on her face, but I can see enough from her body language. There's a spring in her step that isn't usually there.

Look at her, I think bitterly, *strutting around like she's just won the lotto.*

It hits me then and I don't know why I never thought of it before.

His staff. They must know about it if she's openly visiting Dad at work. Does everyone know?

I must be the only one who doesn't.

I think back over the last few months; over the disintegration of my relationship with my father and his anger when I brought up the topic of my mother.

I can't think of a good reason for them to keep their relationship from me—but I can think of a very bad one.

What if I'm thinking about this all wrong and Dad knows nothing about my friendship with Steph? What if she's fed him a whole load of bullshit about needing to keep it a secret from his daughter without revealing she knows me?

I stumble backwards and grip the railing of the building behind me to steady myself.

What if she's been playing the two of us off against each other in the hopes of driving us apart permanently and getting her hands on his money?

She's gone now, but the more I think about it the more it makes sense. Even last night she was so dismissive of me when I told her I was looking into what had happened to my mother.

My eyes widen.

She knew I wasn't going to get anywhere because she knew Dad had told me a false name.

And why did he do that?

By the time I walk into the lobby at work, my head is pounding from trying to make sense of this.

At least I'm on time. It's becoming more and more clear that this job is the only half-decent thing in my life and I can't afford to let my performance slip any further.

———

After the first couple of calls, I'm consumed by the need to delve deeper into the past. I have something to go on now. A name. I thought I had that before, but I didn't: not really.

I resist the urge. Every time I think about searching 'Josephine Kent', I glance at Jason's office. He hasn't spoken to me yet today and I don't want him to either.

I've got to stay on track.

I throw myself into my work and promise myself I can do all the research I need to do on my lunch break.

———

I dash out of the office to get a sandwich to eat at my desk. I need to eat as quickly as I can so I have more time for research.

Thankfully Jason isn't in his office—I saw him go out earlier with a load of people from a different team—so I don't have to watch out for him. It doesn't matter that it's my lunch break and I'm allowed to use the internet—I don't want to risk another confrontation where he flies off the handle before I can explain I'm on my break.

I look around. The office is quiet. It seems like lots of people in my team have gone out for lunch too. I don't care —I'm past the point where it bothers me that I don't get invited to these things. In a way it's good: I don't have the money to spend on whip-arounds and birthday lunches and all the other pointless events they seem to have around here.

I finish my sandwich and wipe my fingers on the rough napkin that came with it.

At first I don't know where to start: the present or the past. Then Steph's smug face and designer clothes pop into my head and I know that's where my focus needs to be. What if she's trying to rip him off?

I hesitate for the thousandth time today. Am I seriously thinking about protecting my dad, the man who lied to me about who I am and what happened to my mother?

No, the first thing I need to do is find out what happened to her. Who poisoned her? There has to be a record of that.

I hiss out a breath and type in the name from the documents I found this morning.

Josephine Kent.

There's nothing. I grit my teeth when I realise why: there are a lot of people called Josephine who live in Kent. That gives me an idea.

Josephine Kent Hull.

I sigh as I skim through the results and see there's nothing relevant.

I sit back and drink some water from the bottle I keep on my desk. There's a lump in my throat and I don't know whether it's from eating too fast or for different reasons.

I don't know what to think about anything anymore.

I replace the cap on my bottle.

Josephine Kent death.

Josephine Kent poisoned.

There's nothing. No outpouring of grief. No sentencing of whoever was responsible.

I try **Eleanor Kent.**

I hold my breath expecting that there must be something. But there's not. I sigh. The trail is just as cold as before. How can that be?

As I type in Steph's name, I realise how little I know about her. I never asked prying questions about her life in case she did the same to me. I realise that she probably knows all about my past.

Unlike my mother, there are lots of pictures of Steph online with her equally glamorous friends down in London.

The most recent ones are from only a few months back, right before she started chatting to me at yoga.

Why, is all I can think. Why did she move here? Was it because of Dad?

I slam my hands on the keyboard as I tap in my next search query.

Steph Price golddigger.

There are some pictures of her in the image results, including one of her with an older man. I click on it, but it won't let me open the website it's linked to.

I grit my teeth and look for others. Is he her last boyfriend? He looks like he's in his fifties and judging by the big gold watch on his wrist, he's loaded.

I sigh.

I need to calm down and think. Knowing she's gone out with rich men in the past isn't going to solve anything. I try to remember the name of her company, but I can't.

I sit back heavily, frustrated now.

John Cartwright Steph Price.

There's nothing nothing nothing. I can't stand it anymore. I'm exhausted and I have no idea what's going on all around me.

The worst thing is there's one place I can go that might be able to help.

But I swore I'd never set foot in there again.

———

I lose my nerve long before I get to the police station. I try to convince myself that it might be different now; that there are lots of officers who work there and I might not necessarily see the same ones.

It doesn't work.

All I can remember is being sneered at; the detective's anger when I suggested that maybe the reason he was shielding Mikey had something to do with his rugby connections.

I stop outside the building and stare up at it, telling myself it's just a building and they're just people; that I've done nothing wrong.

In the end, it's my obsessive need to find out what happened that drives me through those doors even though it's far more tempting to scuttle back to work. This place brings back too many bad memories.

The last time I walked in here I was on crutches for my broken leg and every time I so much as grazed against a door or wall the pain made me wince. Those bruises and breakages have long since healed, but there are other scars I'll never be rid of.

I still don't understand why he did it. All he had to do was tell me to leave him alone. Having his heavies from the club follow me and intimidate me was unnecessary then, just as it is now.

I clench my fists as I walk into the reception area.

My anxiety has spiked since I walked through those doors. I'm not reporting Mikey, I'm just trying to find out more about my mother, but tell that to my pounding heart and clammy palms. This place will forever be linked in my mind to discovering that the system was rigged against me.

The officer behind the desk looks up and relief floods through me. I've never met her before.

"Can I help you?"

She's my age or a little older. I relax a bit. I wasn't sure what to expect but now I realise I didn't think I'd even get this far without them turning me out of the place and telling me I'm a liar.

Just like the last time.

I wince. *Do you know the penalty for wasting police time, Miss Cartwright? Or for making a false claim about an innocent man?*

I wasn't just angry, I was humiliated too. Weren't my

bruises and broken leg proof enough?

"Can I help you?" she asks again. This time there's an edge to her voice.

I nod quickly. I've got to get a grip. "Yes. I'm hoping you can help me. I'm trying to find out more about what happened to my mother."

Her eyes scan my face. Her fingers hover over her keyboard. "I'm going to need some more information."

"Yes, of course. Her name was Joy…" I stop and clear my throat. "Josephine Kent."

"Okay. I'll have a look. Do you have any ID on you?"

"ID?"

"Yes."

I shake my head. "Just my bank card. Will that do?"

"Does it prove your relationship?"

I'm confused for a moment and then I realise what she means. "No," I whisper. "No, it doesn't. I have a different name."

I frown as I run through how that can have happened. How can my bank account be in the name of Ellie Cartwright when my birth cert says Eleanor Kent?

"I'm afraid I'll need something," she says.

"I don't have anything," I whisper. "I don't even know why our names are different. Oh wait. I have my birth cert. Are you able to look up the records, see if my father officially adopted me or something?"

She looks up at me and I see that something has closed off inside her. My heart sinks as I realise she's written me off as a crank—one of those people who go around wasting police time with stupid questions. "You'll have to contact Births, Deaths and Marriages, I'm afraid."

"Please," I hiss. "I have her death certificate here. I'm sure it has all the information you need to find her files."

She shakes her head. "I can't do that. I can't give out personal information."

I'm about to argue when I catch sight of the clock above her desk. It's ten past two. I need to get back to work.

CHAPTER 20
MIKEY

ikey's phone buzzed in his pocket. He pulled it out, hopes rising that this might be the call that got him on the front of one of the women's magazines and catapulted him into the A-list.

It wasn't. He groaned when he saw Graham's name flashing on the screen.

"What now?" He sighed. "I told you, I think I've strained a muscle in my groin. You don't want me straining it further, do you?"

He rolled his eyes. Graham should know by now that he was a hundred percent dedicated to his career. He wasn't going to make up an injury to get out of training and it offended him that Graham would call to check up on him. He was probably listening like a hawk for pub noises in the background.

But Graham didn't start bawling him out. He just sighed like this call hadn't been an easy one to make.

Mikey was immediately on edge. "What is it?"

"I thought you were going to sort things out." There was an edge of disappointment to the older man's voice.

"I did." Mikey didn't need to ask what he meant anymore. They'd talked about *her* more than they'd talked about rugby lately—or that's what it felt like anyway.

"How'd you explain the phone call I've just had then?"

"What phone call?" Mikey's stomach churned and he was starting to feel queasy. He'd been too patient with her. He'd suspected as much, but he'd been powerless to change. He loved her, simple as that—and he always would. "What's happened?"

"She's gone to the police, Mikey. I bloody told you..."

His coach's voice faded. It was happening again, just like it had before. He groaned. "Jesus," was all he could manage to say.

"Jesus won't help you now."

Mikey rubbed his chin. "Can you?"

"I'm afraid not. You'd best get down there yourself. Find Hobson. He's a good lad. He'll sort you out."

Mikey frowned. "Was it him that called you?"

"I can't say. And it doesn't matter. Just be thankful I've got eyes and ears all over this town."

"But Graham," Mikey muttered. "What am I going to say?"

Graham cursed under his breath. "Make something up. Just be convincing. She doesn't have an ounce of credibility left after the stunts she's pulled."

"I know, but—"

"She's not just your problem, Mikey," Graham snarled. "She's mine too." He cleared his throat then muttered something Mikey couldn't catch. He ended the call before Mikey could ask him to repeat it.

Mikey lay back on the couch and groaned. How had it come to this? Why the hell was she going to the police? He thought he'd taken care of it.

Mikey spent the whole drive into town dwelling on his actions. He'd obviously not been as subtle as he thought. What was he supposed to do? They'd been together for years. Was he supposed to not care about her all of a sudden? That didn't happen overnight. All he'd done was care about her. Yes, he'd lost his temper and reacted in the heat of the moment, but he hadn't meant to.

He parked the car and turned off the engine. There were lots of people around but he couldn't see her. That meant she'd gone. He was sure of it—he'd recognise her no matter how big the crowd.

He shook his head.

No.

No, he wasn't going to the police like Graham wanted. That was only asking for trouble.

He'd sort this out his own way.

CHAPTER 21
ELLIE

At six on the dot, I throw off my headpiece and log out of the system. I've been thinking about it all afternoon and there's only one thing I can do.

I've got to confront Dad about what I found in his house.

Dad wouldn't tell me anything before, but this is different. I have physical proof. If he denies he lied, I'll refuse to leave until he tells me the truth. The first thing I did when I got back to the office earlier was scan the certificates to myself so I'll always have proof even if he tries to take them away from me.

I hesitate as the lift doors open in the lobby. Will he try that? Do I need to be worried? He's my father, but if Josephine Kent was my mother—and I'm pretty sure she was—does that mean he was the one who hurt her?

I knead my temples as I make my way to the door. I just can't believe he could have hidden something like this.

I decide it's best to get a taxi. That way, I can get the driver to wait outside for me. Thankfully it's not raining so I'm able to flag one easily enough.

It doesn't take long to get to Dad's—we've pulled up before I know it.

The driver turns around. "That'll be ten pounds, love."

I reach in my bag for my purse and hand him the money.

Beads of sweat break out on my forehead as I remember the reason why I decided to get a taxi in the first place. "Would you mind waiting for me?"

He frowns. "How long will you be?"

"I don't know. I've just got to pop in and speak to my father."

He reaches into the console. "Here's our card. You can call the company when you're done and dispatch will send a car."

"But I…" I sigh. There's no point in arguing. I don't really believe Dad is capable of hurting me, do I?

———

I get within two paces of the door when I hear them.

Voices.

Raised voices.

I tiptoe closer to the door and crouch as low as I can, aware that someone in the hall might be able to see my shadow through the glass. I push my ear against the letterbox.

My dad is speaking. I only catch the end of what he's saying. "Mikey."

Now that I'm closer, I can hear them clearly, though I have to hold my breath. I close my eyes. They're in the dining room, I think. It sounds like the door from the dining room to the hallway is open.

"She needs to know," a woman says and my blood runs cold.

Not because I think they're talking about me, though I'm certain they are. It's because I recognise the voice. That's Steph talking: I'm certain of it.

"Nonsense," Dad mutters.

"It's not nonsense. You need to take this seriously. We've got to, John. She needs to know."

"It's not that simple."

"She needs to know, John. She has no idea."

"Well we've got to keep it that way. She's got issues. There's no telling how she'll react."

"I know that," she says patiently. She mutters something else I can't catch.

It doesn't matter. I've heard enough.

What I've just heard changes everything. They're talking about me like I'm crazy. Why are they doing that?

Tears sting my eyes as I scramble to my feet as quietly as I can.

For the first time I'm afraid. What kind of trap are they setting for me? That's the only explanation I can think of for what I just heard. She's convinced him I'm crazy—but why?

I'm so distracted by what I've heard that I pay barely any heed to my surroundings. So much so that I almost don't see the huge figure in the gateway, blocking my exit from the house.

I open my mouth to scream, but no sound comes out. I try to change course but there's nowhere to go. The trees are too tall and thick to get through. I try to barrel past him, but I'm no match for his strength.

CHAPTER 22
ELLIE

My breath is ragged in my throat. I try to catch it and scream, but by the time I've got enough air in my lungs, a huge hand is clamped over my mouth.

"Just be quiet! Don't make a scene."

My heart pounds and time seems to slow down.

Think!

My instinct is to bite his hand, but I hesitate. That's not going to be enough. He's holding my arm with one hand and his other hand is clamped over my mouth to stop me from screaming.

I inhale, trying not to retch from the smell of stale smoke on his hand.

He shifts position and pushes me forward. He's still holding me in the same way, but now I'm facing out onto the street. My handbag is still shoved up on my left shoulder, where I usually carry it. Good. My phone.

"Go on," he hisses. "Move." He shoves me forward. Oh God, he's trying to kidnap me.

I need to do something now, before it's too late. I bite down as hard as I can on his hand, while at the same time I lift my foot off the ground and slam it blindly towards his crotch. He groans heavily and loosens his grip on me.

As soon as he does I tear off into the darkness. My mind races with different routes I could take back to town. I've got to get out of sight. He looked like a big bloke, but I know nothing about his fitness and I'm not very fit myself. I'm out of breath already, but that could be down to being frightened.

I blink. It's no time to think about it now. I've got to get to safety.

I duck down the first side street I come to and run as fast as I can in the middle of the road, knowing there's another street off to the left after about fifty yards, which bends sharply and then lets out onto a busier village area.

It's all fine in theory, but I have no idea how fast he is or if he's run back to get a car. I don't dare look back.

I change my plan.

I've been assuming I know the area better than he does, but what if I don't? It's been a long time since I lived around here.

I run faster, crossing to the left hand footpath. I don't take the first left, though. I keep running until the entrance to the park, but I change my mind about that too. What if he's right behind me? The grass could be slippery and I can't use my phone in the pitch darkness in case he sees the light.

I gasp for breath as I try to picture the streets around here. There's another left coming up and I take that at a run, even though it's a straight road to the shops without any bends. I'm just going to have to rely on the kindness of strangers to help me if I can get to them, because there's nothing else I can do—I can't keep running forever.

I'm immediately on edge. This street is better lit. While there's less chance of me tripping on a bad section of pavement, it's easier for him to see where I'm going. I don't know what to do.

My lungs scream with the pain of running for my life when I'm not used to running at all. I see the little cluster of shops up ahead—it can't be more than a hundred yards.

I've got to make it.

I've got to.

As I get closer, I remember this place. There's a pub we used to go to with an outside area that has an exit onto a side street. I aim for that, passing the first shop and takeaway and barreling towards the door of the pub. I stop abruptly when I see the bouncer.

I've never been so relieved to see a bouncer before.

"Please," I say before he can say anything. My words come out in juddering gasps. "There's a man following me."

I force myself to look back, convinced now that the man is gone.

But he's not. I watch as a shadowy figure comes to a stumbling halt further down the street.

"That's him," I hiss, pointing.

"Right," he says. "You get in. I'll call the police."

"No. No, not the police."

"Your call," he says with a frown. "Know him, do you?"

"No," I mutter, embarrassed now. "Look, I'll call a friend to get me. Can you please just not let him in here?"

He shrugs and I push open the door to the inner part of the pub.

There's only one person I can call now, and I'm not sure how pleased he's going to be to hear from me—that's if he even answers.

CHAPTER 23
ELLIE

Nathan arrives within five minutes. I've got to hand it to him—he was frosty when he answered the phone, but once he heard that I was in danger he told me to hold on and he'd be there in a few minutes.

He looks around the bar and his brow furrows when he sees me.

"I must look a sight," I say when he sits down.

He nods. "I've never seen anyone look so scared."

"Thanks for coming," I say. It's an effort not to cry. "Did you see anyone out there? I asked the bouncer not to let him in but he's not said anything."

He shakes his head. "No. I'll go ask him now."

I reach over and grab his hand. I'm too cold and shaken to worry about calling him after he told me he didn't want to see me anymore. "No, please. Just stay with me will you?"

"I'll get you a hot whisky."

I freeze and look around. It's still early, but the pub isn't that busy. "Should we go somewhere else?"

He squeezes my hand. "We'll be fine here."

"Will we? That guy grabbed me outside my dad's house and tried to drag me off..." I trail off. What was he doing? The important thing is I got away, but I can't help replaying it in my head and wondering how close I came.

"Ah shit," he says, rubbing his face. "I'm sorry, Ellie. I had no idea how shaken you were. We can go somewhere else. Or I can drop you home if you like."

"No," I say too quickly. I flush. "No. The pub, maybe. Somewhere quiet. But not home."

His eyes widen.

"Yeah," I whisper. "You were right. I was preoccupied."

He cringes. "I'm sorry, I didn't…"

"Look, it's fine. I'll explain everything—well, as much as I know. But can we go somewhere else? I'm afraid he's lurking around outside."

He takes my arm and leads me out. My unease returns when I see the bouncer has gone.

Nathan was telling the truth—he's parked only a few paces from the pub. He opens the passenger door for me and closes it again when I'm inside. My heart pounds as he moves around the front to the driver's side and I imagine my attacker jumping out at him.

Am I being crazy? I don't even know anymore.

Nathan gets in and closes the door, rubbing his hands together before he puts the key in the engine. "Right, there's a little pub near me that does a decent roast in the evenings. Sound good?"

I have to stop my stomach from rumbling. I haven't eaten since I had that sandwich for lunch at my desk—which feels like weeks ago now, so much has happened in the meantime. "Yes," I murmur.

———

"The benefit of taking you to my local," Nathan says, holding up his pint. "Is that we can have a few drinks."

I hold my glass to his and mutter "cheers" but I'm not as relaxed as I'm pretending to be. I can't go back to the flat. I've got to sort out a hotel or B&B to stay in for the night. No, not just tonight—how can I go back to the flat after what's just happened?

Nathan's face falls. "What is it?"

I sigh. "I'm sorry. I'm not very good company right now."

"That's no surprise." He puts his drink down on the table. "Who was the guy? What are you involved in, Ellie?"

The hairs on my arms stand on end even though it's roasting in here. "I don't know."

"Was it random?"

I shake my head. "No, that's not what I meant." I take another sip of my whisky. I'd much rather get lost in it than recount what's been happening in my life. But what choice do I have? "I used to go out with a lad called Mikey. He's from around here." I sigh. How do you begin to condense something like this down to a few sentences in a pub? "It was good until it turned bad. His team didn't like the fact that I was with him." I flush. The catalyst was that night I got drunk at a team event, but I still think they overreacted. "His coach had a quiet word with me. Told me there'd be consequences if I didn't leave it." I pick up my drink and take a large gulp. I hadn't meant to, but this is harder than I thought. I wince. "Anyway, I was foolish. I thought he loved me and it was just the others that wanted to break us apart. Graham had someone follow me. I don't know, to threaten me? I never knew. Because before I could ask Mikey about it, he attacked me in the pub we used to go to every Saturday. That was almost a year ago. And for some reason he's back at it again. I thought it was because I was seeing you, but..." I dip my head, embarrassed now that I've had to go running to a guy who doesn't want to have anything to do with me. "Anyway," I say. "I can't believe you never heard this. Everyone I knew stopped speaking to me. It's such a mess."

He looks away and grimaces. "I'm not exactly Mr Popular here."

I resist the temptation to point out that he can't be more unpopular than me.

"Do you want to go to the police after this?" He gestures to the table, where we each have about half a drink left.

"No." I shake my head and—to my alarm—tears well up in my eyes.

"Why not, Ellie? If this guy is harassing you—"

"I just can't," I hiss. "I went to them before and they didn't do anything."

"Have you talked to your family?"

I'm not fast enough to stop the sob escaping my throat. "Oh God," I wail, burying my head in my hands. "You must think I'm a complete mess."

"No, I..." he pulls a face. "Okay, I can't lie. You're a bit of a mess but I won't hold it against you."

I can't help but laugh. "Thanks, Nathan. I really appreciate this. If my psycho ex wasn't enough to deal with, I've just found out my father is going out with my friend and he's signed his company over to her. And he lied to me about my mother."

"Wow."

"I know." I take a sip of my drink and stare at the glass, suddenly very self-conscious. Only a few days ago, Nathan decided he didn't want anything to do with me. Now I'm landing all of this stuff on him and I haven't even told him the part about the documents I found in Dad's house. I swallow. I really don't want to say what I'm about to say next, but I feel like the only decent thing to do is to give Nathan an out. "I really appreciate you coming to get me. You didn't have to." My hands are shaking. "You can walk away if you want."

He frowns. "Do you want me to?"

I look away. Of course I don't. I'll be on my own if he does and I can't stand that thought. But I also can't stand the idea of him getting involved in this out of pity.

"It's not about what I want. It's... this isn't your fight. And," I lower my voice because I don't trust my emotions anymore and the last thing I need is for him to think I'm even crazier than he already suspects. "You were going to walk away before, remember? That text you sent? You still can. I just want you to know that you shouldn't feel obligated—"

"Is this you telling me you're not interested?"

"No," I say through the tears I can't hold back anymore. "No, I'm not saying that at all. Look at us! This is only the third time we've been out together. I can't stop crying and you had to come and rescue me from some random pub after a stranger tried to grab me."

Nathan watches me for a while and then shrugs. "It's not perfect, but that's life." He leans closer. "Look, I have a spare room. You're welcome to stay for a bit until you get this sorted out."

I stare at the table. I shouldn't, I really shouldn't. I should book a hotel or a motel and stand on my own two feet, but a little voice in my head screams at me to accept his offer. I can't afford to move into a hotel. "I don't know how long it's going to be for, Nathan." I shiver. I don't really want to tell him what I'm about to tell him, but I don't have a choice. "This may have all kicked off because my ex found out I was seeing you. You've got to be aware of that. This could be dangerous for you."

Nathan smiles.

"It's not funny!" I hiss. "I'm serious. I'd be putting you at risk."

He takes my hand. "It's sweet of you to worry about me, but I'll be fine."

"But he's dangerous, Nathan."

He grins and picks up his pint, finishing the rest of it in one long gulp. "So am I. Now, can I get you another?"

I find myself nodding, even though I can't stop thinking about what he's just said. Nathan? Dangerous? I hadn't thought so, but how well do I really know the guy? As messed up as it is, I find myself hoping that it's true: I could do with someone dangerous on my side—that's how serious this has become.

CHAPTER 24
ELLIE
FRIDAY

I roll over and I'm immediately on edge when instead of rolling onto the cold and empty side of the bed I collide with a warm sleeping body.

I sit up quickly, alarmed at first but then it slowly comes back to me.

Nathan puts his arm around me. The tension flows out of me and I lean into him.

"Sorry," I whisper. "Did I wake you?"

"It's fine," he says, rolling out of bed. "I have to get up and go to work soon."

My heart sinks. I want to tell him to stay here with me, but I don't. I've been needy enough already. The last thing I want is to drive him away. "What time is it?" I've just realised it's still dark outside.

"Just after six."

My eyes widen. No wonder he's always been so eager to meet early in the day. I've bitched to him about my job, but I don't know a whole lot about his. "Do you always start this early?"

He nods. "Got to. I'd get the sack if I wasn't on site by seven at the latest."

"Wow."

"Don't let that scare you. Feel free to have a lie-in. I'll

leave the spare key on the table and I'll make coffee if I have time."

"There's no need, I—"

He kisses me. "Of course there's a need after the week you've had. Right, I'm jumping in the shower."

As soon as the door closes behind him, I'm hit by a wall of absolute despair. I try to cocoon myself in bed, but it's no comfort.

Josephine Kent.

Joy Cartwright.

Dad.

What the hell happened?

I think about getting up and going to confront Dad, but that resolve lasts as long as it takes to remember the conversation I overheard between him and Steph last night.

They think *I* have issues?

That's rich coming from the man who's been lying to me my whole life and the woman who pretended to be my friend so she could get her claws into his company.

That's the part I don't get. Why bother? She could have told me who she was or else avoided me. What did she gain from making friends with me? It's not like I hold any sway with Dad.

The door flies open. Nathan comes in with a plate in one hand and a mug in the other. "Breakfast in bed. It's not much."

I smile as I take the plate from him. It's toast smeared with butter and jam. "Thank you."

"I'll leave your coffee here. You have a nice lie-in and I'll see you later on."

"Thanks, but I think I'm going to get up and get to work early," I say, sitting up.

"Whatever you like. Give me a call if you want me to pick up anything on the way home or if you want a lift from work."

I smile, feeling a little awkward. "Thanks, Nathan. I'll be out of your hair soon, I promise."

He leaves and a few moments later I hear the door closing behind him. I'm on my own again, but I feel safer now. No-one knows I'm here.

———

I open my eyes and yawn so hard it makes my eyes water and almost causes my jaw to lock. My head is fuzzy and disoriented and there's a terrible headache building at the base of my skull.

I smack my lips. There's a terrible taste in my mouth too. I look around, half in a daze until I realise how bright it's gotten. I gasp and feel around on the bedside table for my phone. There's no sign of it. I cup my hand around the bottom of the mug and frown. It's cold even though it's still half full. How long have I been asleep?

I jump out of bed and the pain in my head intensifies. I'm suddenly conscious of being naked, so despite the urgency of finding my phone I scramble around retrieving my clothes from around the room. There's not much to see in here—there are minimal furnishings and decorations, but it's not tidy like Dad's place. It's an old house but it's been renovated recently and there's no trace of mould. The room is toasty and warm.

I shake my head. Now is not the time to snoop around Nathan's place—not when I suspect I've slept far later than I should have.

When I open the door to the living room, I realise why I woke when I did. Nathan's sitting at the kitchen table eating a sandwich.

"Ellie," he gasps. "You frightened the life out of me."

"Sorry. Any idea what time it is?"

He glances at his watch. "Just after eleven."

"Shit!" I cry. "Shit! I overslept."

"Oh no," he says, putting down his sandwich. "I just thought you'd forgotten your key and phone."

"My phone—where is it?"

"Charging in the kitchen," he says. "Where I left it. Are

you sure you're alright?"

"No," I hiss, shaking my head. "My manager has already bollocked me out of it once this week about timekeeping and now I'm going to show up late and," I bend my head and sniff my top, "wearing yesterday's clothes that probably smell like a brewery, as he'd put it."

Nathan runs a hand through his hair. "Okay, calm down. You made a mistake. You were up earlier than usual and you dozed off."

"I know, but you don't understand—"

"I could talk to him! Explain—"

"What good would that do? You don't even know him." I turn and pace back to the bedroom. "No, I've got to get showered and get in to work straight away. I don't even have time for a shower." I realise then that I don't even have a toothbrush.

"I'll give you a lift."

I start to say he doesn't need to, but he does need to or else it'll be after half past by the time I get in. I don't say anything.

"I'm heading back to work anyway. It's a good thing I popped back for lunch."

The only good thing I can think of is that I'm now well and truly distracted from all the other stuff going on in my life, but is this really what I wanted? I feel on the verge of a panic attack: now, more than ever, I can't afford to lose this job.

I hurry to the bathroom and spray deodorant under my arms. It's that awful supermarket stuff teenage boys spray liberally all over themselves and I retch when the smell reaches my nose, but it'll have to do. I've got to get in there as soon as I can.

"Are you ready?" I say when I return to the kitchen and unplug my phone. It's switched off—it must have died last night, but that doesn't matter. There's no time for me to check messages anyway. "I can walk if you'll be a while."

He stands up. "No, I'm ready. And don't say that. After

what you've told me, it's not safe for you to wander around on your own. Let me protect you."

I turn away so he doesn't see the way I recoil a little when I hear this. He's only trying to help and it's ever so sweet of him, but it annoys me that I need protecting. Why can't Mikey just leave me alone?

———

As soon as we're in the car and all of Nathan's attention is taken up with driving, my thoughts begin to swirl around again. I bury my head in my hands. It's all too much—I just can't understand it. Even though I've had plenty of sleep, it's just too much to get my head around. I thought it was yesterday's exhaustion that stopped me from being able to process it, but it wasn't.

Why wouldn't Dad tell me we used to have different names? And why did he change them?

And her cause of death… If Josephine Kent was my mother, who poisoned her? Was it Dad? Did he change my name and go on the run so he wouldn't be caught?

"Penny for them," Nathan mutters.

I shake my head. "You seriously don't want to know."

All too soon we pull up outside my office. I kiss Nathan and get out of the car. I stop on the pavement and take a moment to compose myself before going in. It's twenty past eleven. I'm almost an hour and a half late—which wouldn't usually be the worst thing ever, but this week it is. Jason will think I'm testing him, and I'm not.

There's a knocking sound behind me. I spin around to see Nathan knocking on his window. "Are you okay?" he mouths.

I nod and force a smile. Of course I'm not bloody okay—everything's falling apart.

I walk in the door and straight to the lift, relieved there's no-one else waiting. I couldn't face small talk right now—I don't have the space in my head for it.

CHAPTER 25
ELLIE

"Where the hell have you been?" Jason snaps.

I shake my head, trying to get rid of the dull fuzzy feeling. This is serious—why do I feel so numb? Jason called me into his office before I could even log in to the system. I haven't even thought of what I'm going to say to him yet.

"I'm sorry, Jason," I whisper. "I've..." I think about lying and telling him I was ill. Then I imagine his response. There's no way he'd believe me. "I overslept. It just happened."

He looks astonished. "It just happened, did it?" He makes an exaggerated sniffing sound and my heart sinks. Why did I bother with the deodorant? If anything, it's just highlighted the fact that I didn't stay at my own place last night. "Big night, was it?"

I take a deep breath. "No it wasn't."

"Do you seriously think I'm stupid?"

Panic rises in me. I've got to convince him that I'm not taking the piss, but how? If I tell him the truth he'll assume it's a lie. I would, if someone had told me a similar story a year ago. "No, I don't think you're stupid. I've just... there's some personal stuff going on right now that I'm struggling with." I close my eyes. No. I can't let it slip out.

"What personal stuff?"

I shake my head. "It doesn't matter."

He snorts. "Does it have anything to do with the bloke whose car I just saw you get out of?"

I curse myself for being so stupid as I look past him to the window. We're on the third floor: Jason has a perfect vantage point of the pavement outside the building from the floor-to-ceiling window beside his desk. Why didn't I think of that when I was giddily kissing Nathan before I got out of the car? And then just standing outside like a fool? What must he think of me?

I take a deep breath. "He's a friend who's being kind enough to help me out right now, that's all."

Jason shakes his head. "I don't have time for this. You turn up smelling like a locker room and plead personal problems —which are vague enough that I can't possibly catch you out in a lie. That's convenient, wouldn't you say?"

"No, I—" I close my eyes. This isn't the place to talk about what's been happening to me.

"You what?" he sighs. "Look, I don't want to do this, Ellie. I warned you earlier in the week. I've got to give you a written warning. It'll be on your desk by the end of the day."

"Please, no. Don't—"

"You've left me no other choice, Ellie."

"Please! I need this job. Things are messed up. I can't even go back to my flat. I…" I grit my teeth and stop talking. What am I going to tell him? That my ex is stalking me and my friend is secretly going out with my dad, who I think may have killed my mother? He'll think I'm losing my mind. "Fine," I say, turning to leave. "It won't happen again."

It won't—I'll make sure of it.

I'm shaking with dread and disbelief as I make my way back to my desk. This is completely my own fault—I know that. Even so, I wouldn't be in this position without the actions of a few people.

Mikey.

Steph.

Dad.

They're the ones who really deserve my anger. I've got to remember that.

CHAPTER 26
ELLIE
SATURDAY

jerk awake. This time there's no confusion about where I am but I'm troubled by the dreams that were swirling around in my mind just before I woke up.

I lie in bed staring into the darkness. At first I assume the faint light is coming from outside, but then I turn my head slightly and realise it's coming from my phone.

I don't want to move and wake Nathan even though I'm overcome with curiosity. I go back to staring at the ceiling, but adrenaline is pumping through my body now.

I grab my phone and tiptoe towards the door.

"I've got to get up for work anyway," he groans, his voice hoarse from sleep. He flicks on the light.

"I'll make us some coffee," I say.

I throw myself down on the couch after I've flicked on the kettle. This whole thing is so big I can't think clearly.

When I unlock my phone, I see that I have four missed calls from Steph. I have new messages in WhatsApp too—no doubt from her. I open the app and then pause.

Do I really want to read them? What can she possibly say to justify what she's done?

In the end, curiosity wins out. I haven't looked at my phone since I got back from work yesterday. I didn't want to —I was sick of them all. I'm surprised there's been nothing from Dad. Hasn't he seen his home office since I was in there on Thursday?

I shake my head. I don't care. He's not the wronged one here. If he hasn't called, it's because he feels guilty—like he should.

I sigh and open Steph's messages.

Hi Ellie, haven't heard from you in a while. Do you want to meet for a drink?

It was sent at half six. Did she not have plans with my dad last night, I wonder bitterly.

I'm leaving work now.

Sent at seven.

Helloooooo?!?

Sent at eight. I grimace when I see that. She's not in a position to give me shit after what she's done. Why does it matter to her if she has me onside—she's got what she wanted.

The kettle clicks off and I get up. I've got to stop thinking about Steph and Dad. When I think about it, it's not that unusual, is it? It's greed and stupidity, that's all. He met her, he was flattered by the attention and she convinced him to sign the company over to her.

Before I realise what I'm doing, I've squeezed the cup in my hand so hard that the handle comes clean off and the body goes smashing to the floor.

"What's happened?" Nathan comes barrelling into the room.

Despite my anger, I can't help but smile at the protectiveness and aggression in his voice. It feels good to have him on my side.

"Sorry," I say. "I broke your cup. I'll get you a new one."

"Hmmm." He takes the broken china from me. "I don't

know. It was Mum's."

I gasp as the horror of what I've done hits me. "Oh Nathan, I'm so sorry." I shake my head. "I had no idea."

"You wouldn't, would you? I'd not said anything."

I turn away, ashamed of myself for breaking something so important to him—I was indulging my anger, that's all it was.

"Oh Ellie, come here. It's fine, honestly. I have other ones. Look."

But I barely hear him. It's not the bloody cup I'm crying for but his mum and my mum and him and me.

He squeezes me into a hug and I'm dimly aware of the strength of him. Everything else is a fug of such deep sadness I don't know where one part starts and one part ends.

"Why won't he just leave me alone?" I gasp, struggling to get the words out between huge racking sobs. "I don't have the headspace to do my job, let alone figure out what happened to my mother." I groan. "Oh God Nathan, I'm so sorry. I broke your mum's cup and here I am sobbing about my mum."

He pulls away. "For fuck's sake, Ellie, if you apologise for the cup one more time I'll start crying myself."

I look up to see him grinning and it has a strange effect on me: suddenly I can't stop laughing either. He leans over to grab some kitchen paper from the holder by the cooker and that makes me laugh even harder. I must look like such a mess, sobbing my heart out in this man's kitchen.

"I'm so—"

"You're not allowed to apologise anymore," he teases.

I snort.

"I'm serious." He pulls me into his arms again. "You know I'm messing with you. But look, I need to leave for work in a few minutes. Do you want me to call them and say I'm ill?"

I shake my head. I'd love for him to do that, but I've messed up my own career enough—I don't want to jeopardise his too. "No. Please don't do that for me."

"You sure?"

"One hundred percent."

"Okay." He looks thoughtful for a moment. "The least I can do is make you breakfast."

I smile. I'm not going to argue with that.

———

A shadow comes over Nathan's face as he's cracking eggs into the pan.

"What is it?" My heart starts to race. What if he's having second thoughts about getting involved with me?

He turns to me. His face is more serious than I've ever seen it. "I've been thinking, Ellie."

No, no, no, my heart screams.

"Look, don't take this the wrong way or anything…"

My pulse roars in my temples. This is it. I knew it was coming, didn't I? "What?"

He turns back to tend to the pan. "Are you sure you won't go to the police about your ex?"

"Eh?" Even though it's a topic I don't even want to get into, I can't hide my relief. He's not fed up of me—not yet, anyway.

"What's the harm in trying? You're so wound up. They can't just ignore you if he's a threat."

"They can and they will," I say, squeezing my eyes shut. "Don't you get it? Last time I went to them, I had broken bones and bruises all over my body."

He winces. "I'm just trying to help."

"I know," I whisper. "But I've tried. I told you that." I sigh. There's one thing I haven't really told him—the thing that's been eating away at my soul for the last year. I've got to tell him now. I need to get it off my chest because the guilt and shame are killing me. "They took the fact that I'd been drinking and couldn't really remember what had happened and they used it against me."

There.

As wretched as I feel, it's a relief to have finally said it to someone else out loud.

CHAPTER 27
ELLIE

stare at Nathan, waiting for the judgement to come. How can I forget something that's had such an impact on my life? I remember the hours leading up to the pub. The way I debated with myself whether or not I should just leave it. Going to the Builder's Arms was a statement: that was our place. I should have accepted that he was done with me; that the team was always going to be more important than me.

I was so frustrated with him. In my warped frame of mind, I thought I'd go in there and everything would be right again. Instead, I stood on the edge of the group, not really having anybody to talk to. That's probably why I got so hammered: I was knocking back the pints of cider mainly so I'd have something to do.

And that's it. That's my memory of the night my life changed forever. One minute I was drinking a pint of cider trying to edge my way into a conversation with some of the lads and the next I was waking up in hospital.

Nathan sighs and shakes his head. "It wasn't your fault, Ellie. Just because you were drunk, it doesn't mean he had the right to hurt you."

I grit my teeth. Logically I know that's true, but I've been living with the pain for almost a year. Everyone else seems to think it was my fault so I've accepted that too.

"I really think you should go to the police, Ellie. I'll come with you. For support."

I grimace. How can he even say that after what I've just told him? I tell myself to stay calm. There's no point in having a go at him. "Maybe later or tomorrow."

"Good." He kisses me. "I'd best get going."

"You're not going to eat?"

He shakes his head. "I'll grab something on the way." He jerks his head towards the toast and eggs he's prepared. "Enjoy."

———

As soon as I've eaten, I become more restless than I've ever been—and that's saying something. I just want to do something instead of being cooped up in here, but what? It's not even been two days since Nathan rescued me from that man.

Ugh.

I cringe as I look down and catch sight of yesterday's clothes. No, they're not even yesterday's, they're from the day before.

I've never felt so grubby. I've been in some low places in my life, but I've never felt this bad. Thank goodness for Nathan. I barely know him and he has so much patience for my craziness—I still can't believe it.

The TV isn't distracting me, not when I feel so unclean. I decide to have a shower and put my things in the wash. I'll borrow some of Nathan's clothes until my own things are dry —I'm sure he won't mind.

I get up and return to the bedroom. I pull open the wardrobe and stare into it, looking for anything that'll fit me. T-shirts aren't the problem—he has lots of those. And boxers. It's trousers I'll struggle to find. In the end, I grab two pairs of gym shorts, unfold them and choose the longest one with drawstrings. It's not like I'm planning on going out so what does it matter what I'm wearing.

I'm going to have to ask Nathan to come back to the flat

with me before the weekend is over. I need more than one outfit for next week.

I check my phone. There's nothing from Dad or Steph. I still haven't replied to her messages from last night and I'm not sure I will either. Isn't it easier if I let them realise that I know what's going on? Surely that's better than keeping up the pretence that everything is fine between us.

When I eventually find a fresh towel, I wrap it around myself and throw my clothes in the washing machine. I can't go on like this. This isn't my home. I don't know where anything is. I hate rummaging around his house to find things.

I double-check the front door is locked before I get in the shower. Thankfully the hot water is on so I don't have to faff around trying to figure out how it works.

I step underneath the torrent and my exhausted body finally starts to relax. That feeling lasts until I start to lather my legs and realise they're like two hairy forests.

I cringe. What must Nathan think of me? I look around but instantly dismiss the idea of using his razor. That's just too nasty. I'll pop out to the shops and buy one later.

I brighten at that thought. Nathan won't be back for hours —I can go to the shops and get some essentials like shampoo and shower gel that doesn't smell the same as Nathan's teenage boy body spray.

———

I end up leaving the house sooner than I'd planned. I sat down in front of the TV after I showered, but Saturday daytime TV just doesn't appeal to me today. I don't want to watch anything. I have enough drama going on in my own life. The moment I sit still I start to get back into the loop of thoughts that have been plaguing me lately: Mum, Dad, Steph, Mikey. I can't bear to think about it anymore.

I jump to my feet and go to Nathan's bedroom. I didn't think I'd seen a full-length mirror in there and I don't find one now. I glance down at myself. I must look ridiculous in his t-shirt and shorts, but my coat is long enough to almost hide the shorts and my hideously hairy legs. It's not as if I have to go very far either: there's a shop a few streets over. With any luck, I can get there and back without anyone I know seeing me.

I grab my bag and shove on my coat.

I lock the door carefully with the key Nathan gave me. It's so freeing to walk up the path and into the open without having to be afraid there's someone watching me, but I warn myself not to relax too much: this is a small town. Mikey could easily track me down and I've got to remember that.

I clench my fists. He's obviously keeping tabs on me if he reappeared as soon as I started seeing Nathan. Why? What's his problem? Why hasn't he moved on by now?

I start to walk faster. I don't want to think about him now —not when I'm out alone. The shop is further away than I thought and my shoes are uncomfortable with no socks or tights on. I feel the telltale chafe of blisters before I'm even halfway there.

I try to keep up my pace, but I've got to slow down: my feet are too sore.

When I finally reach the shop, I'm in a horrible mood, wondering whether it would just have been better to go back to my flat.

I put that thought out of my mind. Sore feet are so much better than... I shudder as I think of what could have happened if I hadn't managed to get away on Thursday night.

I hurry through the shop, rattled now and eager to get back to Nathan's. I grab a pack of razors and a bottle of shower gel. I get some crisps and a bottle of wine. I quickly grab another—I don't care if it's unhealthy, I want anything that's going to make me feel slightly better.

As I'm dumping everything onto the counter, I feel a hand on my shoulder and it almost makes me jump out of my skin. I try to jerk away, but I can't without knocking over everything that's halfway between my arms and the counter. It's ridiculous—some strange sense of politeness kicks in harder than any safety instinct and by the time I manage to react appropriately, his grip on my arm is too strong.

I turn. It's a tall man dressed in black clothes and I just know in my heart that it's the same man who's been following me. His face isn't covered this time but I don't recognise him—not that that means anything. The rugby club has enough goons hanging around who'd do anything for Mikey.

"I need to talk to you."

I shake my head and snap my head around to the man behind the counter. "Please help me."

I stumble backwards and realise the counter is too long for him to get out here and help me in time. I open my mouth to scream, but nothing comes out—it's the sound of a cornered animal when it knows it's well and truly screwed.

Why hasn't he covered his face? Doesn't he care that I'll be able to identify him?

The man pulls me closer and I flail around desperately for a weapon, but all I can grab is a can of tomatoes. It's no use—I swing it, but my angle is all off. He grabs it out of my hand before I can hit him and his grip on my other arm doesn't waver.

"Enough," he snarls.

I glance at the guy behind the counter, who's as rigid with fear as I must be. Do something, I try to tell him, but what?

Is this man armed?

Is he going to kill me?

I turn and look at him, screwing up my face in terror. "Please," I whisper. "Please don't hurt me."

I hear the sound of sirens in the distance and I look at the shopkeeper. I know from the way he blinks that he's set off a silent alarm and I'm almost giddy with relief.

Until I look back at my attacker.

Does he fear the police? Does he even hear the sirens?

My relief evaporates. He's watching me strangely and I'm terrified of what he's going to do.

"Listen to me," he hisses. "I'm your father."

I shake my head. "No."

"It's true."

"Why would you say that?"

"Because," he says, shaking me. "Because it's the truth!"

I stare at him, dumbfounded.

"I've called the police!" the shopkeeper cries and I cringe as I wonder what this man will do to him.

But he doesn't react in the way I would have thought. There's no aggression. Instead, his face crumples. "I just wanted to see Joy's little girl."

I shake my head. "No. You can't. It's not…" I stare into this stranger's eyes, desperately looking for something familiar. There's nothing.

"Your name is Kent. Did you know that? Look it up. He changed it when he took you away from me. Do you know how long it's taken for me to find you?" There's desperation in his eyes now and as mad as his story is, my gut says he's telling the truth.

"It was you. On Thursday. Why didn't you say then? Why did you let me think you were going to hurt me?"

He lets go of my shoulders and mutters an apology as he steps back towards the door. The sirens are getting closer.

"Call them off," I tell the shopkeeper.

He shakes his head. "I can't. It's tamperproof."

"Wait!" I say to the man who's been following me. "Please wait."

"I can't." His face falls. He glances back to the door as if to explain. No police.

"Wait," I say again, shaking my head. "Why? If he took me away, why are you the one who's afraid…" I stop. He's almost gone now. "What's your name?" I whisper, moving towards him now.

"Tony Kent." It's the last thing he says before he bolts.

CHAPTER 28
ELLIE

I try to follow him, but it's no use with blistered feet in these awful shoes. By the time I make it out of the shop, he's disappeared. With the web of side streets around here, I'll never be able to find him.

I sigh.

I got this so wrong.

The sirens are screeching now and it shakes me to my senses. How can I explain what's just happened to the police?

"Can I pay?"

The man nods his head, still as shaken as I am, I guess. "You'll wait for the police?"

I jerk my head. "I can't. I can't..."

"Go then," he says dismissively. "The number of bloody questions I'll get for a false alarm. You might as well take the lot without paying."

"Sorry," I say, leaving twenty quid I can't even afford on the counter out of guilt.

I hurry out of the shop—well, stumble is more accurate. The pain is my feet is unbearable now and I realise I should have bought some plasters. It's too late to turn back—the police will be there any moment.

I duck down the closest side street to stay out of sight. I'd love to take off my shoes but there's likely to be broken glass on the footpath so I leave them on and stumble on as best I can.

I half expect that man to be waiting for me when I turn down the next street, but he's not.

Nor is he outside Nathan's house when I finally turn onto his road.

Tony Kent, I think, reciting that name over and over in my mind.

Is it true?

How can it not be?

The only other explanation I can think of is Dad knows I've been in his office and he sent someone after me to tell me a load of lies—but why? I can't imagine him asking someone to pretend to be my father.

I look around before I let myself into the house, though I'm not as afraid as I was before.

My fear has been replaced by total confusion. Was that man telling me the truth? Is it possible that the man I've always thought was my father is a stranger? The mad thing is it sort of fits with what I found out on Thursday.

Twenty minutes after I left the shop, I'm rummaging in Nathan's kitchen cupboards looking for a wine glass. Finding none, I settle for a normal glass. It'll have to do and I don't much care. I'd drink the wine from the bottle if I needed to.

I pour a large glass of wine and pop an ice cube in on top to try and cool it. I wander back to the couch and sit down.

What does this mean? Is he actually my father?

I sigh.

I don't know what's true anymore.

I take a gulp of wine and let it sit in my mouth, relishing the way it makes the insides of my cheeks tingle. The events of the past week flash through my mind. I've been so tired and distracted it's a struggle. Everything seems hazy like it happened years ago, not days.

The man following me.

Someone breaking into my house.

My eyes widen. Was that him too? But why? Why would he do that?

No, that has Mikey written all over it.

I take another large gulp of wine.

But this guy Tony was following me.

The wine is going straight to my head, but I need it. Nothing makes sense anymore and I just want to switch off for a bit.

But it's no use.

Tears well up in my eyes. It's not from disappointment—it's something far more complicated than that.

All along, beneath my fear and anger, there was something else too. This great big sense of shame. Because even after everything—after Mikey put me in hospital and turned everyone I loved against me for daring to report him—I still loved him.

I sigh and rub my eyes with my coat sleeves. I can't bear to take it off even though it feels like it's confining me.

None of it makes any more sense than it did at the time. There was that awful chairman's dinner. That's when it began. I had a few too many drinks and got a bit lairy. Mikey was so dedicated to rugby that I suppose looking back on it I was a bit jealous. I had nothing. So I threw all that extra energy into nights out. Possibly a bad idea, but I can't do anything about that now.

I was just letting off steam. I assumed after a year or two, when he got picked up by one of the big clubs, we'd get married and have kids. His success was a sure thing—he had the earning power for both of us. And I'd had such a cold upbringing that I'd always craved a big family to spoil.

I close my eyes and take a deep breath. I've suppressed these memories for so long that it's painful to think about them now.

Mikey was transferred to a club in France only days after that night out where I made a fool of myself. I missed him like crazy, but I didn't think anything of it. I certainly didn't think it was an attempt by the club to get me out of his system.

He was away for a few months. The first inkling I had that something was wrong was when our friends casually mentioned meeting him for drinks at the weekend. Because he hadn't contacted me to say he was back. That's when Graham had someone start following me too. I knew it was Graham's doing, but it still rattled me. I reported it to the police but of course nothing ever happened. No proof, they said. Like he'd bloody walk in there and just confess to intimidation.

So when I finally worked up the courage to go to the Builder's Arms a few weeks after Mikey got back and he still hadn't been to see me or returned any of my calls, I was a ball of nerves from everything—the intimidation and the non-contact from Mikey.

I stifle a sob. I wish I could remember that night. What did I say to make him flip? I know I shouldn't blame myself, but I do. I can't help it. It was so out of character. One minute I was standing with him and the next I was in hospital.

My glass is empty now so I reach for the bottle to top it up. I stop myself. The washing machine has just beeped so I jump up to hang out my clothes. It's good to have something to do that's not sitting around dwelling on everything that's happened. I know in my heart that I shouldn't be drinking, but it's the only relief I can get—my GP prescribed sedatives but they're so strong that I can't function when I take them and I need to be able to work.

I turn on the TV, but instead of absorbing me it only seems to heighten my restlessness.

My phone buzzes and I pick it up, thinking it might be Nathan—he's due back soon.

I unlock my screen and feel a rush of dread when I see I've got a new text message from Dad. He never texts.

That's the only reason I open his message.

Ellie, are you coming for lunch tomorrow? We should talk.

I stare at his message in disbelief. *Now* he wants to talk?

What about? How you're not my real father?

My heart pounds as I wait for his reply. I realise I'm holding my breath; willing him to tell me that I'm talking nonsense. Even better yet—to call me and scold me for saying something like that.

We'll talk tomorrow.

I stare at his words in disbelief. That's all he can say? I can't believe he'd sit on the fence like that—does he have no consideration at all for how I feel? Is he not even curious about how I found out?

I sigh.

Sorry. Can't make it.

I think about making a snide comment about his gold-digging bitch girlfriend, but I decide against it. If he accused me of being childish right now I don't know how I'd react.

I throw my phone onto the chair and it lands face down.

Good.

There's nobody I want to speak to or message right now.

The door opens and my heart leaps. I instinctively slam my glass down on the table, but use a lot more force than I intended to and it makes a loud bang.

"You're back!"

"Wow," he says, dropping some bags on the kitchen table. "That's a nice welcome."

"What's in the bags?"

"I picked up some food and wine. I thought we could have a lazy afternoon and watch movies." He stops. "What the hell are you wearing?"

I look down, feeling awkward all of a sudden. "I raided

your wardrobe. I hope you don't mind—I took the first things I found."

"That's fine," he says. "I should have offered."

I sigh happily. Despite my earlier frustration at not being able to find stuff, I'm starting to relax here.

He bends over to kiss me. "How was your day? I hope you've not been bored."

I can't help but laugh. I was bored earlier—that was before I ventured out to the shops.

"What's so funny?"

"Just that question." I wrap my arms around him. "I popped out to the shops."

His demeanour changes instantly. "You did what?"

"Relax," I whisper. "You'll never guess. The man who was following me appeared in the shop. I thought he was trying to hurt me, but he told me he was my father."

"And you believed him?"

I shrug, feeling foolish. "I didn't know what to believe until I got a text off Dad—you know, the man I thought was my dad. He wanted to know if I was coming for lunch so I tested him. I asked if it was so we could talk about how he's not my dad."

Nathan's eyes are as wide as saucers. "And he admitted it?"

"He didn't deny it." I sit back into the couch and stare straight ahead. I still can't really believe it. I just feel numb.

"Forget him," Nathan says passionately. "He obviously doesn't give a shit about you."

It's painful to hear the truth said out loud like that, but he's right. And I can't deny that the way he said it made my heart stir. I was wary of Nathan at first after how he tried to end things, but he cares about me and it feels good to know at least someone has my back.

"Thanks," I whisper. "I don't know what I'd do without you."

I cringe when I hear myself say that—talk about over-keen. But Nathan doesn't shrink away or cringe. He just smiles as he gets up to find plates for our food.

"Come on. You'll feel better after you eat. Oh and Ellie?"

"What?"

"Don't take this the wrong way, but those shorts look mental on you."

I snort.

"Did you seriously go out to the shops like that?"

"Afraid so."

"I think I have some old jeans that might fit you. I'll have a look."

I start to relax. Things are bad but they're not the worst. I have this thing with Nathan that's going from strength to strength.

"Will you put the food and drinks out?" Nathan calls from his bedroom. "I'm absolutely famished."

I get up, smiling to myself. He's always bloody famished.

CHAPTER 29
JOY
TWENTY-ONE YEARS AGO

"Where are you going?"

I spin around. I've been so caught up in getting ready that I forgot to even mention to him that I need him to babysit. "Just out for a bit. Can you mind Ellie?"

"You're joking, right?"

"No," I say breezily, checking my lipstick in the mirror. "Why would I joke?"

There's a loud bang right beside me. My heart races so hard it makes me lightheaded. I turn around, openmouthed. John is not a violent man but he's just punched the mirror and shattered it inches from my face.

"John, Jesus! What the hell?"

I expect him to be embarrassed; to tell me he's sorry over and over and to ask if I'm okay. I look around l in shock: there's glass all over the floor, but none of it hit me, thank goodness.

John says nothing. He just stares at me with a look I've never seen before. Then, to make things worse, the baby starts to cry.

"Oh for fuck's sake," I mutter, stomping off towards her room.

"Wait," John snaps. "Wait. I need to talk to you."

"That's no reason to go shattering mirrors in my face. I need to settle her."

"Don't worry about her. I'll do it." He closes the gap between us and grabs my arms. I pull away from him, hating him more in this moment than I ever have done. Judgemental bastard. It's easy for him to look down on me—he always had it easy.

"Get off me. You could have killed me."

"So?" His face is deadly serious. "It looks like you're dead set on doing that yourself so what do you care?"

"This again? I don't have time for this. I can't handle you being so protective all the time. You're not my keeper." I turn away and walk towards her bedroom. I'm already late as it is and this isn't helping. "I'm sick of this, John. She's always crying. You don't see it when you're at work. I'm stuck with her and her tantrums. It drives me crazy."

"She's a little girl. How can you say that?"

"There's something wrong with her. I'm sure of it."

His face falls. "Listen to yourself."

"It's the truth. You don't see it. I just need… I need some time to myself for once."

"She needs you."

I clench my fists. I wasn't expecting that. I knew they were demanding when they were little, but she's not a baby anymore. She can walk but she still goes apeshit whenever I leave her alone for a minute and she's still in nappies. It feels like this will never end. "There's something wrong with her. I can't handle this."

"Yes, there's something wrong with her. Her mother isn't doing what she's supposed to be doing. Can't you think of somebody but yourself for once? She's a little girl."

"She's a monster!"

"Joy!"

"What?" I snap, grinding my teeth so hard I wouldn't be surprised if they started to crumble. I feel like a caged animal, trapped here at the mercy of his moods. He doesn't get it; he just doesn't. "I just want to have a little fun. Is that too much to ask? A night out with the girls, that's all."

He shakes his head. His expression's full of disappointment. It's a look my dad used to give me when I was a kid and it turns my stomach that John thinks he can control me like I'm a little girl. I'm not a child. "Do you think I'm a fool?"

His voice is so cold that I don't turn around. I'm not telling him the whole truth, but there's no way I'm going to admit that. I just need some time to myself, that's all. What's so wrong with that? I fiddle with my sleeves. I hate this. I hate being judged. I'm also terrified of what he'll do.

"You've got to try harder, Joy. You promised you would."

"I know," I say, sniffing into my sleeve. I'm an emotional wreck these days and he's the one to blame. I look like shit too. Things have changed. I miss my old life. It's not the same now.

"You've been seeing him again, haven't you?"

"Who?"

His eyes narrow. "You know who. Tony."

My blood runs cold. How does he know? "He's my husband, John."

"He has a funny way of showing it."

"Things are different now."

John stares at me for a long time. I think he's going to start lecturing me again, but he doesn't. "Why don't you take off your coat and I'll order us a takeaway. Eh? How does that sound?"

I'm about to turn around and tell him where to shove his takeaway when an idea starts to form in my mind. Recently he's become very careful about hiding his money from me. It's just another way of controlling me and making sure I can't do anything he doesn't know about. I'd search his office, but he always keeps it locked during the day. He's so regimented that way. Now, though… this isn't like him. He's not the type of bloke to get takeaway dinners every week. He's just come downstairs from his office. There's a good chance he's not locked the door.

Seizing my chance—maybe the only chance I'll ever get—I put on the performance of a lifetime. I smile and shrug off my coat.

"Mammmmmma," the child screams, and I do my best not to wince. Instead I giggle. "That sounds great, John. You know what, I'm so tired. You're right. If you get food I'll go settle her and then we can relax."

I want to shoo him out the door but I turn away and go to the baby's room instead. He's too clever: if I show too much enthusiasm he'll know I'm up to something and he'll lock that damn door. I can't let him do that. He's got a stash of cash somewhere in this house and I've searched everywhere else. It's got to be in his office.

It's got to be.

I need that money. It's the only hope I've got. I don't need much. Just enough to get away from here and make a new life for myself.

The child cries again and it's all I can do not to scream back.

"Okay, I'll pop out now. What do you want?"

I think about it for a moment. "We haven't had Chinese in a while. I'd love some sweet and sour chicken."

I will him to agree with me. The Chinese takeaway is the furthest away from here and there's never parking outside it. If he goes there he'll walk. That'll give me time.

"Great," he says. He walks out the door.

I turn and stare after him. It's a strange feeling to know that this might be the last time I ever see him.

CHAPTER 30
ELLIE
SUNDAY

I open my eyes and immediately regret it. I close them again but it's too late. The pounding in my head makes it feel as though my whole body is pulsating. As soon as I swallow I realise it's worse than I first thought. I sit up and blink. I'm in Nathan's living room. That's all I have time to register before I have to dash to the bathroom. I sink to my knees in front of the toilet just in time.

Oh God.

I was so weirded out by my encounter with that man in the shop that any sense of moderation went out the window last night. I think at one point, I insisted on going out for more wine. An uncontrollable sense of self-loathing washes over me at the thought that I allowed myself to get into this state.

There's a knock at the door. "Are you okay in there?"

I can only grunt as my stomach churns again and I retch. All that comes out is bile. It's so bitter it makes me wince.

"Do you want a glass of water?"

I lean back so I'm sitting on my feet with my eyes closed. I breathe as shallowly as I can and will the panic to pass. Why did I drink so much? My memory of last night is hazy too, which I can't stand. I hate the loss of control that comes from not being able to remember the whole night.

"No thanks," I murmur, looking around. I want nothing more than to rest my head on the cold floor tiles, but they're grubby looking. I've got the same terrible headache as a few days ago—the kind that feels like it'll never go away.

I shake my head. This is pathetic. I get to my feet on shaky legs, ignoring the swell of nausea it causes—not to mention the pounding in my head. I can get through this—I'll happily put up with it if I can just get rid of the panicky feeling that something terrible is going to happen.

I open the door. Nathan is leaning against the wall opposite, bleary-eyed and pale. "What have we done to ourselves?" he mutters.

I scan his face for any trace of judgement, but there's none. Just exhaustion—the same as me. I can remember us deciding to watch the Godfather trilogy, but at that stage it was still bright outside.

"What time did we go to bed?"

He shrugs and immediately winces, like even that slight movement is too much for him. "I went around seven. I was pissed."

I flush. "Why didn't you wake me? I'm stiff all over from sleeping on the couch."

"Wake you?" He laughs. "You weren't asleep. I said I was tired but you were all on for staying up and getting more wine."

The hairs on my arms stand on end and panic washes over me again. I hate to be reminded of my seemingly limitless capacity for alcohol once I get started.

Nathan pulls me into a hug. "Stop giving yourself a hard time. You've been through a lot. You were just blowing off steam." He pulls away. "Jesus, Ellie, what did you do when I went to bed?"

I follow his gaze and groan. The panic was starting to ease, but it's back now and worse than ever. There's mud smeared all over one side of my jeans, mainly on my right calf. I shake my head. "I don't know... You said I was going out to get more wine. I..." I shake my head, so overcome with anxiety and shame that I can't talk. "I'm going to go lie on the couch."

I need to talk some sense into myself. I can't keep doing this. It might feel good at the time to lose myself completely, but that's purely short term. If my liver doesn't pack in first, the guilt and shame will kill me.

"I'll make breakfast," Nathan says.

I say nothing. I'm too wrapped up in trying to figure out what happened last night.

I open my eyes as Nathan puts two plates on the coffee table. My stomach turns at the sight of the greasy fry-up, even though it's probably exactly what my body needs right now.

I've got to eat something, though—if only to avoid hurting Nathan's feelings after he's gone to the bother of cooking for me. I force down a sausage and a few bites of toast.

"Is that all you're having?" he asks, when I put my plate down.

"I need a shower," I mutter. "I'll have a bit more after."

He turns his attention back to his phone and I get up. I've got to get out of these clothes. It's bothering me that I can't remember how the jeans I'm wearing got all muddy. I find the same towel as I used yesterday and shut myself into the bathroom.

How many times have I stood in the shower and vowed to myself that I'll never drink again and that I'll turn my life around?

I twist the tap and step into the shower, gasping as the hot water hits my skin.

This time will be different. This time I *will* change. I'll start going to the gym several times a week instead of only making it to the occasional yoga class. I'll start eating better. My stomach somersaults. I can start today: there's no reason for me to stay away from my flat now.

I stay in the shower for far longer than I need to and I'm

finally starting to feel better when I step out. Finding that my trousers haven't fully dried yet only dampens my mood slightly—it feels good to be back in my own clothes again, even if they are work clothes.

I scoop up the clothes I borrowed from Nathan and go through to the kitchen. He's still sitting in the same position when I pass the living room. I chuck the pile onto the ground so I can put a laundry tablet in first. I'm surprised he uses the expensive liquid ones, but it doesn't matter: even with home comforts like this, I'm still looking forward to being back in my own space.

As I pick up the jeans, I notice for the first time just how much mud there is. This wasn't a splash—it's literally caked on.

I cringe, hard. What was I doing? I don't have any bruises or cuts: I'd have felt them in the shower.

I sigh and try to accept the fact that I'll probably never know—and it likely doesn't matter. The important thing is I've made a decision and I'm going to change my behaviour.

I select the hottest, most heavy-duty cycle and hope the mud comes out. Otherwise I'll have to buy Nathan a new pair of jeans.

But that's okay, I tell myself. I'll deal with that.

"Do you think I need to have a relationship with that man?" I ask Nathan as I return to the couch and sit down beside him. "You know, if it turns out he really is my father?" I frown. "That reminds me, have you seen my phone?" I look around. There's no sign of it anywhere. The last place I remember seeing it was on the arm of the chair, but that was yesterday. Where did I put it?

Nathan puts his arm around me. "Just relax, would you? If you ask me I think you're doing the right thing not going to your dad's today. And you're probably better off not looking at your phone too."

I turn and smile at him. He's right, I realise. "Thanks, smarty. And what about the other guy?"

He shrugs. "Today is not the day you should be making

decisions like that. Today's a day for leftover takeaway and relaxing. You can decide all that tomorrow. One more day won't make a difference."

I smile and cuddle into him.

"Where's the remote?"

"I don't know," I say into his chest.

He moves and I swear under my breath because I don't know how I'm going to get as comfy again as I was just now.

"I'll make some tea," I mutter. I get up and go into the kitchen.

"Jesus," Nathan mutters.

I sit the kettle back into its housing. "What?"

"Look at this. A woman killed."

"Oh," I say, only half paying attention. "What happened?"

He turns back to me. "Ellie. It was right here in town. Look."

I hurry over and lean against the back of the couch.

A local reporter takes up most of the screen. It looks like she's really having to shout to be heard and she's losing a battle trying to control her hair in the wind. I stare at the words at the bottom of the screen.

Breaking: woman's body found. police suspect foul play.

"Murder?" I gasp.

"Yeah. What did you think I meant?"

"I don't know," I say, hurrying back around and sitting beside him. "That someone had been killed, you know. An accident or something. Who is it?"

"They've not said."

I sigh. "Poor woman. Turn it up will you?"

He turns up the volume. It takes me a few seconds to tune into the frantic voices of the reporter on the scene and whoever is speaking to her from the studio. The reporter takes up ninety percent of the screen. The camera moves a bit to capture two police officers in white overalls as they walk past in the background. Police tape flaps in the breeze behind her.

"As you can see behind me," the reporter is saying. "The

forensic team are making their way into the building now. The police have so far refused to release a name. All we know is the body of a woman was found this morning in suspicious circumstances." She stands aside and the camera zooms out a bit. "As you can see behind me," she says as more people in white suits walk towards the door of a modern building. "More forensic officers have just arrived here at the Rose Court complex."

"Fuck," I hiss as I realise exactly where she is. "That's Steph's building."

"It's a big complex," Nathan says. "It's probably someone else."

"It's not." I shake my head, still unable to fully take it in. "I recognise the door to her building. It's blue, see? They're all different colours." I shiver as I think about it properly. There are only eight apartments in each of the low-slung blocks. "Jesus, Nathan, what if it's her?"

"Relax. The chances of it being her are tiny."

"No, they're not!" I snap. "I can't remember who she said lives in all the apartments in her building, but I know two of them are rented by single male doctors. Out of eight apartments, there's a one in six chance it's her, Nathan, that's big."

He rolls his eyes. "It could be a girlfriend of one of the doctors. It could be anyone. Come on, Ellie, what does it matter even if it is her? You've only known her a few months and you've been cursing her name ever since you found out she's involved with your dad."

I stare at him in disbelief. "How can you say something like that?"

He pats my knee. "Please, Ellie, I didn't mean it in a bad way. I just don't want you to freak out when there's no need. If it was her, someone would have called you."

I stare at him and I see the realisation dawn on him at the same moment it hits me: I haven't checked my phone today. I jump off the couch and look around the room. Where the hell did I leave it?

"Can you please call me?"

He looks like he's about to object but he says nothing and takes out his phone. I hold my breath, waiting to hear a faint buzz—I always have it set to vibrate.

But there's nothing.

"It must be dead," he says, looking worried now.

I pull the cushions off the couch, getting more and more desperate by the second. I hiss out the breath I've been holding. It's there, hidden under one of the big cushions. I pull it out and press the button at the side that activates the screen.

Nothing happens.

I hurry over to the kitchen and shove it into Nathan's charger. I turn it on and wait—every second feels like an hour. I need to know. I need to know if it's her.

Finally, after what feels like forever but can only have been twenty seconds or so, my phone loads up fully. I stare at the home screen, waiting for dozens of missed calls to register.

But they don't. There are no messages either.

"That's weird."

"See?" he says. "Nothing."

I stay standing over my phone. Even though Nathan thinks I'm freaking out about nothing, I can't relax.

An elderly woman appears on the screen and my heart sinks. I recognise her from visiting Steph. She lives downstairs and is always complaining about Steph thumping around on her ceiling in heels.

"Fuck," I mutter as it becomes real for the first time.

The old woman—I can't remember her name, and she's only identified on-screen as *victim's neighbour*—clutches a tissue in one hand, which she dabs her eyes with every few seconds.

"She was such a nice girl," she sobs. "She'd always say hello."

"And you heard noises upstairs last night?"

"Oh yes," the woman says. "It was early on in the night and I hadn't taken out my hearing aid. It was an awful racket." Her face screws up. "I only wish I'd thought to call the police or noise control now. It might have saved her."

The camera switches onto the reporter and I stand there staring at the screen, in absolute shock.

"It's probably not—"

"It's her," I snap. "That's her neighbour."

My pulse gets louder and louder—it's like a constant buzz now.

What the hell is going on?

Yesterday I thought everything was fine—messed up, but fine. The man following me was my real father, not some thug Mikey had hired. Totally bizarre, but not exactly a dangerous situation. Steph and Dad? Well, I was pissed off at them, of course I was. But this?

Steph is dead.

I start to hyperventilate.

"You don't know it's her," Nathan says, getting up and coming over to me.

"I do," I hiss. "There are only eight apartments and that woman talked about noise upstairs. She's Steph's downstairs neighbour, for fuck's sake, Nathan, it's her."

"Calm down. Please."

"I'm sorry," I say, gasping for breath. "But someone's murdered my friend. How the hell am I supposed to calm down?"

"Your friend?" he says dismissively. "I've only ever heard you slag her off." He pauses. "Oh, Ellie, I'm sorry."

I stare up at him. I saw the look that flashed across his face a moment ago. He camouflaged it well, but it was there. I know what he was thinking.

My heart starts to pound.

He's right.

Only yesterday I was cursing her.

Now she's dead.

And I can't remember what I did last night.

CHAPTER 31
ELLIE

t's like I'm in a terrible trance. I stare at the TV even though the words across the bottom don't change.

Steph.

It can't be. It just can't.

Nathan has retreated into himself and maybe I'm being selfish, but I'm a little disappointed in him. It's like he's annoyed at me for being upset about her death just because I've been complaining about her for the past few days. But that's only a few days. We were friends.

We were.

And we'd probably have gotten over our differences if this… this…

My stomach plummets and fresh tears come to my eyes as I remember how angry I was at her and Dad.

"You still don't know it's her, Ellie."

I close my eyes and take a deep breath. I realise that in all my panic I didn't think to call Steph.

I scroll down and find her name, but something makes me hold off on making the call.

I open WhatsApp.

Steph's name is top of the list of my conversations. That's not a surprise, but what does send a jolt of fear through me is the preview text below her name with two blue ticks beside it.

Let me in

My blood runs cold.

The fact that there are ticks beside it means that I sent it, but I have no memory of texting her that. The last messages I remember were from her trying to get me to go for a drink on Friday night.

I suck in a breath and tap the conversation.

I have to scroll a long way back up to get to the messages from Friday night. In my impatience to get them, I end up going back too far; back to when things between us were normal. But there's no time to get nostalgic.

I scroll forward slower, trying to read the dates but not the messages. My heart is pounding now and my headache is back, preventing me from being able to think clearly. This is bad. This is really bad. This isn't hungover paranoia. It's real.

Finally I get to the right place. Steph's message saying **Helloooooo?!?**. By now my breathing is ragged, like I've just been running as fast as I can. It's like I've woken up in a bad dream except it's not a dream and by drinking so much last night I've effectively handicapped myself from being able to deal with it properly.

Fuck.

I realise now that my vow to stop drinking might have come too late.

Focus, Ellie.

I take a few deep breaths.

"Are you alright?" Nathan asks.

I ignore him and sit down at the table. I've got to—my vision is starting to blur at the edges.

The next message is from Steph at around five last night.

Do you want to meet up later?

And another just after six.

What's going on? Why are you ignoring me? I can see you've read my messages.

My heart pounds and a cold sweat breaks out on my skin. I have no memory of reading that, but I must have. I cringe when I see my reply. The timestamp is only a few minutes later and my words radiate bitterness.

U know what's going on. Do u think im stupid?

I can't remember sending that but it resonates with me all the same. I may have been drunk, but my reaction was in line with how I've been feeling.

There are three missed calls in the app from Steph then, all within the space of a few minutes.

Ellie, I'm really confused. Can you please just call me?

I shake my head, feeling annoyed all over again before the sinking feeling hits and I remember that in the grand scheme of things, none of this matters. I'd certainly never have wished harm on her.

She tried to call me twice more.

Jesus, Ellie. Please just answer the phone.

And then a short time later:

Last chance. I don't need this in my life.

I grit my teeth. Just reading that makes my blood boil and I know if it pisses me off now it must have really wound me up yesterday if I was so drunk I blacked out.

U dn't need this n ur life? Are u fuckin jokin?

I wince. I don't normally use textspeak and there's a stark

difference between my first message and the one I've just read. I was obviously getting very drunk very quickly. I scroll down quickly, filling with dread at what's to come. Because I know what the last message in the chain says. My mind is racing as I try to think of reasons I might have said those words that don't involve me being right outside the door of a girl who was murdered last night.

There's another missed call and then:

You're pissed, aren't you? I should have known.

I shake my head. Why would she say that? Why would she goad me like that if she was trying to make peace? But then I don't know that. Was she trying to make peace? Or was it about something else?

Fuck off

Nice. That's really clever. You're not making this easy.

I grimace. How can she have been so self-righteous? Is it possible she didn't know that I knew about her and Dad? But she must have known. Who else did he think broke into his office?

Ur used to havin it easy u gold digging cow

What the hell?

There's no response from me.

Ellie, I meant what I said. I really don't need this in my life. There's only so much I'm willing to put up with for the sake of our friendship.

Friendship? Fuck u. Using bitch

That makes me wince. I had a legitimate reason to be angry at her so why did I have to resort to abusive language like that? My head is throbbing again now and there's a stabbing pain in my throat.

You know what? I'm done.

I sigh with relief before I remember that this wasn't the last of it. Perhaps I should have read the messages from newest to oldest, but I've started now. There can't be much more—the slider bar on the right hand side of the screen is almost at the bottom.

I replied straight away:

No i am. With 2 o u.

What???

Tell dad he can fck of 2

OK I don't know what you're talking about.

I swallow. I'm afraid of what's to come. Seeing her pretend there's nothing happening is pissing me off even now I know what's happened to her. I suck in a breath and scroll down.

I can't even look. I close my eyes. These messages are from around eight last night. There must be a mistake. Maybe I'm misinterpreting. Let me in could mean a lot of things.

I groan.

I'm lying to myself and I know it.

I open my eyes and try to fight back the feeling of butterflies in my stomach.

BULLSHIT!!!!

I mean it, Ellie. Look, whatever it is you think I've done,

you're wrong. I've just tried to be your friend. I'll call you tomorrow and talk when you're sober.

2face bitch! U sedced dad 4 $ ur no frnd

"Jesus," I mutter. I don't remember any of this. I can't even interpret what my messages are supposed to mean.

"What is it, Ellie?"

I shake my head.

There's no reply from Steph, just another message from me.

U gona dny????

Steph didn't reply to that one, but then I didn't give her a chance. Two minutes later, I followed up with:

Cmin ova. C if u cn deny 2 my face

"Oh no. No, no, no," I groan.

But I've reached the end and there's no way to twist the truth now. *Let me in* meant exactly what I thought it did; what I hoped it didn't mean. The last message was sent fifteen minutes later at half-past eight.

Let me in

"Ellie, what is it?" Nathan gently takes my phone out of my hand. I look up at him numbly.

Do I tell him?

Can I tell him?

I shake my head. This makes no sense. It can't have been me.

"Should I call her?" I whisper. "Just to make sure?"

"What, you haven't tried already?"

I shake my head, second-guessing myself now. No, I can't. I shouldn't.

But won't it look suspicious if I don't?

But what if the police answer and they start to investigate me?

My stomach plummets.

Calling isn't going to make any difference. If the police have her phone, they'll have access to our WhatsApp chat. What the hell are they going to think when they see that?

"Ellie, please talk to me. You've gone really quiet."

I look up at him. How can I tell him? He's not going to believe me. I'm not sure even *I* believe me.

CHAPTER 32
MIKEY

Mikey shoved open the door of the toilets and groaned when he saw who was waiting outside. He should have expected as much. He knew from one glance at her glazed red eyes that she was already far to pissed to even be served, but then that was why the team loved this place: they didn't care how drunk you were.

This was different though.

"There you are," she said, moving towards him.

Mikey cringed. They'd had so many nights out together where it was hard to tell who was more pissed, but it was different tonight. He'd been mulling over what Graham said to him the other day. He'd been trying to decide what to do. Not only that, but he'd been struggling to recover from injury and it was bothering him. He'd been bored out of his mind all evening and he'd started to wish he'd gone home.

Now he wasn't sure what he wanted.

Graham had warned him over and over again about her, but she looked so beautiful despite her drunkenness. Would she ever bloody learn? After the stunt she pulled at that party —getting pissed and falling all over the chairman of the club —Mikey was lucky all that had happened was being sent to France for a few months whilst Graham smoothed things over.

He gritted his teeth and hardened his heart. She could destroy her own life, but he wouldn't let her ruin his too.

"Ellie, I've told you before. This has got to stop."

"But we're supposed to be together," she whispered.

Mikey looked away. He may have been sober, but it wasn't enough. Even though logically he knew he was better off without her, he still loved her. He probably always would. "Look, Ellie—"

"Don't *look Ellie* me! You went away for months! And you never even told me you were back. What the fuck, Mikey?"

He shook his head. She always had this effect on him. For the last few months, all he'd heard was Graham ranting and raving about how she was a loose cannon; how she'd be the ruin of him. Now, standing before her, things looked a lot different. She was so vulnerable. That was how they'd always been: he was the dependable one who'd always looked out for her.

Things were more complicated now, though. He had to remember that. "You went to the police about me. What the hell were you playing at?"

"What?" she slurred, holding her hands out and staggering closer to him. She stroked his face with her fingertips and part of him melted again.

But no. He had to be strong.

"You went to the police. You were seen."

She pouted. "Only because you had that asshole Graham follow me."

"What?"

"You heard me. Graham's been following me. Creepy prick."

"But he wouldn't." Mikey shook his head as he recalled his last conversation with Graham. The guy had been so angry at her. Could he... No. But he could have sent someone else to do his dirty work—Mikey wouldn't put it past him.

Mikey swore under his breath as he started to make sense of it. Bloody Graham had had it in for her from the start. Everything was black and white for him. He saw it clearly now. It wasn't her drinking Graham cared about—not really —it was the fact that Mikey spent so much time looking out for her; staying up with her when she woke herself up screaming in the middle of the night. She wasn't screaming at him. He had no idea what was going on in that mind of hers, but it was something from way back. He'd tried to ask her about it but she had no idea herself and he'd never warmed to her father.

How could he just walk away?

He'd get her a therapist.

He'd find out what was causing the dreams.

They'd quit drinking together. Being sober wasn't so bad. It was such a double standard anyway: Mikey had done way worse things than Ellie ever had, but he got away with that because he was a bloke.

Something moved in the corner of his eye as he was reaching for her and Mikey spun around. There was a man with them on the narrow landing. Mikey hadn't noticed him before, which was odd, but then his attention had been fully absorbed by Ellie and the realisation that he'd been a right shit to her, only thinking of his career when she needed him.

At first Mikey assumed the guy was on the phone, but he wasn't. He was standing there, watching them.

"Oi, what's your problem, mate?"

The guy looked at Ellie. "He's treating you like muck," he slurred. "You deserve better."

"What?" Mikey laughed. "You? Get out of here you twat."

The bloke turned and stomped to the toilets. Mikey considered going after him, but he soon dismissed that thought. There was something familiar about him, but Mikey couldn't place it. He shook his head. Probably some local troublemaker who'd tried to rise him before. It happened to the lads all the time: local hard lads who thought fighting with a rugby player made them tough. Mikey wasn't one for pub fights—especially not sober.

He turned to Ellie. "Let's go." He tried to grab her arm but she stood firm—which was an achievement given how unsteady she was on her feet.

"No!" she cried. "No! He's right. I have let you treat me like shit."

Mikey was about to argue, but he hesitated. It was true, wasn't it? He glanced down the stairs. All he wanted to do was get her out of here and get her sober so they could talk. There was so much to say.

Nothing else mattered—nothing except him and Ellie. He'd let Graham twist the truth to keep his little whipping boy loyal. Well that was the end of that. Mikey would find another club if he had to. They'd move. For all of Graham's big promises, none of the big clubs had made him an offer yet and time was moving fast. Perhaps it was better if he moved. They could start a new life…

A movement beside him and a strange sort of whooshing sound made Mikey flick his head round. There was no time to react. Something heavy—something impossibly heavy—collided with his face and the next thing he knew he was flying through the air, then bumping, bumping, bumping. There was a scream just as he landed hard on the ground and the most intense pain he'd ever felt tore through his head.

CHAPTER 33
ELLIE

"Ellie!"

I take a deep breath. This looks bad—really bad. I've got to try and calm down; to figure out what's going on here.

"I'm upset, Nathan," I manage to say. "My friend's been murdered."

"How do you even know? You haven't tried calling her."

"You're right." I take the phone off him and turn away so he can't see the panic in my eyes. I find her contact and hit the call button. It rings—to my surprise—but there's no answer.

In my heart, I already know the truth.

Her voicemail message plays and the sound of her voice takes my breath away. My gut tells me to hang up, but I don't.

"Steph, it's Ellie. Call me. I've just seen the news—they're at your apartment block. Just let me know you're okay, will you?"

I hang up and drop my phone on the kitchen counter like it's contaminated. Did I do the right thing?

"No answer?"

I shake my head. Part of me wants to spill out all my fears to him, but I hold back.

He pulls me into a hug and I relax into him—but not fully. I can't turn off my frantic mind.

"It's usually the boyfriend or husband, isn't it?" he mutters into my hair.

I start to nod, about to agree when I realise that that would mean my Dad is behind this. How could he be?

But then I think of the death cert I found and the man who said his name was Tony Kent.

It's the same name: Tony Kent. Josephine Kent. Eleanor Kent. How can it be a coincidence?

I've got to face facts: Dad's been lying to me my whole life and there's a chance he's the one responsible for my mother's death. Why else would he take me? Why else would he take those certificates?

But why would he kill Steph? He signed the company over to her only a couple of months ago.

"Ellie, stop freaking out and talk to me, will you?"

The washing machine starts to spin—it's so loud that it sounds as if it might tear itself away from the wall. Nathan's whole body goes rigid. My heart starts to race.

"Your jeans," he mutters.

"*Your* jeans." My head's in a spin.

"You know what I mean. Why were you so eager to wash them? That mud—where did it come from?"

I shake my head. "I wanted to give them back to you. If it doesn't come out then I'll get you a replacement pair."

"It's not about the jeans!" he shouts, slamming his hand on the counter. "What did you do last night?"

"What do you mean?" My pulse is buzzing in my ears.

"You *know*." He won't meet my eyes.

I try to focus on my breathing. It's impossible. I'm on the verge of panicking.

Do I tell him?

Do I show him the messages?

How can I expect him to believe me? We've known each other for less than a month.

I look up at him. There's such concern in his eyes and I'm so tired. I can't do this on my own.

My hands shake as I hold my phone out to him. "I found these just now. I have no memory of sending them."

Nathan looks confused at first but then he takes the phone from me. His eyes widen as he scrolls through. "Jesus, Ellie," he gasps as he hands the phone back to me.

"I know," I say miserably. "What do I do?"

He exhales heavily. "Right, Ellie. Okay." He paces back to the couch. "Have you checked your purse for receipts?"

I shake my head. I hadn't thought of that. My handbag is sitting on one of the kitchen chairs. I pull out my purse and look inside. There's nothing in there, just my bank card. I zip it closed again and put it back in my bag. I wouldn't have gotten a receipt from a little corner shop anyway, but I had no cash left after earlier in the day so I'd have had to use my card.

I open my banking app on my phone. It takes a few goes to get my password right. My brain is so clouded and fuzzy, today of all days when I could use some clarity. But then if I wasn't hungover, I wouldn't have this problem. I'd *know* what happened last night without having to try and figure it out. I blink back tears. *Not now*. I need to focus.

There are no new transactions since the last time I withdrew cash. I frown. So I can't have gone to the shop and I didn't get a taxi. Wherever I went, I walked.

I think of the time between the second last and last messages I sent to Steph. Fifteen minutes. It takes me roughly ten to walk to her house if I'm going as fast as I can, so fifteen sounds about right for being incredibly drunk.

"No receipts," I whisper. "And no card transactions either."

I run through the facts in my head.

I was so drunk I can't remember what happened.

I was angry at Steph and there's a message trail between us to prove that.

"Talk to me, Ellie."

I shake my head. "I don't know what to say. This looks

bad, Nathan. So bad. I don't remember anything. And you were asleep."

He folds his arms across his chest and watches me silently for a long time. "You wouldn't do something like this, Ellie."

"I know, but that's not the point. How's it going to look?"

He pulls me into his arms. "I'll tell them I was with you," he says desperately. "I'll say we popped out to get wine and you decided you wanted to see Steph. I'll tell them I drove you to her apartment. She didn't answer the door so we came back here."

I cling on tight to him. I know I should shut up and accept his help, but I can't. I don't understand it. "Why? Why would you do this for me?"

He kisses the top of my head. "Because I know you didn't do it."

I close my eyes. I want to ask him how he can be so certain, but I don't. I say nothing. I need him in my corner because there's nobody else there.

CHAPTER 34
JOHN
MONDAY: SIX DAYS EARLIER

Monday

Six days ago

John flicked his indicator to turn right off the main road down the long and winding driveway. He steeled himself. It was time.

As the imposing red-brick mansion came into view, Tony shifted in the passenger seat beside him.

"I thought we were going somewhere quiet we could talk. What is this?"

John sighed. There were no signs at the entrance so he could understand the other man's caginess. This place was discreet. Expensive.

"Just wait."

"Is this some sort of trap?" Tony snapped. "Because you don't want to fuck with me. Not after everything you've put me through."

John focused on the road. There wasn't much of Tony in Ellie, but sometimes he caught glimpses that were enough to put him on edge. He supposed he shouldn't judge too harshly: he wasn't perfect either.

He often wondered where it had come from, the streak of madness. There must have been one. People didn't just turn into liars, cheats and addicts, did they? John had reflected on that a hell of a lot over the past twenty years, and he still hadn't found the answer.

"John," Tony said, knocking him back to reality. "What is this?"

"You'll see soon," he repeated. "Please, just be patient."

Even if he wanted to explain, he couldn't. Tony wouldn't believe him. Not until he saw for himself.

John parked the car and got out. Tony lingered, taking what felt like an age to unbuckle his seatbelt.

"Come on then," John snapped. This place always put him on edge and it was even worse today. He preferred when he could come here in silence and not have to talk to anyone. They understood that here. They didn't force cheeriness on you like they did in other places. Because who wanted that?

Tony snarled at him as he got out of the car.

John bit his tongue. What was the point in having an argument out here? He looked at the other man. His jeans and fleece were clean and tidy, but there was still something unkempt about him, like it was the very essence of him that was wrong. But he found he couldn't hate Tony. Not today. Today he almost pitied him for what was about to come.

They crunched across the gravel. There were only a few cars about and it wasn't because it was a weekday. This place was always quiet.

John hurried up the steps and pushed the doorbell. There was a discreet brass sign beneath the buzzer, but Tony was too distracted to notice. He'd turned around and was looking back towards the main road and the town. Probably realising how sheltered this place was from the road.

The door opened and they both stood up straighter at the sight of a middle-aged woman in a stern-looking suit. Her expression grew a touch less severe when she saw John, but she said nothing to him, only nodded. Her attention turned to Tony.

"My brother-in-law," John said.

He felt Tony's gaze switch to him, but the other man said nothing.

She was already standing back and pulling the door open. "Of course. Come on."

They stepped through the door and John was aware of Tony tensing. He understood why. The place wasn't what you expected. From the outside it looked like it must be lavish, but inside it was the same as any big institution.

"What is this place?" Tony muttered. "It looks like a hospital. Smells like one too."

The woman raised an eyebrow but didn't say anything. "Go on up," she said, pointing to the staircase before disappearing through a door near the entrance.

They started up the stairs.

"What the hell—"

"Not now," John muttered. He couldn't. No matter how many times he came here, he could never get past the sense of doom that came over him when he was inside these walls. He'd never get used to it. Never.

They got to the top and walked along the corridor. The lino hushed their footsteps. John stopped at the fifth door along. It was closed, just like the others. Always closed. The place was always silent. He didn't know whether that was a good or a bad thing. Perhaps some people found it relaxing. John didn't. The silence seemed to haunt him.

"John, I—"

He held up a hand to silence the man. He'd always been afraid of Tony, but something had shifted during the car journey. Did he really have anything to fear anymore? His life was in tatters anyway, what more could Tony possibly do?

"Close the door," he said when they'd entered.

He swallowed and huffed out a breath.

"What the hell is this, John? Who's he?"

John made himself walk to the side of the bed and look down at the young man who'd once had such a promising future.

"He's in a vegetative state," he said, almost to himself. "The doctors say there's little chance of him ever regaining consciousness now."

"Okay, right," Tony said impatiently. "Lots of people are. It's sad. But…" He didn't seem fazed by it at all, but then he didn't know the truth.

Yet.

It was time.

"This is Mikey Grant, Tony."

Tony curled his lip and leaned closer. "Is this some kind of threat, John? Because you know that's not a good idea. Who is this kid? And why do you think I care?"

"He's Ellie's ex."

All of the hairs on John's body stood on end and tears came to his eyes. Saying those words out loud made it different somehow. He'd been stuck in this nightmare for almost a year, but it was easier when it was left unsaid.

"What's your point? You think showing me this lad is going to put me off seeing her? She's my daughter. You took her away and changed her name and—"

"I did that for her," he snapped. "I uprooted her whole life to bring her here so she wouldn't have to live with the stigma of what her mother was." He huffed out a breath. They hadn't come here to talk about that.

Tony glared at him. He seemed about to launch into another attack.

Enough, John thought. He had to get this over with. "It was Ellie. She attacked him."

"Bullshit."

John sighed. "I wish with all my heart that it was. But she did."

"She can't have."

John felt a pang of sympathy. He remembered his own reaction and all the confusion that had fogged his mind until he accepted the truth. Of course she was messed up in ways he couldn't understand. Look at the start she'd had in life.

"I'm sorry, Tony. Truly I am. We've had our differences in the past." He stopped, deflated.

"No." Tony scratched his jaw with such force that John

wondered if he'd draw blood. He'd never seen the man this agitated. "No, she can't have done this."

"You don't even know her, Tony." He regretted saying that as soon as the words were out of his mouth.

But Tony didn't take the bait. He looked crestfallen.

"There'd been a bit of trouble between them before," John said, even though Tony hadn't asked him to. He was talking to fill the void and he knew it, but he couldn't stop. He'd carried this load alone for the past year and now here was someone who might understand why he'd have done whatever it took to protect her. "They'd broken up and she hadn't taken it well. She hit him over the head with an old shoe last that was being used as a door stop. He was thrown down the stairs by the impact and she must have lost her footing and stumbled after him. Their friends rushed in as she was falling but they didn't get there in time to stop her landing on him. The doctors reckon it was only the fact that her blood alcohol level was so high that saved her from more serious injury."

"But why would the police let her go if she did it?" Tony's expression grew dark and John remembered himself going through a similar process of denial.

"It's true."

"It can't be."

"Look around you. Why would I pay for this place if she wasn't responsible?"

Tony jerked his head up. "She has no idea about me, does she? You haven't told her."

John looked away. "It never…" he sighed. "As she got older, we became more distant from what happened. It never seemed to be the right time. And then all this happened…"

Tony's face fell. "You talk about it like it's normal. It's not. She had a decent upbringing. Do you reckon I… that it's in her blood?"

That same thought had gone through John's mind countless times in the past year, but something inside him had changed. Tony didn't even know the girl but he cared about her enough to track them down. That wouldn't have been easy. "You did what you did because of what he'd done to Joy."

"He was our dealer, man. It could just as easily have been me who gave her that shit."

"You were upset. It…" John shook his head. It was complicated, so complicated. He understood Tony's grief because he'd felt it himself, but he couldn't console him. There would always be a part of John that hated Tony for getting Joy onto that muck and treating her so appallingly.

"I want to be a part of her life," Tony said suddenly.

John groaned. He couldn't deal with this. Not now. How the hell would Ellie react if he told her that her mother had been an addict and he wasn't her real father, but her uncle? She'd never forgive him. No, it would make a volatile situation even worse and he couldn't do that to her.

"No."

"She's my daughter."

"I said no, Tony. And I meant it."

CHAPTER 35
ELLIE
SUNDAY

The washing machine beeps to indicate that it's finished and I reluctantly pull away from Nathan. Even though I feel far better than I did a few minutes ago, I'm grateful to have something to do.

I pull open the door of the washing machine so roughly that there's a loud crack.

"Sorry," I mutter.

"It's fine," Nathan says. "I'll hang those out."

"No, it's okay. I need something to do."

"I'll put the kettle on then. There's a dehumidifier in the wardrobe in the spare room."

"Thanks," I say, taking care to shut the washing machine door more gently than I opened it.

I shuffle to the spare room with the wet clothes bundled up in my arms. It doesn't take long for my uneasiness to return. The police will want to question me as soon as they see those messages. It's good that I got my muddy jeans into the wash early, but there are still so many ways I could mess this up.

I bite my lip and dump everything on the wire clothes horse.

What if I did this? That's all I can think about. Because who else would have? Steph didn't mention any enemies.

Nathan said it's usually the boyfriend or husband, but that would mean Dad.

I think about calling him, but I dismiss that idea immediately. What good would it do? It's not like he'll admit it even if he is the killer.

Which he can't be. He just can't.

I take a deep breath and sink to the ground. It was either Dad or me. Neither makes sense. The only other possibility is that I was right about Mikey being back. Would he have killed Steph to spite me?

I shake my head.

I just can't make sense of this.

"Tea's ready," Nathan calls.

I jump to my feet. I have got to relax. I'm going to get through this. "Coming."

I quickly hang out the clothes and remember what Nathan said about the dehumidifier. I groan when I see that it's buried under a pile of old blankets and bed linen—I can just make out the water container but when I pull on the power cable, it doesn't give easily because there's too much sitting on top of it. I don't want to force it and break anything. For a moment I forget my current problems and think about how nice it will be to be back in my own space again. If we ever decide to live together in the future, we're going to have to figure out a way to deal with each others' messes.

I start pulling things out and look around. I realise for the first time that there's no bed in here, just a camp bed in the corner that hasn't been assembled. I hesitate before chucking the blankets on the floor—it looks like it hasn't been vacuumed in a long time. Instead I shove them up on top of the wardrobe. Did he just pile all this stuff in here on the night I came? I can't really judge: my flat is pretty messy.

My arms ache as the pile on top of the wardrobe builds up with ragged towels and old backpacks. Is Nathan some kind of hoarder? I'm starting to seriously believe it. I lift out the dehumidifier and plug it into the wall.

I have bigger problems right now than Nathan's hoarding. He's standing by me—I can handle a bit of mess in return.

I try to tidy up the pile on top of the wardrobe: there are bag handles and bits of bed linen sticking out all over the place. Just when I've nudged it into something half resembling tidiness, something slips off the other side and falls to the floor.

"Shit," I mutter, hurrying over to pick it up. I expect Nathan to come in and see why I'm muttering to myself, but the dehumidifier unit is so loud he probably hasn't even heard. Good—I don't want him to have second thoughts about me.

It's a crumpled up photo that must have come from one of the backpacks I pulled out. My first reaction is relief: at least I haven't broken something. Before I can stop myself, I smooth out the scrunched up heavy paper, curious as to why he's done that: why destroy a photo?

It takes a few seconds to realise what I'm looking at. When I do, my heart accelerates to the point where my vision goes spotty.

Nausea rises in my throat.

It's me.

It's a picture of me.

One that I've never seen before, but I'd recognise the bar in the background anywhere.

It's the Builder's Arms.

I haven't set foot in that place for almost a year—so why on earth does Nathan have a photo of me from months before we ever met?

"Ellie?" Nathan shouts. "Your tea is getting cold."

I stare at the door, desperately trying to figure out what to do.

CHAPTER 36
ELLIE

My pulse blares in my ears as I try to make sense of how a guy I only met a couple of weeks ago would have a picture of me that's at least a year old hidden in his flat.

And why is it all scrunched up like he'd thrown it away? I pull all the stuff down off the wardrobe to try and see if I can find its source, but I can't. I shove it all back in the wardrobe and think about plugging out the dehumidifier and putting it where I found it.

Because what's he going to do if he realises I've found the photo?

I stare at it.

It was taken in the Builder's Arms. I'm leaning against the bar laughing. There's someone standing close beside me. I'm blocking them, but I don't need to see his face to know who it is. I can see his hair. His shoulders.

It's Mikey.

Why would Nathan have this?

I shake my head. All I can think is that he's the one who broke into my flat, but I don't think I've ever seen this photo in my life. The ones I've printed off over the years tend to be posey ones. I don't look particularly good in this one—I have my head thrown back, laughing.

I shiver. Why does he have this? Where did he get it?

Looking closer, I see that I'm wearing the pink floral top I used to love. I can't remember the last time I saw it.

I close my eyes. The headache isn't helping things: I can't think straight. There are a few people in the background, but there's no-one I wouldn't have expected to see. It could have been any Saturday night in the Builder's Arms.

But it was at least a year and a few months ago.

"Ellie?"

I shake my head, willing myself to snap out of this stupor and figure out what's going on. I've got to get back to Nathan even though I don't want to face him right now. He's going to get suspicious if I stay in here much longer.

"Coming. I'm just popping to the bathroom."

I think back to last night. We drank so much. Nathan egged me on. But I egged him on too. He didn't force me to get drunk.

I close my eyes. There was Monday evening. He was so adamant that we had to meet at three—even when I said I couldn't get off work.

Then there was Friday morning. He made me coffee and I fell into a deep sleep after drinking half of it. I never do that. Plus I woke with a pounding headache. Did he slip something in my drink?

It seems crazy to think like this, but Steph is dead. I have the same headache this morning and can't remember what happened last night.

How many times have I asked him how we can be from the same town and have never met? He had loads of chances to tell me he knew me. But I didn't know him…

Was he stalking me? Why else would he have a picture of a random stranger in his flat? My blood runs cold. Is Mikey behind this?

I fold the photo carefully and shove it in my pocket before I walk out of the room. I have to force one leg in front of the other—I can't face him.

I stop in the hallway. Nathan's jeans are where I left them, drying in the spare room.

What if he's setting me up?

No. It's too messed up.

Isn't it?

I take a deep breath. Can I afford to take any chances?

I hurry back and grab the clothes. How can I know for sure that there isn't DNA on them?

What has he done? What have *I* done?

I sink to the floor and try to get my breathing under control.

Get it together, I tell myself. There might not be much time.

I leave the clothes in the narrow hallway while I go and fetch my handbag. Nathan's watching TV. I quickly check that my purse and keys are in my bag.

"There you are." He frowns. "Your tea will be ruined."

"I'm just popping out to get some paracetamol," I say, making my voice as hoarse and hungover as possible. "I'll make some more tea when I get back."

"Oh." He turns and looks at me, frowning. "I think I have some paracetamol."

Panic rises in me. What if he tries to stop me from leaving? He's not as big as Mikey, but he's still far stronger than me. And he's been lying to me. I don't know what he's capable of.

"Oh, thanks. Well, I fancy some crisps so I might pop out and get some. Unless you have a stash?"

He shakes his head. I don't like the way he's looking at me. "Are you alright?"

"Yeah, I'm fine. I'm just a bit shaken about Steph. Do you want anything?"

"No thanks."

I hurry out, closing the door behind me and grabbing the clothes. I wonder if I should wrap them in a bin bag or something, but no. I need to get out of here quickly and stop wasting time before I find myself in serious trouble.

I hurry out the door. At first I go to Nathan's bin, but I

hesitate. It's better if I use one down the street. I'll have to choose carefully because the last thing I need is a nosy neighbour getting suspicious and calling the police.

I shake my head. Am I going crazy? Maybe there's a far simpler explanation. Maybe I didn't even get as far as the corner shop last night. Maybe I fell over and told Steph I was outside just to piss her off.

It doesn't add up, though. Steph is dead. Someone was there. If not me, who? She didn't answer my last messages. Did the killer come just after she'd seen them?

I shudder. Was I there at the same time as him? What if I saw something?

But wouldn't I remember if I'd seen something important? Surely that would jolt me out of my drunken state?

I'm so deep in thought that I don't register the police car at first. It's only when it's turned onto the street and about five houses away that my heart starts to beat faster.

I keep walking. I'm amazed I'm able to. I've got to act normal. If I start running now, they'll know something is wrong.

The car skids to a halt alongside me and the air fills with the stench of burning rubber.

Act normal.

Fuck.

The clothes. They're still in my hand and I can't drop them now.

I glance at the car but I don't stop walking. Normal. Like an innocent bystander would.

I *am* innocent.

This is a headfuck. I can't deal with it.

"Miss Cartwright."

Two car doors slam.

I try not to react. I turn, slowly, telling myself to breathe.

"Yes?"

I start to second guess myself. I've already tried to call Steph. Shouldn't I be more concerned? Should I acknowledge that they're probably here about Steph so I shouldn't be all that surprised to see them?

"Constable Roberts and Constable Jameson. Would you mind coming down to the station with us?"

"Oh God," I say, staggering against the nearest wall and subtly dropping the clothes on the other side. "It's Steph, isn't it?"

The two officers exchange glances.

"Please, just tell me. She's my friend." I'm very careful to use the present tense. "I recognised her apartment building on TV."

"This would be easier if you came to the station with us."

"I was just on my way home," I say, as a whole fresh batch of worries starts to run around in my mind. Like why did they come here? How did they know I was here? "Do you mind if I come down later?"

They look at each other again, and I get the feeling it's some tactic they've been taught in police college. I feel wrong-footed by it. Why do they feel the need to play games with me?

"Actually, it would help if you came now."

The other one nods. "Unless you've got something important on that can't wait."

I shake my head. They've got me. What can I possibly have planned that's more important than helping to find my friends killer? I can't explain that I need some time alone to figure out why my new boyfriend has a picture of me from way back when we've only just met.

Nathan.

My blood runs cold.

I see his promises in a new light now. What's his game? Why was he so eager for me to believe he wanted to help me?

"Can I go and let my boyfriend know I'm going with you?" I falter. Is that a weird thing to say considering I've already left his house? Even if it is, I've got to keep going with it now. He's the last person I want to see, but this is important. How can I face their questions if I don't know what

Nathan is up to? "He was going to come and meet me at my place. I don't want to leave him waiting."

They look at each other again. Why do they keep doing that? "You can text him from the car."

I force a smile as I walk towards the police car, but inside I'm a wreck. I can't send what I need to say to him in a text.

CHAPTER 37
ELLIE

stare out the window, trying to appear calm and not let them know that I'm driving myself crazy trying to figure out what's going on. I've been feeling groggy and disconnected all morning, just like I felt on Friday. That's not helping, even though it is starting to make sense.

Has Nathan been drugging me?

I run my tongue along my bottom teeth, and try yet again to put what's happened into some sort of order, but it's a jumble of seemingly unconnected things.

Dad lying to me about my mother and signing the company over to Steph.

That guy Tony saying he's my real father.

The photo I found in Nathan's flat.

Steph.

I take a deep breath.

"Alright back there?"

"Yeah," I say, feeling rattled. So much for hiding my emotions from them. "I'm just struggling to take it in."

It didn't seem real until the police came to take me to the station. Part of me hoped it was a mistake. I wanted to believe what Nathan said—that it was somebody else who lived in Steph's building.

Who would murder Steph? That's what I can't get my

head around. And why would they choose last night of all nights?

There are three possibilities that I can see.

One, Steph's murder was nothing to do with me and my messages to her were just incredibly badly timed. That seems unlikely—too much of a coincidence.

Two, someone knew I went to see her and killed Steph to frame me.

And three, the one that I just can't get my head around: I did it.

What if I'm being framed? I think of the photo in my pocket. Why did Nathan have a picture of me from long before we met? There's only one reason I can think of: someone gave it to him. I always thought it was strange that a guy who grew up here in town could be so distant from everyone our age that he never heard Mikey's rumours. I massage the back of my head trying to ease the throbbing pain.

What if I wasn't drunk? What if that's just what he wanted me to think? He had so many opportunities to slip something into my drink last night. That would explain why I feel so weird today.

A picture slowly forms in my mind. Mikey, biding his time and waiting until I'd stopped being scared of my own shadow; sending Nathan to get close to me and find an opportunity to destroy me.

My eyes widen. Perhaps I was right before, that Mikey wasn't pleased about my new relationship—I just got the relationship wrong. He was pissed off about my friendship with Steph, not my relationship with Nathan.

It sounds absolutely mad, even to me. How can it be true?

I stare out the window. I've got to face facts. Steph is dead. I'm in a police car on the way to the station. I've got to convince the police that I'm not responsible for this. But how? I know why they came to find me: they saw the messages between me and Steph. So they know I was probably there last night.

I can't rely on Nathan's alibi anymore. Was he trying to lull me into a false sense of security?

My skin crawls with the memory of his hands on me. To think I believed he was some sort of saviour who'd fix my broken life. I should have known no-one around here would be genuinely interested in me.

We stop at a red light and I can see the police station up ahead. We're almost there and even though I have a good idea of what's happened, I have no idea how to deal with it. I can't just tell the police the truth: last time I tried that I had a broken leg and bruises all over my body and they still wouldn't believe me.

I take a deep breath.

"We're almost there."

I ignore them. I've got to stay focused because soon they'll be asking me questions. I need to be ready for them. There's only one positive in all of this: I found that photo before I spoke to the police. I have time to prepare myself for what's to come.

Any bravado I felt in the car evaporates when I'm led into the station and come face-to-face with Detective Sergeant Hobson. Even though almost a year has passed, my heart begins to pound and my gut screams at me to get out. I force myself to meet his eyes. I've done nothing wrong and I have no reason to feel ashamed. That's how he makes me feel: ashamed. I've never been able to understand why he hates me so much.

I didn't hurt Steph—I know I didn't. I've got to cling to the facts to get me through this.

But the facts don't reflect well on me, do they? The messages I sent to Steph last night were filled with such rage and hatred I don't know how I can possibly spin them to make me look innocent.

The police station is busier than I've ever seen it. I'm led through a door in reception and along a corridor to an interview room. I think it's the same one as I was in before—the last time. I spent so much time here this time last year. First when I tried to get them to take me seriously that someone from the club was trying to intimidate me and then again after Mikey attacked me.

"Thank you for coming in to talk to us, Ellie. I'm DC Stevens."

I nod at the female detective sitting beside DS Hobson. She looks professional in a neat black suit jacket with the sleeves rolled up over a crisp white shirt.

"And you know DS Hobson, I believe."

I try not to make a face. How could I forget the man who made my life a living hell last year?

"Let's get started," she says. "How did you know Miss Price?"

Should I ask for a solicitor? It was different last time—I was the one reporting a crime, they just made me feel like a criminal. But they've not arrested me this time—not yet, anyway. I don't want to ask for a solicitor in case they use it against me.

I blink a few times, trying to clear my head. What I really need is a strong coffee, not a grilling by a man who hates my guts for some reason known only to him.

"She's my friend."

"Where did you meet?"

"At yoga. We got chatting after class and started meeting for coffees."

"I see," she says. "When did you last see her?"

I swallow. I wasn't expecting that so quickly and I haven't figured out yet what I want to tell them. "Wednesday evening," I say, and my voice comes out as a pained wheeze that reflects my indecision. Shit. Why didn't I say I called over yesterday? They've seen our messages: they're going to know I'm lying. "I went to her place last night but there was no answer."

My heart races. Do they know I'm lying? Can they tell? I

try to relax. For all I know I'm telling them the truth. Sweat breaks out on my forehead. I still haven't thought of a way to explain those nasty things I said to her.

"Can you tell us some more about that? A planned get-together, was it?"

I take a breath. "No, not exactly. I found out during the week that she was involved with my father. I wanted to talk about it."

The detectives exchange looks.

Did they already know? Is this news to them?

DC Stevens clears her throat. "Were you angry?"

I nod. It goes against every instinct I have, but it's the right thing to say. If they don't already have our messages from WhatsApp, they will soon. "Yes. He's my dad. She's my friend. They didn't tell me and that hurt."

"How did you find out if they didn't tell you?"

"I saw them together." I don't elaborate.

"That must have made you mad?"

I sigh. "More sad than mad. If they'd just come to me, I'd have given them my blessing. Steph's..." I lower my head and close my eyes. I feel like a horrible person for hamming this up, but what choice do I have? I did everything by the book last time and look where that got me. I clear my throat. "She was a lovely person and my dad has been alone for as long as I can remember. He deserves to be happy."

Those last words stick in my throat, but I don't think they noticed. I'll tell them whatever I have to tell them to get them off my back. They should be out there looking for the real killer.

It flashes through my mind that the simplest explanation is that I did this, but I brush that thought aside. I can't afford to dwell on it right now.

DS Hobson opens the plain brown folder in front of him and shuffles through the printed sheets inside. He pulls one out and clears his throat before he begins to read.

I try to keep it together when I realise he's reading out the message chain between me and Steph from last night. I knew the police would get those messages, but it's still a shock to hear them being read aloud. I cringe as he deliberately makes a big fuss out of trying to understand the later messages—the ones that even I struggled to decipher when I saw them earlier.

He puts the sheet back in the folder. "You sounded incredibly angry to me. And drunk."

I flush despite my best efforts not to. I make myself count to three before answering. The worst thing I could do right now is fly off the handle. That's what he wants.

I need to sound plausible.

"I'd had a few glasses of wine," I say as calmly as I can. "And I decided to go over there and confront her."

"What happened?"

"She didn't answer the door. I pressed her buzzer a few times and then gave up."

I do my best to steady my nerves. It doesn't help that they're both watching me impassively and I have no idea what they're thinking. Was it a bad idea to say that? I don't know what evidence they have from Steph's building, but they can't have anything too incriminating because they would have arrested me. Wouldn't they?

"You didn't try to call her?"

Damn it, why didn't I anticipate that question? I shake my head and hope they can't see how stressed I am. "No. We used WhatsApp mostly. Like I said, I'd had a few drinks. I wasn't feeling very sharp. I was starting to sober up and get sleepy. I just wanted to get home."

"So what happened then? Where did you go?"

"Home. Well, back to the guy I've been seeing's flat."

"What did you do then?"

I shrug and force a smile even though my heart is pounding. I thought Nathan was my knight in shining armour. Instead, he kept me close so he'd know exactly where I was at any given moment. "I snuggled up to him in bed and fell asleep."

"What time was this at?"

I shake my head. "I don't know. Around nine? I didn't check the time on my phone and he doesn't have a clock in his bedroom."

A uniformed officer comes in with a sheet of paper and hands it to DS Hobson, who glances at it and frowns. My heart skips a beat but I try my best not to show it. They're trying to trip me up, I tell myself. I've got to rise above it.

As soon as the door is closed, Hobson leans his elbows on the table. "Tell me, Ellie. Why would you dump a set of damp clothes in a neighbour's garden?"

do my best not to panic. I should have chucked them in Nathan's bin. How was I to know that the police were already on their way?

I take a breath. I could lie and say I have no idea how they got there, but what if the police car had a dashcam? The last thing I need is for them to catch me in a lie. This is all starting to look very bad for me. "Nothing dries in Nathan's house. I was taking them back to my flat to put them in the tumble dryer. I got a fright when your officers pulled up. I must have dropped them."

"And why were you going back to your flat?"

"To pick up some fresh clothes. To shower."

"To hide the murder weapon?"

I snort as if that's the craziest thing I've ever heard, but inside it sets off a panic. Why didn't I think of this? Whoever did this won't just rely on me incriminating myself because I was drunk last night and told Steph I was going to her place. They'll have done something else.

I have got to get to my flat and search the place from top to bottom.

"No, of course not. I'd have it now, wouldn't I? You can search me if you want." I stop talking. Did they ask me that to see my reaction to being falsely accused? I need to keep my interactions with them limited. I look Hobson in the eye. "I came here because your officers asked me to. I don't think there's anything I can say that will help you find who did this to her, but I feel bad about sending her those awful messages. I'm sure you can appreciate that this isn't a good day for me. Can we move on to the questions about Steph so I can get out of here and go check on my father?"

At first I think I've won; that I've put him in his place and he's going to start asking me the questions he should be asking me.

But then DC Stevens looks at him strangely and I realise I haven't beaten him, he's just so angry he can't speak. His nostrils flare. "Your father? What do you care about your father?"

I flush. I expected him to treat me unfairly, but I wasn't expecting hostility like this. I turn to DC Stevens. "I came here to do what I can to help you find Steph's killer. Not to be abused. I'm leaving." I turn to Hobson before I can stop myself. I'm so angry I have no control over what I say anymore. "Perhaps you should look a little closer to home. Like your precious rugby team for a start."

"Excuse me?" Hobson's voice is dangerously quiet, but he's pushed me too far. I can't stop myself.

If he set out to push my buttons he's succeeded in doing just that.

I reach into my pocket and throw the photo of me on the table. "I found this in Nathan's house. Someone is setting me up for this. I'd bet everything I own that it's Mikey Grant. Nathan claimed he didn't know me when we first met, but this picture is from ages ago. I wouldn't expect you to believe me, though. I'm not your rugby mate."

I start to get up but freeze when I see the look on Hobson's face. I don't think I've ever seen anyone so angry.

Well I'm angry too. I'm sick of people thinking they can treat me like shit and expecting me to take it.

"You're a bloody sociopath," he snarls.

DC Stevens snaps her head around. "Sir."

"You didn't see it, Linda. I've had enough. Just enough. It was bad enough that she wriggled out of it last time without this. The poor lad can't even feed himself and you're coming in here suggesting that he's behind—"

"Sir," DC Stevens says again.

He doesn't even hear her. "Your father got you out of trouble last time, Ellie, but I doubt he'll be so eager this time—not if what you told us about their relationship is true."

All of the warmth leaves my face. What does Dad have to do with what happened? "What are you talking about?"

"Don't pretend."

"Sir, I think we should move back to the case at hand—"

"You don't know what it was like," he says. "That poor lad. She ruined him. But there was nothing we could do. His mother said she'd go to the press and call it a miscarriage of justice if we pressed charges."

"Yeah," I snap. "Because how could she? He put me in hospital and tried to claim he was the victim."

"He claimed nothing, Ellie." He gets up and goes to the door. "Keep her here, I'll be back in a moment."

I shake my head in disbelief. I want to tell her that they have no right to stop me from leaving if they aren't arresting me, but I don't. It could be a trick, but even so, I'm intrigued by what he's saying.

No-one's ever actually come out and told me what I'm supposed to have done to Mikey that's so bad and who could I ask? I only found out this week that Dad had heard the rumours too. The truth is I didn't really want to know. His story must have been terrible if it turned all my friends against me—do I really need to hear the details of what I know is a lie?

But that doesn't explain DS Hobson's reaction. It's been nearly a year. Why would he even remember me, much less be angry? He's a police officer—he must have seen some terrible things.

DS Hobson storms back into the room and throws several

folded sheets of paper on the table. "I know exactly what happened even if there's nothing I can do about it."

"What is this?"

He laughs bitterly. "Why pretend, Ellie? I know the truth."

I pick up the paper. I recognise the name at the top. It's an exclusive clinic on the outskirts of the town that no-one really knows much about. There were rumours that it was a rehab for celebrities but I've also heard that it's a mental hospital.

I blink a few times because what I've just seen doesn't make sense. The exhaustion must be playing tricks with my eyes.

The bill is addressed to John Cartwright and the patient's name is Michael Grant.

My blood runs cold.

"This is a trick," I mutter. "It's got to be. It's Photoshopped."

"Who would bother?" Hobson growls. "The only trick is on your father's part, using his money to trick Mikey's mother into giving up on justice for her son."

It's an invoice. The whole page is rows and rows of medicines and treatments. I turn the page and see more of the same.

"It goes back almost a year," I whisper, more to myself than to them.

Hobson snatches the invoice away.

"Someone's made this up. They must have." I take a deep breath and hiss it out just as quickly. I can't get enough air. "Call the hospital. They'll tell you it's not real."

"It is real," he snaps. "Do you want to see pictures?"

This time, DC Stevens puts her hand on his arm. "Sir, please stop. I can get one of the others to take over."

I stare at him in disbelief.

Mikey.

I close my eyes. I've spent so long trying to understand why he'd snap and hurt me, but that's what he did. I didn't hurt myself. How can he be hurt too?

Who the hell did this? The police obviously don't know or else they wouldn't have given me such grief last year.

A surge of nausea judders through my body and I can't stop myself from retching as Hobson's words sink in.

"What's wrong with him?" I whisper.

"Oh, you suddenly care, do you?"

"Sir!"

"Tell me!"

"He's in an unresponsive state."

I shake my head. "No. No he can't be." I've spent the past year hating him. And hating myself for pining for the man who ruined my life. I assumed he'd gone off to a bigger club like he always wanted, or a foreign club like he did when we had that blowup over me getting drunk at the club party.

I had no idea.

I can't breathe. I'm gasping for air, but no matter how many deep breaths I take, it doesn't help. I'm choking. The edges of my vision go fuzzy. I try to ask them for a glass of water but my voice is clumsy and it sounds like it's coming from very far away.

CHAPTER 39
JOHN

John's phone buzzed in his pocket. He took it out, hoping it might be Ellie. He'd half expected her to show up for lunch even though she'd never answered him. Of course she hadn't. He had to face the fact that she knew the truth now and it was just as he'd feared: she'd chosen to have nothing to do with him.

It was an unknown number. He was tempted to cancel the call, but what was the harm he supposed? It felt like forever since he'd spoken to someone outside of work. That didn't bother him in the past but it all seemed futile now when he didn't even own the company.

"John Cartwright speaking."

"Ah," said a cold voice. "Mr Cartwright. This is DS Hobson."

A shiver ran down John's spine. He knew the other man well, though they had never been—and would never be—friends. "To what do I owe the pleasure?"

He shouldn't have been rude—it wasn't like him—but he couldn't help it. Hobson had come very close to undoing everything he'd done to protect Ellie. He might not be her birth father, but he felt just as protective of her as if he was.

"I'm calling about Stephanie Price."

"Oh," John said. "What about her?"

There was a sudden tension on the line. "You haven't heard?"

"Heard what?"

There was a pause. "Mr Cartwright, what is your relationship to Ms Price?"

John shook his head. "Relationship?" he said, puzzled now. "I wouldn't call it that."

"No?"

"No. I sold my company to her father. He has a good reputation. I didn't realise he was setting his daughter up in her own little offshoot."

"I see. You weren't happy about that, I take it?"

"No, I bloody well wasn't. The girl is barely out of university. It's galling to watch her trying to slash costs in the company I've spent my life building up as though it's some two-dimensional case study in a textbook."

"I see."

"What's this about, DS Hobson? I doubt you called to get my opinion on company management."

"Ms Price was murdered last night. I have reason to believe your daughter was involved. She seems to think the two of you were in a relationship."

"Oh Christ," John groaned. "Oh no. No."

"Mr Cartwright, I—"

John hung up. He needed to think.

He got up and poured himself a whisky. Stephanie Price had come to him on Thursday, complaining about the terrible position she found herself in. It was only then that he'd learned she'd sought Ellie out and befriended her.

He groaned and sat back down on the couch. What had she done? She could have chosen any other girl in the town to make friends with, but she'd picked Ellie. And then she'd had the cheek to insist he tell Ellie the truth about how he'd sold the company.

But how could he have done that?

To top it all off, Ellie had found out about their involvement anyway. He discovered that on Friday morning when he found his office torn asunder. Now it seemed she had jumped to the wrong conclusion. How could Ellie have thought…

His phone started buzzing again, but he ignored it. Hobson could come over here if he wanted to talk to him and even then John wasn't sure he'd bother letting him in.

What had Ellie done?

Someone started banging on the door.

Was it Hobson? He could bloody wait. John didn't want to speak to him. Not now his heart was breaking.

He'd done everything right. She'd never wanted for anything, that girl. John had wiped himself out financially trying to make up for her mistakes, and now look what she'd done. With Mikey, he'd always assumed there must have been a reason she'd lashed out. Now?

He couldn't believe it. He would have been the first to admit that Stephanie Price was pushy and entitled, but she certainly hadn't deserved to die.

There was another loud thump on the door.

"Who's there?" he called.

The letterbox rattled. "It's about Ellie."

John sighed. It wasn't Hobson at all. It was Tony. The man he'd despised for most of his life who had now turned into a strange sort of brother in arms.

He got up and shuffled out of the room, aware that Tony would smash the door in if John didn't open it. He opened the door and Tony pushed past him.

"Do you know what?" he said miserably, turning to go back to his drink. "Forget everything I said before. Go and spend as much time with her as you want. Because I'm done with her."

The other man lunged forward, grabbed him and slammed him against the wall.

John blinked as the pressure on his neck made it difficult for him to breathe. "Go ahead," he squeaked at the man who had caused him so much pain. "Do it."

Tony let go of him without warning. John crumpled to the

floor. "I'd love to, believe me. They've taken her in, John. The police."

"I know that," he spat, rubbing his neck where it felt like the other man had crushed it. "And I'm glad. She's turned out just like you despite all my efforts to raise her right."

Tony's hands tightened into fists. John watched with detached interest. Because what did it matter what Tony did now?

That girl was dead because of John. If he hadn't stepped in and bought the Grant woman's silence, Ellie likely would have been pursued for what she did to Mikey. She'd be in prison now.

He sighed. It broke his heart to imagine her in prison, but maybe that was the best place for her.

He'd tried his best to raise her well. He'd been strict and he'd sent her to good schools. Whenever he so much as suspected that she was hanging around with unsavoury characters, he'd found an excuse to stop her from spending time with them outside of school hours.

He'd tried everything.

It had been exhausting.

And it hadn't even worked.

It was galling to discover that nature meant far more than nurture.

"You don't seriously think she did this, do you?"

John bowed his head. He was exhausted. He just wanted to be alone with his regrets. This was the last thing he needed. "What does it matter what I think, Tony? If the police think she did it then that says a lot. She had a motive. She thought I was involved with that woman. And she has issues. You know that as well as I do. You saw what she did to that young lad, and now this."

"So what are we supposed to do?"

John sighed. "Let the justice system do its job."

"Like you did before?"

John flushed. "I tried to protect her and look what happened."

Tony hunkered down in front of him. "She didn't do this. She can't have."

"You don't even know her, Tony."

"I talked to her yesterday. Told her who I was. She was terrified at first. Thought I wanted to hurt her, for some reason. Why would she think that?"

John shook his head. "Who knows. She's not… She said something last week that was strange. I let it go at the time, but I can't help wondering now if I should have pursued it. She seemed to have no idea about what had happened to Mikey even though she's the one responsible."

"I don't care about him, John. I care about her," Tony said fiercely, and just for a moment, John could have sworn he was looking into Ellie's eyes. Strange. He'd always thought she took after his and Joy's side.

"I care about her too, believe me. But I have to draw a line somewhere. She'll destroy us all."

Tony lunged for him again before he could get out of the way. "Do you hear yourself? Ellie's locked up and you're giving up on her! What the hell is wrong with you?"

"You don't know her like I do."

"That's true. I haven't had the chance. But she's not violent. She's not aggressive."

"How can you say that for sure?"

"Because I followed her a couple of times before I worked up the balls to speak to her. When I tried to approach her here the other day she was terrified."

John looked at the other man. "Here? What are you talking about?"

"It doesn't matter. I'm just telling you, she's not aggressive. She's not a killer."

John stared into the other man's eyes then down at the hands that trapped him against his own hallway wall.

Tony let go.

"She's violent. Perhaps it's the alcohol that sets her off. It's in her nature, her genes."

Tony shook his head. "You have to help her."

"Why? What am I supposed to do? Get her off so she can kill someone else?"

"Believe her. Trust her. I don't know. You're a clever man. Talk to her. Find out what's happening."

"I can't talk to her." John shook his head. He was exhausted, but he'd never get to sleep after this. "I don't want to talk to her. I had a call from DS Hobson down at the station just before you came. He was of the belief that this girl Stephanie and I were involved in a relationship because that's what Ellie told him. She has her own reality." He put a hand on Tony's shoulder. "We've had our differences in the past but I'm telling you this now: I know you want to think the best of her, but you don't know her like I do. Just leave it, Tony. I know how you feel. It's breaking my heart, but the best thing we can do now is let the system do its job: I won't have another person's blood on my hands."

CHAPTER 40
JOHN

"Two calls in the space of a week, John. What can I do for you this time?"

John resisted the urge to point out that the other man hadn't done much for him last time. He didn't have time for this. "She's gone and killed someone."

There was silence on the other end of the line.

"Are you there?" John asked, irritated.

"Ah… I'm sorry. What did you say?"

"You heard me. Ellie has killed the Price girl."

"Why would you think that? That would be a dramatic escalation."

"Because the young woman came to me on Thursday. She was concerned about Ellie's mental state."

The other man sighed. "What do you want me to do about it?"

"I don't know, Alan," John snapped. "You're the bloody solicitor. Can't you do something?"

"There's no need to react in that way. It's not my area of expertise, John."

"That didn't stop you when I needed new names and documents."

There was a long pause. Alan's voice had a new edge to it

when he finally spoke. "That was a long time ago, John. I can't believe you'd throw that back in my face."

John sat down and squeezed the bridge of his nose. That was a low blow and he knew it. Hadn't he been the one who begged Alan for his help? Alan had been reluctant even then, but it was the only way John could have been sure of keeping her. Even though at that point Ellie had lived with him for most of her life, he was only her uncle. He hadn't been able to stomach the idea of having to hand her over to Tony's mother to raise.

"I'm sorry. This has hit me hard. That's all."

Alan sighed. "I understand. Believe me. How do you think I can help?"

John thought back to their last conversation; to Alan's insistence that he get her off the scent before it was too late and she found out what had happened in the past. It all seemed so trivial now. He'd been so worried that she'd follow her mother's footsteps that he hadn't noticed her taking a completely different—and even more destructive—path.

"I know I ought to wash my hands of her, but I can't." He closed his eyes. Regardless of what he'd said to Tony, he couldn't just leave her alone to face something like this, could he? "Shouldn't I try to help? I don't know, to get her out of it?"

"Did she do it?"

John closed his eyes.

"She has form," Alan said softly. "Just look at what happened when you tried to step in the last time."

"So you're saying I should cut her loose? I don't know if I can be that cold."

"What if you come to her rescue again and she hurts someone else? Could you live with yourself?"

John fell silent as he pictured Stephanie Price, lording it over him as she swanned into his office like she owned the place—and thanks to him, she had owned it. He hadn't liked her, but it didn't mean he wanted her to come to any harm. He was the reason she'd moved here. If he hadn't sold the company, she'd still be alive. He'd struggle with that for the rest of his life. He couldn't let it happen again, no matter how much he loved Ellie. His first instinct had been right—even if it was hard for him to accept.

"No," he whispered.

"There's your answer then."

John hung up. There was little more to say. Until last year, he hadn't spoken to Alan for almost twenty years. He'd been the only one who John could turn to. He'd understood John's need to make sure the past stayed buried.

Now?

It didn't matter anymore, did it? Not when John had raised a murderer. He deserved whatever punishment might come his way once the police learned who Ellie really was and what John had done all those years ago.

CHAPTER 41
ELLIE

I open my eyes and groan as my surroundings come into focus. My mouth is dry and there's a pounding pain in my temples. I blink hard. It looks like I'm on a floor I don't recognise.

I turn my head and the room spins. I snap my eyes shut and swallow.

"Ellie," says a woman's voice. "Ellie, it's DC Stevens. I have some water here for you."

She helps me into a chair and I try to open my eyes again. It's far clearer this time. I take the paper cup of water and take a long sip.

"What happened?"

"You fainted."

I'm about to ask her another question when it all comes back to me. I bury my head in my hands.

Steph.

Mikey.

Mikey, especially.

I can't believe it.

Who did this?

I groan. The pain in my head is replaced by a gnawing sense of loss. When I got out of hospital I retreated into my shell and hated everyone for not believing me. I don't understand how Mikey could have been so seriously hurt if he was the one behind the attack.

I squeeze my eyes closed and will myself to remember, but I can't. All I have is the faintest memory of the upstairs landing in the pub, outside the toilets. Talking to Mikey. My heart surging with happiness as he took my hand. And then pain.

I don't even know if it's real or a dream I had in the months since.

"I didn't know," I say, looking up at her. "I didn't know he was hurt."

She watches me for a few moments but doesn't say anything. "Is there anyone I can call for you, Ellie?"

The buzz of the fluorescent light overhead becomes deafening in the silence that falls. I understand perfectly well: she doesn't believe me and she doesn't even want to hear it.

I shake my head. No. There's no-one.

"Right then. Well, in light of what's happened, we'll ask you to come back tomorrow."

"Wait, what?"

She looks at me with such contempt that I realise I shouldn't stick around here questioning why they're letting me walk out of here.

I should go.

Now.

But I can't. Not after what they've just told me. It could have been a tactic to mess with me, but I don't think it was. It wasn't the invoice that convinced me, it was the look in DS Hobson's eyes. This was never about him thinking I made up my accusations last year. He thinks I hurt Mikey and got away with it.

"I need to talk to you," I say urgently. "This is so messed up. You've got it wrong. I didn't hurt Mikey. I didn't even know he was hurt. I was attacked. I thought he was the one who did it, but if he wasn't—"

"We have a murder to investigate." She moves to the door, clearly waiting for me to leave.

This is what I wanted, isn't it? To get out of here? But everything's changed.

"But I'm in danger," I hiss. "You have to help me. What if whoever hurt Mikey is the same person who hurt Steph?"

DC Stevens narrows her eyes and I know what she's thinking. They think it's me. They think I'm the one responsible.

I shake my head. "I didn't do this. I didn't."

"I've got to get back to work." She doesn't meet my eyes.

She's not saying they think I did this, but she wouldn't, would she?

But why would they let me go?

"Come on."

My heart pounds as I get up. What do I do? Where do I go? Dad's not going to listen to me if he thinks I did this, no matter how hard I try and persuade him it wasn't me.

The photo of me is still on the table. I grab it. It's the only concrete thing I have left.

"Look," I say breathlessly. "You still haven't explained this. Why would Nathan have had a picture of me when we didn't know each other back then? I haven't been in the Builder's Arms for a year." I stare at the picture and trace Mikey's outline with my fingertips. All this time I've hated him and he's a victim in all of this.

"I have no idea," she says drily. "Why don't you ask him instead of wasting police time?"

"No, it's not that. You don't understand. There's something going on that's…" I trail off as I realise that no matter what I say, they think I'm guilty.

I shove the picture in my pocket. It's the only physical proof I have that there's more to this than meets the eye. I keep my fingers wrapped around it like it's a precious jewel.

DC Stevens leads me along the corridor and presses the door release button to let me out. I hesitate. I would have given anything to be released without charge when I arrived here, but now I'm not sure. Am I better off here for my own protection?

Or is it best if I get the hell away from here as fast as I can? I've got to try and get one step ahead.

She holds the door open for me. "Off you go."

I take a deep breath. As tempting as it is to ask them to keep me here for my protection, police custody is not something I should be aspiring to right now. Not until I know for sure that I'm not responsible. There are two possibilities here: I'm guilty or I'm in danger.

I walk out the door and she slams it behind me.

I freeze.

Nathan is sitting in one of the chairs opposite the desk.

My stomach lurches and I grasp at the edge of the desk for support. What the hell is he doing here?

"Hi, Ellie." Nathan stands up and walks towards me.

All I can do is stare at him. "What are you doing here?"

"I came here to get you."

"But…" I shake my head. "How did you know I was here? I didn't tell you my plans changed."

He smiles. "I heard brakes squealing outside. I thought something had happened so I looked out the window. I saw you getting into the police car."

"Oh," is all I can say.

I wrap my arms around myself. The photo in my pocket is the only proof I have that something's not right. It's the only thing that stops me from accepting that I'm the one who hurt Mikey and killed Steph. The police won't believe me and now the man who had that photo is standing here in front of me.

"Come on," he says. "Let's get out of here."

I stare at him. He's got an almost manic look in his eyes like we're off to a party he's been looking forward to for ages. Why does he look so pleased with himself?

"What?"

He smiles conspiratorially. "Come on. Let's go back to my place. There's something I've got to tell you."

My fingers are still wrapped around the photo in my pocket. Nathan's eyes are so kind and full of warmth, but this picture tells a different story. He's a liar. And he wants me to go back to his place?

I glance back at the duty officer behind the reception counter but she's typing noisily and not paying us any heed. I look behind me. The door I've just come out of is closed. There's no sign of Hobson. Even if he was here he wouldn't listen to me if I begged him to arrest Nathan and question him. By insisting an injured man was setting me up, I've destroyed any credibility I had with the police—and I didn't have a lot to begin with.

I can't think straight. Does he seriously think I'm going anywhere with him?

But what else am I supposed to do? Go back to my flat alone and wait for him to come for me? Nathan is not what he seems and I don't know what he wants from me. I can't call Dad. I can't go back to my flat.

I take a deep breath. My heart is pounding so hard I'm worried I might pass out again.

"Don't you want to know what I've got to tell you?" Nathan asks, eyebrows raised.

He's getting suspicious of how I'm acting. And even though my gut is telling me to get as far away from him as I can, I've got to be careful.

The fog in my brain clears a little as I realise how serious this is. This isn't about keeping my head down and saving money to move away anymore. I've got to get the hell away from here if I don't want to end up like Steph and Mikey. I don't know what he's planning. I don't know what he wants from me.

"You know what?" I say, linking my arm through his even though touching him makes me want to scrub my skin until it's raw. "I think I need a drink after all that. Can we go to the pub first?"

CHAPTER 42
ELLIE

Nathan puts his arm around me as we walk into the pub and it's all I can do not to shove him away. It's Sunday night—there's still a crowd but it's far thinner than it would be on Friday or Saturday as people filter off to get an early night before work on Monday.

Work.

So much has happened this weekend that I haven't even thought about work. Friday seems like a long time ago now. I was so terrified of losing my job—that seems trivial now after everything that's happened.

It's too hot in here. I tug at the neck of my coat. I can't take it off in case I need to get out of here quickly. Panic rises in me as I look around. It feels like everyone is watching me. Do people know the police wanted to speak to me about Steph?

Nathan smiles at me. "You find a seat. I'll get the drinks in."

"No," I say quickly. "No, let me. I must owe you ten rounds at this stage."

I try not to let him see that I'm watching him like a hawk. I need to buy the drinks tonight. I need to be in control. Nathan nods and I hurry to the bar.

"A double vodka soda lime and just a soda with lime."

The barman nods. "Sure, love."

I stare into the mirror behind the bar. My heart pounds.

The barman comes back with the drinks. "This one's got the vodka."

"Thanks," I mutter. I'm struggling to breathe properly. I have three pills left in my bag. My emergency supply of sedatives. If I crushed up one or two and dropped it in Nathan's drink…

I take my change and pick up the drinks, reminding myself that my drink is in my right hand. What am I thinking? Am I seriously planning on drugging Nathan to stop him from coming after me?

What if he catches me? Even thinking about it is making my hands shake so hard that the drinks are sloshing around. I've got to try and calm down.

The more I think about it, the more I realise it's what I have to do. It will be a lot easier to slip something into his drink than it will be to get him out-of-his-mind drunk.

And anyway, I think, recalling the weird fog in my brain on Friday and this morning: it's not like he thought twice before drugging me.

"Thanks," Nathan says as I put the drinks on the table and slide the one in my left hand towards him. For a moment I worry that he's on to me; that he's going to take the one with no alcohol in it.

He doesn't.

My hands shake.

"What's this?" He lifts the glass to his nose and sniffs it.

"Vodka," I say as theatrically as I can. I make a big show of gulping down half the contents of my glass. "I need something stronger than beer."

For a horrible moment, I wonder if he's going to reject it and go up for a pint, but he doesn't. He smiles at me and tips half the glass down his throat. He winces. "That's strong."

"Yeah, well. I need strong. After what happened to Steph."

"Really?"

I look up. He's smiling.

A shiver runs down my spine. "Of course. She was my friend."

"You weren't saying that on Saturday. You were cursing her for lying to you and ripping off your dad."

My cheeks flush. "I was just mouthing off."

"Don't worry," he says. He leans forward and his hand creeps up my leg. "Your secret's safe with me."

I pick up my glass and gulp down the rest of it. God I wish there really was vodka in it, but I can't afford to get pissed right now.

"What do you mean?"

He shifts in his seat. The smile never leaves his face. "I told them, didn't I?"

"Told them what?"

"That you were with me all Saturday apart from when you popped to Steph's and she wasn't there. Just like I said I would."

"Right." My pulse is roaring in my temples and it's a struggle to fight back the feeling of nausea.

"I said you came back and we made love for hours."

The thought would have delighted me just days ago, but now it's about the most repulsive thing I can think of. I want to puke. Who is he? Who is this monster that I allowed into my life? Is that his game? He wants to hold this over my head; to own me?

Nathan frowns. "You don't look very happy considering I've just saved your arse."

"Thank you," I say, forcing a smile. "I just really need a wee, that's all. I'll pop to the loo and get us some more drinks."

He doesn't object. Good. I need to get as many of these rounds in as I can even if it makes a dent in my savings. This is a necessary expense to make sure I can get out of here on the first train tomorrow morning.

I hurry past the bar and into the toilets. I use the pill bottle to crush up two of the pills onto a piece of toilet paper. When

I'm done, I wrap it carefully, as though my life depends on it —which it just might.

————

"Same again?" the barman asks.

I nod. I realise I've been a bit stupid. What if Nathan had gone to the bar and realised I was getting doubles for him and sodas for myself?

I take the drinks and return to our table. "This place is dead," I say, casually taking a gulp of my drink. "We should go somewhere busier."

He shrugs. "Maybe we should go back to mine. I've got to work at six in the morning."

No, that's absolutely the worst thing we could do. "I can't," I whisper, forcing tears to my eyes. "That's where I was when I found out about Steph."

Nathan looks at me and I can tell he's not impressed. I don't know what other excuse to give him. I'm not going to his house. No way. He's been playing me all week and now it's time for me to play him.

"Come on," I say. "I'm going somewhere else. You can go home if you want."

A strange look crosses his face. His cheeks are flushed from the alcohol but I've got a long way to go yet to get him where I need him, and I need to be careful. "Why aren't you frightened? You were afraid to leave my flat yesterday and the day before."

"It was my real father who was following me."

"Yeah I know," he says, pronouncing the words carefully. "But what about what's happened to Steph? It's not safe for you."

I grab his hand even though touching him makes my skin crawl. "Thank you. It's so good of you to look out for me. Do you know Mikey Grant?" I stare at him, stunned. I don't know where that came from. I suppose the need to know the truth is too strong for me to suppress. Why would he hurt Mikey?

He flushes. "What?"

Fuck. I need to keep him on side—just for tonight. "Mikey Grant," I say, waving my hand. "Sorry. I must be getting pissed. I just don't know why he'd do this to me. I wish you could understand what he's like."

He shakes his head. "I'd have told you if I knew him. I don't know many people here, I told you."

How did I fall for that? It's unbelievable to me now. I was so desperate for love that I was willing to believe it. What an idiot.

The photo I found in his flat is burning a hole in my pocket. I want more than anything to slap it on the table and ask him to explain why he had it, but I can't let him know I suspect him.

I drain the last of my soda and lime, wishing I had a better idea of what to do. My plan has so many holes in it. I massage my temples with my knuckles, kneading harder and harder until I'm causing myself actual pain.

"Come on," he says. "We should go. You have a headache."

"Do you know the best cure for a headache?" I ask, raising an eyebrow.

"Ellie..."

"What? I just want to have a little fun after the craziness of today."

"Are you sure that's a good idea?" he nods at his glass. "I still have half my drink left and you've polished off yours."

I poke my tongue out at him. It kills me to flirt with him, but I've got to do it and it's got to be convincing. "Well finish it then. Come on. Or else I'll finish it for you."

He frowns, but he lifts his glass to his lips all the same and drinks from it.

CHAPTER 43
ELLIE

"Come on," I say, trying to stop my voice from shaking. "Let's go to the Dog and Duck."

He grabs my hand. "Why don't we just go back to my place. I don't want to be tired at work tomorrow."

I think about it for a moment. I could bide my time and run when he's at work. Maybe it's a more sensible plan than the one that's currently forming in my mind, but I can't. I can't go back there with him and pretend that everything is okay. Who knows what he'll do to me if I slip up and he knows I've seen through his act?

"Just one more," I say. "I'm buying."

"Okay, fine."

———

An hour later, I'm starting to think this plan might work. I had a quiet word to the barman when Nathan went to the toilet. I told him I was pregnant and that I haven't told Nathan yet, so he's been giving me cokes and pretending they've got vodka in them.

Nathan's stopped telling me we should leave, which is encouraging. He's on his fifth double vodka now and he's starting to slur. I don't know how far I'm going to have to go to get him absolutely wasted.

He gets up to go to the toilet again and I seize my chance. His drink fizzes up when I pop the crushed up pills in and stir it with my finger. I keep a hawk-like eye on the door to the toilets to make sure he doesn't pop out and catch me.

———

"Shots?" I say, widening my eyes and grinning across the table at Nathan.

He smiles. His pupils are dilated and his cheeks are pink and blotchy.

Have I done enough? It's impossible to know.

I order two tequilas knowing mine will be water. Still, I go through the pantomime of putting a pinch of salt on my hand and then sucking the piece of lime when I've had my fake shot.

"Last orders, folks," the barman says to the thinning crowd.

Shit. I hadn't realised it was that late. I shake my head. Even though I've stayed sober, there's so much noise in there at the moment that it's hard to think clearly. I've also got a headache.

We drink up and go outside before I've thought of a plan. Nathan takes my hand and I start to panic. It's cold out and I could do without that—I don't want the cold air sobering him up. Why is he still standing? Do those pills have the opposite effect when they're taken with alcohol?

I look around. I no longer fear the man in the shadows—I need him. But there's no-one there.

Damn it.

I could really use his help right now. He doesn't know me —so he might just believe me.

There's one place I know will still be open, but I can't bring myself to go there—or can I? This isn't about keeping my head down anymore. It's about my safety.

I close my eyes and try to fight back the tears that are coming.

"I know where to go."

I drag him along the street towards the Builder's Arms.

———

"I love this place," Nathan says as we walk in the door.

I wrench my hand away, filled with a stronger hatred than I've ever felt for anyone. I bet he loves this place. I used to love it too until my life changed forever. Just in here. I glance at the door that leads to the toilets. That's one place I can't bring myself to go—it's a step too far.

Nathan walks towards the bar.

"No," I say, "I'll get them. Let's sit over there where it's quiet."

We can't sit at the bar. Not in here. I know too many of the regulars and I need Nathan off their radar so I can feed him as much booze as I can get into him without anyone refusing him service.

Thankfully I don't recognise any of the bar staff. I make my way over there and upgrade Nathan to a triple vodka. I don't have much time. I need to make this count. I get us two drinks each.

I have around four hundred and fifty pounds in my savings account plus another two hundred which is all that's left of next month's rent. By running away I'll be forfeiting my deposit, but I'm going to have to forget it. I can't risk my life for the sake of that crappy flat.

It doesn't seem real yet. In less than twelve hours I'll be leaving here for good.

I shiver. That's if everything goes to plan.

By now, Nathan is struggling to lift his glass without sloshing the contents all over the place.

"We should get food," he slurs.

"Lightweight," I say, laughing.

That laugh is hollow. I always thought going out to pubs

was fun, but tonight has been the most dreadful night of my life. It's made me even more determined to quit drinking. I don't even envy Nathan his vodka anymore.

Our conversation has been going around and around in circles for some time. I've been tempted to try and find out what his motivations are, but I've stopped myself. I can live without knowing the why's if it means I can get away safely.

When the pub closes and we have to leave, I call the number of a taxi I found on a poster behind the bar. Nathan is half-leaning on me for support and I get the horrible feeling once again that he's putting on an act to get one over on me. I don't see how, though. I sat there and watched him drink those drinks, including the one with the sedatives.

I turn around and look up at the Builder's Arms as we wait for the taxi. I've avoided even looking at this place for the past year, but it's transformed again. Now it makes me feel sad. I've been so angry at Mikey all this time and he's been lying helpless in a hospital bed.

But I can't afford to lose myself in the past—not now.

I snake my hand around Nathan's hips and slip my fingertips into the pocket of his jeans. I half expect him to grab me in a headlock but he doesn't even flinch.

The taxi finally pulls up as I'm shoving Nathan's phone and wallet into my handbag. I help Nathan into the back and give the man the address.

The short drive to my flat feels like it takes forever. I have to keep elbowing Nathan to stop him from snoring and making the driver suspicious. The last thing I need is for him to insist on Nathan getting out at my place.

I watch the dark streets, desperately hoping to see the man who said he was my real father. This time tomorrow I'll have disappeared—I hope. I don't just need his help, I have so many questions for him.

We pull up and I feel a shiver of fear when I open the door. I thank the driver and then make a great show of pretending to put cash in Nathan's pocket.

The taxi driver pulls away and keeps going away from the

town. The address I gave him is a short distance away from the police station in the town ten miles away. When Nathan's not able to pay, the driver will drop him off at the police station for the night, where they'll make him sleep it off.

I feel lighter than I've felt in a long time as I cross the road and walk up the path to my flat. For the first time in ages, I don't have the feeling of being hunted.

But I'm not safe yet.

I still have work to do.

CHAPTER 44
ELLIE

The first thing I do when I get inside is take the sim card out of Nathan's phone and break it. I'm tempted to keep the phone—it's a better model than mine—but I resist. I pour salt into a glass and top it up with water. I drop the phone into the mixture. He knows where I live, but I can't risk him tracking me after tomorrow morning.

I open his wallet. He had a hundred pounds in cash and various cards. I take out the cash. I should have gone to the ATM before I got back but I'll do it in the station before I leave tomorrow. I cut up his cards and drop them in the bin. Anything to slow him down and help me get away.

Will I be able to disappear with seven hundred and fifty pounds? I've got to, don't I? It's not safe here.

I sigh as I look around the flat wondering what I'm going to be able to keep. I won't miss this place. I won't miss most of the things in it, either.

I'm hit by the same painful sensation as earlier—that I've been tricked into hating Mikey for a whole year. We had so many good times in this flat and I've been working my hardest to block them out all this time. How many things have I forgotten that I should have cherished?

I close my eyes. The flat is too quiet. I turn on the TV for some background noise, being careful not to raise the volume too high. The last thing I need is the police showing up. I think about going to Nathan's to see if there's anything there that shows me why he's done this, but it's too risky.

I move quickly through the flat, shoving essentials like face wipes and a change of clothes into a small backpack. The reality of this slowly sinks in: this flat is bitterly cold and damp for about ten months of the year, but it's the only home I have. Pretty soon, I won't even have this. Will home be a shelter? A tent? What will I do for food if I can't get a job and my money runs out?

It's unthinkable. I'm about to blow up my life.

But I don't see another way. Steph is dead. Mikey is seriously hurt. The police won't believe me. I can't stay here.

The one thing that stands in my favour is the birth certificate I found in Dad's house. Maybe there's a way I can use it to create a new life for myself—one where Nathan and the police can't track me down. I can't go to London, but maybe I can get myself to France or Holland on the ferries. I'll figure it out in time—for now I've just got to worry about getting away from here.

I finish going through my wardrobe and stare at the piles of paperwork and photos on the ground. Thank goodness I didn't throw them away.

I hesitate.

My heart hasn't caught up with the new information I learned today. I still feel so angry at Mikey, but I have a feeling that will dull with time. I kneel down and pull the pictures of us from the stack.

I can't fight back the tears as I go through them to pick one to take with me. Any doubt in my mind that I was the one who hurt him melts away now: I loved him too much to ever hurt him. My only problem with him was that he was listening to the people who wanted him to distance himself from me.

My hands shake as I look at a picture of Mikey from that chairman's dinner where all this trouble started and I feel an overwhelming sense of shame. I might not have hurt Mikey, but I'm the one who got uncontrollably drunk that night and turned the higher-ups at the club against me.

If that hadn't happened…

I close my eyes. I need to rest before the morning, not sit here beating myself up. I shove the photo in my bag along with the pictures of my mother and go out to the living room to wait.

I sit on the couch and turn on the TV. I know I should get some sleep, but my mind is racing now. I keep thinking there has to be another way that doesn't involve throwing myself into the gutter, but I don't know what that is.

I pick up my phone and find Dad's number in my contacts. That's the one thing nagging me about all this. Even after everything that's happened between us and everything he hid from me, I can't bear the thought of him thinking badly of me.

I press the call button and hold my breath as I wait for the call to connect. It just rings out and goes to voicemail. I think about leaving a message but decide against it. It was crazy to even call him.

I put my phone on the coffee table and lie down. I wish I could switch off but I can't. I can't think straight. I don't know what's worse: my life as it is or my life as it will be, but I don't know how to make my current life better. I have no idea what Nathan's motivation is and it scares me that someone else can have so much control over my life. I'm isolated from everyone I used to know and Nathan made the point several times that he told the police we were together on Saturday night. He thinks he owns me now. It's a horrible feeling.

I sigh and change the channel. There's nothing decent on this late.

My eyelids grow heavier. There's a peace in knowing that Nathan's not going to bother me tonight. And by the time he sobers up and gets over here, I'll be long gone.

———

I jerk awake. It takes me a few moments to remember where I am. The couch in my flat. I gasp in a breath and tell myself to calm down.

I'm safe.

My plan worked.

I look around as I sit up. It's still dark. Disappointment washes over me—I'm impatient to get going but the first trains don't leave until six in the morning.

How long was I asleep for? It feels like I've only just drifted off.

I yawn and reach for my phone, groaning when it's not right in front of me on the table. I must have thrashed around in my sleep and knocked it off.

I lean forward and feel around on the floor beside me. When I don't find it there, I try the narrow space beneath the couch. It's not there either.

My heart starts to race. I know I'm being silly, but I have the strongest sense that I'm not alone in the flat. I take a deep breath and exhale slowly. I'm just being paranoid. I reach for the lamp on the side table before I remember that the bulb blew a few weeks ago and I still haven't gotten around to replacing it.

I stand up and move to the other side of the room where the light switch is. I've walked around the flat in the dark often enough to know its layout from memory, but I keep my hands out in front of me just in case—I can't afford to trip over something and injure myself; not tonight.

I only make it a few steps when my fingers brush off something. At first I think I've gone the wrong way and walked into the curtains, but that thought only lasts an instant because whatever I'm touching is warm. My flat is a lot of things, but warm isn't one of them. What's in front of me isn't a wall or a window.

It's him.

No.

It can't be.

That's not possible.

But then I remember my doubts from earlier. Didn't I wonder if it was all just a big double-bluff? I told myself I was being paranoid, but now it seems I wasn't. I should have known I could never outsmart him.

I hear the slightest snort of air and my heart hammers. He's enjoying this, I think, and that only makes it worse.

I want to scream at him. I want to lash out for all the pain and misery he's caused me, but I hold back. I need to be smart about this. There's only one way out of the flat and that's through the front door.

I'll have to get past him first.

How am I supposed to do that when I'm struggling to catch my breath?

He still hasn't said anything—it's completely unnerving.

I launch myself in the direction of the door, hoping there's enough space to get around him and get away before he can stop me.

It doesn't work like that. The floorboards creak and I collide with a wall of muscle. Fingers close around my upper arms.

He laughs cruelly as he throws me backwards. My head smacks against the edge of the table and erupts in a world of pain.

CHAPTER 45
ELLIE

I open my eyes. The pain in my head is so bad it feels like it must have been split open. No. This is all wrong.

His fingers close around my ankle. I tear it away from him and kick at him.

"No. Get your hands off me," I snap, disheartened by the shooting pain the movement caused in my lower back.

I'm injured. How the hell can I fight him off if I can't move without it hurting? The only hope I have is if I can talk him around. But how? He's been one step ahead of me this whole time.

"Please, Nathan. I don't know why you're doing this. What have I done to you?"

"Just shut the fuck up, will you? You're not going to wriggle out of this one."

My blood runs cold. It's not Nathan, but I know that voice. I've heard it almost every day for years.

"Jason?"

It can't be. How could it? I barely even know the guy.

"You sound surprised."

He grabs my ankles and tugs me towards him before I even know what he's doing. My elbows chafe against the worn carpet. My heart pounds. I'm no match for his strength and how the hell can I try to talk him around when I have no idea what this is about?

"Why? Why would you do this?"

The light flicks on. I wince. My eyes weren't prepared for it. They water and I blink frantically to get them back to normal as quickly as I can. I have enough handicaps right now without being able to see him.

Jason stands over me with a look on his face that I've never seen before.

I open my mouth and scream as loudly as I can.

Jason doesn't even flinch. He seems more amused than anything.

I shake my head. I don't understand. "It was you, wasn't it? You broke in. How did you get in?"

He snorts. "You didn't exactly make it difficult, did you Ellie?"

How can it be Jason? Is he linked to Nathan? I feel a rush of anger. How dare he come into my home and attack me? "Get the hell out of my flat."

He laughs. "Or what?"

I swallow. My resolve vanishes just as quickly as it appeared. He's been tormenting me for over a year and I have no idea why. That puts me on the back foot. I've got to calm down and figure out a plan, but I don't know what to do. I know Jason in a work context. I know he doesn't like lateness and he always has a bag of crisps on his desk. That's it. I can't understand why he'd do this.

I take a deep breath and fill my lungs with air. "Help!" I scream. "There's a man in my house. Please help!"

"Shut up, Ellie," he says, moving to the kitchen counter. "Actually, you can scream if you want. No-one's going to hear you. There's no-one in the houses either side."

My eyes narrow. "How do you know that?"

"Because I know you," he says simply.

He picks something up off the counter. I squint to make out what it is. It looks like a plastic freezer bag with something inside it.

He comes closer and hunkers down in front of me. My stomach lurches when I realise what he's holding.

Inside the plastic is a kitchen knife. There are dark brown stains on it and I gag when I realise what they must be.

"Do you know what this is?" he asks, waving it in front of me.

I close my eyes. I can't look at it.

"Oh, come on. Don't be squeamish. Don't you recognise it? It's one of yours."

I shake my head. "No." It can't be. It can't.

"It's the knife you used to kill your friend."

"I didn't," I whisper.

He frowns. "It's got your fingerprints on it."

This can't be happening. It can't. I thought I was being paranoid earlier when I assumed it was Nathan who was behind this, but the reality was so much worse. It wasn't real before. I know I saw it on the news and was questioned by the police, but seeing the knife he used to kill her…

I can't hold it back any longer. I retch and acrid stomach water comes shooting out of my mouth—there's no food left in my stomach it's been so long since I ate anything.

Jason recoils. "Disgusting."

I wipe my mouth with my sleeve, not caring what he thinks. I could never be as disgusting as him. Pain shoots through my arm as I move it. I must have cracked something as I fell to the ground at a weird angle.

Oh God, I think. How am I going to get out of this?

"Help!" I shout. My voice is hoarse now, from stomach acid and exhaustion and fear.

I'm so tired of this. The one time I thought I'd gotten back in control, I was wrong.

Jason's eyes land on the backpack resting on one of the cheap dining chairs at the kitchen table. "What's this?"

"You don't get to ask the questions," I snap. "We're not in work now."

He unzips the bag and starts to throw the contents onto the floor. He pauses when he gets to the picture of Mikey. His amusement turns to anger. "What the fuck do you want with this?"

"I know the truth," I hiss. "I know you're behind everything that's happened in the last year." A horrible realisation hits me. "And you were the one following me last year. I thought it was someone from the rugby club."

He throws the bag on the ground and crumples the picture in his hand. "So you finally see me, Ellie."

"What the hell are you talking about? I see you every day at work."

He doesn't seem to hear me. I can't look at him—the look in his eyes makes him seem like a different person to the Jason I know from the office. It's creepy.

"You made it so easy," he whispers. "Searching poison. Searching her name." He smirks. "And your father's."

I shake my head. "No. No you can't."

"Why shouldn't I?" He comes over to me again and I can't help flinching. I gasp as the strongest feeling of deja vu I've ever experienced washes over me. Last week when I thought we'd met Jason out in the pub. I was wrong. That wasn't last week.

"It was you," I hiss. All of the hair on my body stands on end and I shiver. "You were in the Builder's Arms that night."

He laughs. "I should have known. Do you have any idea how shocked I was when you told me you'd seen me out? I thought you'd remembered something during the week."

"But how? How could you... what if I'd remembered at the time?"

"I had no idea. I went to ground for a while. Then when I heard you were in hospital and the police hadn't been sniffing around, I realised you had no memory of what happened."

I stare at him in disbelief. "You started those rumours."

He shakes his head. "Not initially. I did everything I could to spread them, though." He grins and a chill runs down my spine. I've never seen anyone so unaffected by the pain they've caused to others.

"Why would you do that?"

"You were being a fool, Ellie. You'd moped around for a month or two, calling in sick and coming in stinking of wine. Then he came back and smiled at you and you were going to welcome him back with open arms. He treated you like shit!"

"No… I…" I shake my head, trying to get my thoughts in order. "What did it matter how he treated me? It was nothing to you."

"I never meant to hurt you, Ellie." He strokes my face.

I recoil. "Get your hands off me."

"Oh don't worry," he spits. "I've wised up. Even when you had no-one you wouldn't even look at me. You wouldn't even open up to me last week when all that family stuff blew up."

"You're my manager! I was trying to be professional."

"So professional." He snorts bitterly. "Coming in late after staying out all night and getting pissed with that idiot. What's he got that I don't? He's a fucking loser. You'd seriously rather scrape the bottom of the barrel than look at me? You're as unstable as everyone says."

I stare at him in disbelief. "I'm not unstable. The only reason people think that is because of what you've done. You're a psychopath."

I'm filled with regrets. If only I hadn't been so cautious. If only I'd gone back to Nathan's house to try and search the place. He wasn't the real danger at all. If anything, he might have helped me.

Jason slaps me across the face and my whole head erupts in pain. I feel like a broken toy, thrown aside. I can't stay here like this. I've got to get myself away.

But how?

Jason moves out of my line of sight. I hear him clattering around in the kitchen.

I test each of my arms and legs and then my fingers and toes, tightening the muscles and moving them just an inch to see if anything is broken. My right elbow is the worst—there's a sharp pain every time I try to move it. My legs feel fine. It's my head I'm worried about, but I've felt it with my hands and there doesn't seem to be any blood.

Jason is still moving around in the kitchen, opening and closing cupboard doors. My blood runs cold. The searches he mentioned earlier. He's going to poison me, isn't he? All this was sparked off because he thought I was starting to remember what happened to me and Mikey.

"I put myself out there," he mutters, when he comes back over to me. "I was the only one who didn't turn away from you after all this happened."

I can't take my eyes off the glass in his hand. "What is that?"

He crouches down in front of me and holds it out. "Drink it."

"What's in it?" I ask, slowly moving forward to look at the glass. Really I'm trying to move into a better position without making him suspicious.

He waves it in front of me. "Just orange juice."

I shake my head as I curl myself into a ball, with my arms around my knees. "The police are going to know I didn't poison myself when they find slap marks across my face."

He flushes with anger. "Not if I burn the place down around you."

All the blood rushes to my head. I don't doubt for a moment that he'd do it. He's crazy. His pupils are dilated. I've never seen him like this. I've never seen *anyone* like this.

There's no point in trying to reason with him, but I'm starting to doubt my plan. Can I really spring up and get out of here without him stopping me?

What choice do I have?

I hold my left hand out.

My heart leaps as he hands me the glass.

I take it from him, fingers clasping the bottom of it.

He watches.

I raise it to my lips.

His eyes move to mine. They're empty: completely devoid of emotion. Why have I never noticed before?

A surge of adrenaline shoots through me as I flick my wrist. Juice sloshes everywhere as I throw all my weight forward and ram the glass into his face. I've not been at the gym in months but the strength comes from some instinctive place inside me. I hurtle forward as he loses balance and falls to the ground.

I run screaming to the door that leads to the hallway. My heart is pounding and I'm gasping for breath. I scramble along the dark hallway, slipping on the lino but there's no time to put on shoes.

I collide with the front door and scramble to unlock it. I throw it open, but I'm shoved into the corner before I can get out.

"You stupid bitch!" Jason screams.

I buck against him but I can't move. He's pinning me against the wall. His hands close around my neck. I try to scream but no sound comes out.

I claw desperately against the door, so close to getting away.

"No," I cough. "How will this look like an accident?"

I try to kick backwards, but I can't reach him and it only hurts my back from where I fell earlier.

He's too strong. No matter how hard I try, I can't get him off me. With the restricted air flowing to my brain, I'm getting weaker and weaker. My vision is starting to blur around the edges and it's just a matter of time before I lose consciousness.

No.

I can't.

It feels cold all of a sudden and there's noise, but I'm too far gone now. Everything is far away. I feel like I'm drifting further and further by the second.

CHAPTER 46
ELLIE

The first thing I'm aware of is the pain in my throat. Then the confusion hits. It's quiet. I try to open my eyes. They're sore and swollen, but they open a crack. It's bright.

I gasp in a breath.

My heart sinks. For a moment I thought I must be in hospital.

I'm not.

I'm lying in the hallway of the flat.

Panicking, I try to roll onto my side to get up, but my whole body erupts in pain. What happened? Did he knock me out and leave me here? I can't hear anything.

"Ellie, don't move."

I freeze. "Who's that?" It's not Nathan and it's not Jason—who else is involved in this?

A moment later, the man who says he's my father comes into view.

"Ellie," he says, taking my hand. "Are you alright?"

I nod. "I think so." My voice is a sharp rasp that hurts my throat. I stare up at him. "You said you were my father."

He grimaces. "We don't have time to talk about that now. Plenty of time later. The police are on their way."

I try to sit up. "No, what? They can't come. They're going to think I did this."

"Don't move. It's going to be okay."

"It's not," I hiss. "He's set up this whole thing. He's framing me for Steph's murder and for hurting Mikey. He was trying to poison me."

"Calm down," Tony whispers. "He's not going anywhere. When the police get here I'll tell them what happened. When they see the bloody state of you they'll work it out for themselves."

I gasp in a breath. "They didn't the last time. He's sneaky." This time I manage to sit up. I've got to see for myself. "Where is he? Are you sure you've got him?"

Tony kneels down beside me. "You're as stubborn as your mother," he says, brushing my hair from my face. "But I've got him. I was tempted to smash that stupid face of his, but that wouldn't do you any good, would it?"

I stare up at him. I don't say anything for a moment as I imagine someone finally giving Jason what he deserves. I shake my head as much as I can without it hurting. "He'll lie to them."

I close my eyes and play back the past year in my mind. Why did I just sit back and accept that Mikey had turned everyone against me? Why didn't I go knock on their doors and insist that they tell me why they'd cut me off? If I had—if I'd persisted—maybe I'd have gotten to the truth a lot sooner and saved Steph's life in the process.

"Hey," he says, squeezing my shoulder. "Don't blame yourself for this."

I take a deep breath. He's right. It's time I finally stopped beating myself up for everything that's happened. "I want to see him," I say.

I need to be sure. It's going to be a long time before I accept someone else's word as the truth again.

"You should stay here until the ambulance comes," Tony says.

But I insist. He helps me to my feet and supports me as we

move into the living room. I gasp when I see Jason lying bruised and bloodied on the floor with his own hoodie and jeans used to restrain his arms and legs. He's glaring at me and there's something so unnerving about those eyes.

"You shouldn't..." Tony starts to say. He glances at me and stops.

"Why?" I ask Jason. "Why would you do this?"

He just smiles at me and it's the most chilling smile I've ever seen.

A shudder of dread contorts my whole body. It's his word against mine, isn't it? It doesn't matter if he's tied up now: he's still a danger to me.

I turn to Tony. "He'll twist it. He'll lie to them. I have no evidence." I close my eyes. What I need to ask him is not something I've ever asked anyone. "Can't you..."

Tony holds his finger to his lips. A warning. "We do this right."

"No, but..."

"Just trust me," he murmurs.

"He'll talk his way out of it. He'll twist it."

Tony shakes his head. "He won't. Not this time."

I tune in to the sound of sirens approaching and everything around me goes blurry again. I try to fight it; I need to make Tony understand, but I can't get the words out.

CHAPTER 47
ELLIE
MONDAY

The next time I wake, it's in a hospital bed. I stare at the ceiling as I get my bearings. There are people here: I can see them in my peripheral vision.

There's movement. My heart flips: my first thought is Jason has somehow managed to wriggle out of this and convince everyone I'm the unhinged one. I move my arms. They're not restrained to the bed.

Tony appears beside me. "You're awake. Let's prop you up so you can see." He pulls me forward and shoves two pillows behind me. "I took these from an empty room," he says, with pride in his eyes. "I thought you'd want to see what was happening once you woke up."

"Careful," says a disapproving voice.

"Dad?" I cough. I'd forgotten about the pain in my throat. It's eased, but it still hurts to talk. I look at Tony. "I'm sorry," I whisper. "I can't think of him as—"

"It's alright," he mutters, squeezing my hand. "Why don't I fetch you a coffee. A proper one. You two have a lot to talk about."

I smile and nod as I try to hold back tears. This couldn't be more different to the last time I woke up in hospital, alone and afraid, with no memory of how I got there.

Dad steps closer as soon as Tony's left the room. "DS

Hobson told me to call him the minute you woke. I should go and do that. But first." He clears his throat and the colour slowly drains from his face. "I'm so sorry, Ellie. I let you down. I should never have..." his lips twitch. "I was trying to protect you, but all I did was put you at risk."

I shake my head. Even though I've been so angry with him all week, I can't bear to see him like this. "I don't want you to feel bad. I just... please just tell me the truth. What happened? Who are you really?"

He sighs. "You're Ellie Kent. I'm John Miller." He shakes his head. "It's been a very long time since I've said that name."

"And my mother?"

A sad look crosses his eyes. "My sister. Joy Kent. Her name was Josephine but I can't remember her ever being called that by anyone."

"You're my uncle."

He nods. "I am."

My back is starting to ache so I try to shift into a more comfortable position. Dad jumps to his feet to try and help but I wave him away. I'm fine, really. Physically anyway, apart from some bruises and soreness. "Why..." I shake my head. I don't even know what I want to ask. I've spent hours trying to make sense of it. "Why..."

He holds up a hand. "I'll tell you everything, Ellie. Just rest. Don't strain yourself. I know you must have a lot questions." He rubs his cheek and I can tell this is hard for him— he's used to keeping secrets. "Joy was a good name for your mother. She was such a happy child. We were close even though I was five years older. I adored her from the moment she came home from the hospital." He bows his head. "Things changed when she was eighteen or nineteen. She got in with a bad crowd. It was just me and her by then. We... I tried to do my best for her, but she was stubborn. She thought I was sticking my oar in when I was only trying to look out for her."

"She moved into a flat and I started seeing less of her. I

was busy setting up my first company so I probably didn't put as much effort in as I should have. I can't tell you how much I regret that now, but I was still young. I didn't realise..." he sighs heavily. "She came over one Sunday and announced she'd gotten married. Just like that." He frowns and looks at me. "Ellie, I don't want to speak badly of your real father, but there's no love lost between the two of us— even now. He wasn't good for her. He was well known around where we lived as a waster. A good-for-nothing. I tried to warn her, but she wouldn't listen. Well, they got involved in drugs." He closes his eyes. "Sometimes she'd come and stay with me if they were having... a rough patch. I thought things had turned a corner just before you were born. She had enough. She came to live with me. I was proud of her. I thought she'd knocked the addiction on the head."

"She stayed clean for a long time. Until you were well over a year old. Then I suppose she got antsy. I was working all the hours I could. She was at home with you and..." he shakes his head. "I'm sorry if this is hard for you to take, but I don't want to spin the truth even slightly."

I nod. "Go on."

"Tony had been begging her to come back to him. She resisted for a while, but the pull was too strong. She was seeing him again. This time it was different. I warned her. She had you to think of. But she was still so young. She just wanted to have fun. I should have been stricter now I think back on it, but what could I have done? Lock her in the house? There was one night when she was particularly antsy. I managed to convince her to stay in. I was so pleased. I popped out to get a takeaway and when I got back she was gone."

I stare at him. "What? She left me on my own?"

The edges of his mouth turn down. "She knew I wouldn't be gone long. That was the last time I saw her. And I..." He closes his eyes. "If I'd known, I wouldn't have lost my temper at her. I was just so angry that she wanted to leave you. She couldn't help it, of course, it was the addiction that controlled her. She'd fought it for so long, but in the end she couldn't resist the pull of it."

"Who poisoned her then? I thought…"

He takes my hand and squeezes it. "I'm so sorry, love. I thought I was protecting you. I should have just told you. She poisoned herself. Not even a week later. It was an overdose. Heroin."

"But her death certificate says…"

"I know what it says. I called in a favour. I didn't want you growing up with the stigma of it. It's true. She was poisoned. She just administered it herself." He sighs and shakes his head.

I stare at him. It seems like a silly thing to fixate on now, but I can't help it. "She wasn't an actress."

He laughs sadly. "I never expected you to remember that. I can't even remember saying it. When you were very small I'd make up stories to calm you when you were crying for her. She was always a princess or an actress or a famous singer."

We sit in silence for a while as I try to remember. There are so many things I need to ask him, but my mind has gone blank.

"We have all the time in the world, Ellie. You should rest."

I shake my head. "No. I need to know. All of it." I take a breath. "Why did you change our names? What was the point in that?"

"People talked. They knew what she was. And I was worried about you. I thought Tony's mother might try to get custody of you and I couldn't…" he rubs his face. "I know it might sound heartless now, but that whole family was plagued by addiction. I'd lost your mother. I couldn't bear the thought of losing you too."

I think about the search results that came up for Eleanor Kent when I was trying to figure everything out a few days ago. "Did no-one come looking for me? There was no missing person report from that time."

He squeezes my hand. "Not long after we left, Tony was

arrested for killing the dealer who supplied those drugs to your mother. He was in prison for a very long time. I suppose in the chaos, his family were distracted." He raises his eyebrows. "But he did track us down, didn't he? It's very strange—it was something I dreaded for years, but if hadn't gone to your flat last night…"

I shudder. I don't want to think about what would have happened if Tony hadn't turned up when he did.

"We mustn't think about that now. You're safe. That's the only thing that matters."

I look up at him. He seems remarkably composed. "I'm sorry about what happened to Steph."

"Ellie, we weren't involved. DS Hobson called to say you thought we were in a relationship."

"But I found that document in your house," I say. "Signing the company over to her."

The atmosphere in the room changes. Dad's eyes flicker away from me. My heart starts to speed up.

"What? What is it?"

He sighs. "I sold the company to her father, Ellie. The Stephanie Price Trust. I should have known he'd put her in charge when I saw the name of the company, but I didn't give it too much thought at the time. I was just glad to have a buyer who wanted everything finalised as quickly as I did."

"I don't understand. Why would you sell the company?" My heart pounds and there's an uncomfortable lurch in my stomach.

"You should rest. Perhaps I can come back later when—"

"No. You said you didn't want secrets. You need to tell me."

He stands up and paces to the window. "It seemed like such an open and shut case, Ellie. You have to forgive me. It's hard for me to say this, but I believed you were the one who'd hurt Mikey. I should have suspected something was off last week when you spoke as if you didn't know what had happened to him, but I put that down to some sort of avoidance. I don't know."

I shake my head. "What's Mikey got to do with this?" I don't understand why Dad is bringing him up. It's too painful for me to think about him just now. I still feel so guilty for shutting myself away instead of asking the difficult questions I should have asked. My eyes widen as I remember the invoice DS Hobson showed me. "The hospital…"

"When I thought you'd hurt him, I went to his mother. I offered to pay for his care." He bows his head. "Yes, it was partly out of guilt, but it also meant she wouldn't push the police to press charges."

"Oh God…"

"It's not your fault, Ellie. It's not."

"You sold the company to cover up what you thought I'd done."

"That doesn't matter now," he says, though he can't hide the pain in his eyes. "We'll figure something out. The main thing is you're safe. I'm so sorry I doubted you."

I close my eyes. I can't stop thinking about the fact that he'd still think I was capable of murder if Tony hadn't burst in and stopped Jason when he did. He would have made it look like a suicide. He came so close to pulling it off.

"Has Jason spoken to the police?"

Dad squeezes my shoulder. "I'll go and call Hobson. He'll be better able to fill you in."

"No." I shiver. "I don't want to talk to him."

"There's no need to be afraid, Ellie. It's over now."

"Is it?"

"I'll go and call Hobson."

My body breaks out in a cold sweat. "Wait." I want to believe him, but I can't imagine the police being on my side. He doesn't understand.

"What is it?"

"I heard you talking about me. On Thursday evening. I went to your house."

His face falls. "I had no idea."

"Steph was saying you had to tell me. I thought it was

about your relationship. But it can't have been. What did she mean?"

"There was no love lost between us, Ellie. I feel sorry for the poor girl, but we weren't friendly by any stretch of the imagination. I didn't even know you two were friends until that night. She came over and suddenly she was your biggest advocate. She wanted me to tell you everything. I didn't think you could handle it—not after she'd insinuated herself into your life like that."

"Do you think she sought me out?"

He shakes his head. "I don't know. Perhaps she genuinely wanted to be friends. Maybe she wanted leverage. Who knows?"

Who knows. It's the story of my life. I have to accept the fact that I might never know the motivation behind the people who've been pulling the strings in my life this past year. It's a hard thing to admit.

"You said I had issues."

Dad closes his eyes and I wish I hadn't said that. "Jason fooled a lot of people, Ellie. Myself included. I'll never forgive myself for that."

———

"Ellie."

My eyes flicker open. I can't remember falling asleep, but I must have because Dad is gone. DS Hobson is standing alone at my bedside.

I stare up at him, not knowing what to think. Is he going to get angry again? I don't think I can handle that right now.

I sigh. The pain is worse now that it was earlier. The painkillers must be wearing off. My throat hurts every time I try to swallow.

DS Hobson stares at my neck and I realise I've not even seen how it looks. "Ellie, I owe you an apology."

Tears come to my eyes. It shouldn't make a difference

what he thinks, but it does. He thought I'd hurt Mikey and Steph. But then so did everyone.

He points at the chair beside my bed. "Do you mind if I sit down? Or would you prefer if I came back later?"

I sigh. It's going to take a while to get used to the fact that the police aren't out to get me. And I owe it to Mikey and Steph to do everything I can to make sure Jason is locked up for a very long time.

"Please," I say, gesturing to the chair.

He sits down and I take a breath. "It was so messed up. I thought Mikey had come back because he was annoyed at me for going out with Nathan. I had no idea what happened to him. As far as I knew…" I stop myself and take a breath. "I'm sorry. It's all muddled up in my head."

"Take your time."

I shake my head. "No. I need you to get Jason. The rest of it doesn't matter. There was that break-in I told you about yesterday. I didn't think anything was missing, but there was. He'd taken a knife from my kitchen. He showed it to me last night—it was in a plastic bag and had what looked like blood on it."

I take a breath, trying not to imagine how that blood got there.

"We can stop and take a break if you want."

"No, I need to do this." I stop and try to collect my thoughts. If only I'd not said anything to Jason about seeing him in the pub. Was that really the thing that set him off? I shake my head. No. Of course not. He set this off himself a year ago when he hurt Mikey. I wish with all my heart that I could remember more.

"I got home last night and fell asleep on the couch. When I woke up, Jason was there. He'd taken my phone so I couldn't call for help. I tried to get past him but he threw me back and I hit my head against the table. He slapped my face a couple of times. He also said he was going to poison me and burn the house down around me." I flinch as I imagine how differently this might have turned out if Tony hadn't come when he did.

"It was in the orange juice. I hope there's still some trace of it left—it spilled when I threw the glass at him. I..."

"Ellie, we'll leave it there for now. This is a hard thing to come to terms with. We're going to do everything we can to get justice for Steph and for Mikey." He gets up and goes to the door. He pauses. "One more thing, Ellie."

"Yes?"

"Your friend Nathan has been into the station wanting us to arrest you."

I groan. "Oh God. I'm sorry. I thought this was him. I got him drunk last night and stuck him in a taxi so he couldn't... I thought he was the one setting me up."

"It's alright, Ellie. I'll have a talk to him."

I worry at the frayed skin around my fingernails. "I can't shake the feeling that he was involved in this," I whisper. "There were too many weird things about him. I didn't see it at the time, but—"

DS Hobson comes back to my bedside and pats my hand. "If Nathan's involved in this, we'll get him. Don't you worry."

I smile, but I can't stop worrying. I know his intentions are good, but I can't just sit here and leave my problems for other people to sort out.

Not after what happened.

When I get out of here, I'll do my own digging.

CHAPTER 48
ELLIE
ONE WEEK LATER

I knock on Nathan's door and wait. It feels weird to be doing this, but I'm sticking to the decision I made when I was in hospital. I'll never bury my head in the sand again. Jason is refusing to cooperate with the police, but from searching his phone and computer records, they're confident he was working alone and that Nathan wasn't involved in Steph's murder. Still, that doesn't explain why he had that photo of me—I'm not going to be able to relax until I find out.

Nathan opens the door. The colour drains from his face when he sees it's me.

"What do you want?" he asks. He tries to close the door in my face, but I'm too quick for him. I shove my foot in the door.

"This won't take long."

"You're not coming in."

I smile tightly. "I don't want to come in. I just need to ask you some questions." Perhaps it was foolish of me to come here, but I'm sick of being afraid and living my life in the shadows.

"You want to ask *me* some questions? After you drugged me and stole my stuff? I had to spend a night in the police cells because of you. When *I* was the victim."

I shrug. Should I feel bad? Because I don't. "I'll pay for a replacement phone when I get the money." It might be some time before that happens: I quit BE Call Solutions as soon as I could. It doesn't matter if Jason is going to prison for a long time. The place will always remind me of him.

Nathan scowls. "It won't make up for the inconvenience."

I reach into my bag and pull out the photo I found in Nathan's flat. "Recognise this?"

The colour leaches from his face again. "Where did you get that?"

"In your flat," I say breezily. "When I was looking for the dehumidifier." I take a step closer. "I only sent you off on that wild goose chase taxi journey because I found this and assumed it was you who was trying to set me up. What were you doing? Stalking me?"

"You had no right to go through my stuff," Nathan says huffily. "And I wasn't stalking you."

"What would you call it?"

He shrugs. "I just found that photo on my phone and printed it to show you. It was a coincidence. There was no need to overreact."

I shake my head. I'm done with giving people the benefit of the doubt. "You didn't just find a picture of me that you'd coincidentally taken a year before we met, Nathan. That's bullshit."

"Oh alright, fine," he snaps. "I knew who you were. I'd always fancied you and I'd heard the rumours. I figured you'd be lonely so I chanced my arm. I pretended I didn't know who you were." He folds his arms and juts his chin defiantly.

I shiver. "You sat there listening to me tell you about how I was scared Mikey was coming for me. You let me believe…"

"I couldn't do anything. I felt bad, but if I told you the truth I'd have to admit that I lied to you."

"You manipulated me," I spit. "You let me believe I was in danger."

"I didn't know you really were."

I shake my head. "It's pathetic. You used the fact that I was afraid—"

"I didn't force you to go out with me."

I sigh. "What about those times you drugged me. What was that about? Control?"

He flushes. "What?"

"You know what I'm talking about. I woke up on two separate mornings feeling like my head was going to explode and with a horrible taste in my mouth."

He shoots me a withering look. "Perhaps if you didn't drink so much you wouldn't have been hungover. I never drugged you." He tries to close the door on my foot again. It hurts, but I don't move it.

"What about when you insisted we had to go to that cafe even though I was in work. Why would you do that if you weren't trying to sabotage me?"

He looks at me like I'm mad. "It was a nice place. I thought you'd like it."

Is this really the truth? Is Nathan just a creep who saw an opportunity? It fits: that's why he told the police he was with me all of Saturday night. He wanted me all to himself.

"What I don't understand is why you texted me to say you didn't want to see me anymore. Why do all this and then stop seeing me?"

His face twists into a grotesque grin. "Treat 'em mean, keep 'em keen. I knew you'd be back and you were."

My stomach lurches. What am I doing here? Nathan's a creep—that's all I need to know.

I take my foot out of the door frame and turn away.

As repulsed as I am by him, it was his actions that saved me. If he hadn't come to the police station and told them we were together, they might have kept me in custody—giving Jason enough time to plant that knife with my fingerprints somewhere the police would find it.

"You're dreaming if you think I'm going to see you again after this."

I shake my head without looking back. "That's absolutely fine by me."

————

"Well? Did it help?" Tony asks as I sit down.

I think about it for a moment. "Yes and no. I understand things a bit better, but the real mystery is Jason, isn't it?"

He takes my hands. It's hard to believe this is the man who was watching me; the man who almost frightened me to death when he tried to grab me outside Dad's house that night. I understand him better now too: he spent so long locked away that he doesn't have the same way of communicating as other people. He was just trying to talk to me but he didn't know how to approach me.

I still haven't worked out how I feel about him. There's a lot of bad blood between him and Dad that I'm just going to have to ignore. There's also the fact that he didn't treat my mother very well. There's only one thing I know for sure—he saved my life. If it hadn't been for him, I can't even imagine what would have happened.

"Some people are just bad, Ellie. I know from being in… you know."

I shake my head. It's not enough. The need to know is consuming me.

Tony squeezes my hand. "You've got to try and let it go."

"What if I can't?"

"You have to try. You spending all your time thinking about him is what he wants."

I shudder. That sounds a lot like letting him win, and I won't do that. "Will you stay for the court case? It could be months yet, but I'd…"

"Yes," he says. "Of course I will. I'll stay as long as you want."

Our coffees come and I empty a sachet of sugar into mine. "Tell me about her, will you? Even if it's something you think is boring. I want to know what she was like."

CHAPTER 49
ELLIE
SIX MONTHS LATER

have my own theories about what drove Jason to do the things he did. And it's looking more and more like that's all I'll have: theories. Jason never spoke to the police. All the proof we've got that he was the one who murdered Steph is what he said to me that night in my flat when he tried to kill me. His fingerprints weren't found on the plastic bag with the knife, nor was there any other evidence to pin it on him.

I had prepared myself for that.

I had also prepared myself for there being no evidence left that it was Jason who attacked Mikey.

But in terms of the case against him for attacking me, I thought it was clear-cut: there was a witness. I was injured—my neck was marked from where he tried to strangle me, for goodness sake. I thought it was a sure thing—my only worry was that he'd be out in a few years.

What I wasn't prepared for was the way his defence team twisted the truth. They said the fact that there was no evidence of forced entry proved that I'd let him in. They said the marks on my neck were from a sex game gone wrong; one that I'd willingly participated in. They destroyed Tony's credibility, painting him as a junkie criminal and they did a similar number on me.

The police weren't sure if Jason would be found guilty on

the attempted murder charge, but now it's looking like he might get off the assault charge too.

I lean my head against the wall and take a deep breath. We've been waiting here for hours for the jury to come back. I've spent a lot of time sitting here lately and I don't care. I need to be here when the jury comes back with their verdict.

Jason was unrecognisable in court. He was never particularly warm in work, but I'd never seen anyone so cold and unemotional. He claimed I'd become fixated on him when he tried to help me through a mental breakdown. He denied everything and painted me as a scorned lover out for revenge.

It was terrifying—he was so convincing.

So why did he do it? I've finally accepted that we'll never get an answer from him beyond what he let slip in my flat that night. The police have had him seen by psychiatrists, but they can't do much when the subject of their investigation stubbornly sticks to his lies. I've gone back over every single interaction I've ever had with him and I'm still none the wiser. He never gave me any indication that he was interested in me. But he must have been on some level.

That's what bothers me. Why did he pick me? What did he see in me that he didn't see in other people?

I don't think he intended to hurt me—that's the impression I got from what he said in my flat that night. I know his word means nothing, but I believe he hurt Mikey in the hope of getting closer to me. I was hurt too, so he had to lay low for a while. There were a few times in his office over the past year where he tried to get me to talk about my life, but I always brushed him off, wanting to keep it professional between us. Then Steph came into my life and so did Nathan. That's why I think he snapped. Even when I was completely alone, I found someone new instead of leaning on him like he wanted.

I sigh. I could be completely wrong, of course. I've got to stop thinking about him. Tony is right: I can't let him occupy my thoughts forever.

He won't.

I won't let him.

Whatever the outcome of this trial, I'm moving on with my life when it's over.

I shiver as doubts start to grow inside me. What if he's found not guilty? What if he gets out?

I've decided not to move away. I've learned the hard way what happens when you're isolated from your support network. Mine may not be perfect, but it's all I've got and I'm trying to mend relationships and build new ones. I've found a new job in a different call centre.

I've also kept my promise to stop drinking. I know what happened wasn't my fault, but that doesn't make it any easier to accept. I made it easy for Jason. I've started Ju-Jitsu training too. It's early days, but I want to be stronger. I still wake myself screaming in the middle of the night. I don't want to be scared anymore.

The door to the courtroom opens and my heart leaps. Without knowing what I'm doing, I reach out for Dad's hand. And Tony's.

"Don't worry," Tony mutters. "He'll get what's coming to him."

I look at him. Now that the moment we've been waiting for is here, I'm starting to wonder if I should have come at all. What if he's let off? Even if he's convicted, how long will he actually serve? I saw how convincing a liar he was when he told the court under oath that he only strangled me because I asked him to and that we'd been having a secret relationship for months. What if the jury believes him?

"Come on, Ellie," DS Hobson says as he passes. "We're all here for you."

There's a lump in my throat as we walk back into the courtroom.

I can't look.

I close my eyes and clench my fists.

"Not guilty."

The words ring out in the courtroom. I squeeze my eyes closed. I knew that. I expected that. There's still the assault charge. They have to get him on that.

"Not guilty."

I gasp. My shock is mirrored on the faces of those around me.

I shake my head.

How?

He got away with it. He got away with breaking into my flat and trying to kill me.

Dad squeezes my hand.

"No. I can't."

I need to get out of here. I need to leave. I can't face Jason. I stand up.

Dad tugs on my arm. "Wait. You can't get up yet."

I sit down numbly. It feels strange to obey the rules of a court that has just dismissed everything I've been through and made Jason a free man.

The judge leaves and I jump to my feet. I don't want to stay in this place a moment longer than I have to.

Tony puts his arm around me as we walk out.

"It's disappointing, I know."

"I should have known."

"You had a right to seek justice."

I snort. "Not according to his defence. They painted me as some batshit crazy loser who was chasing after him." Tears sting my eyes. It was so humiliating listening to them tell the whole court those lies about me and not being able to stand up and scream that they were lying. I should have: the only reason I didn't is that I was scared it might affect the trial.

"It doesn't matter, Ellie."

I stop and look up at him. What is he talking about? "Of course it matters! He's free! I'll be the prisoner now. I won't be able to set foot outside the door and how the hell am I going to sleep? The nightmares were bad enough with him in custody."

Tony looks around before leaning closer to me. "Keep your voice down, alright? That's not what I meant."

I frown. "What did you mean? It sounds like you're saying it's no big deal that he got off."

"Come on," he says. "Keep walking."

"I can't, Tony." The familiar buzz of an anxiety attack begins. I stop and sit down on the nearest doorstep. "I can't. I'll never feel safe if he's free. You and Dad can't protect me all the time and I don't want you to have to do that. I'll have to move away after all."

"Ellie," he whispers. "Breathe. And listen to me. You're safe now."

"But I know that's not true. You know that more than anyone." I stop talking when I see the look that flashes across his face. I frown. "What are you going to do?"

"He'll get what's coming to him."

My eyes widen as I realise what he's talking about. "No. He's already hurt enough people I care about. He'll win if you get locked away again."

He shakes his head. "I've learned my lesson, Ellie. No-one will ever know I was involved. That's why I've held off."

"But Hobson is—"

Tony laughs. "Do you think Hobson will shed any tears over him? I don't."

I shake my head. I don't know what to think. A year ago I would have been shocked by what he's suggesting—by what I asked him to do on the night Jason broke into my flat—but a lot has changed. Jason has cost Mikey and Steph their lives, Dad his business. He almost killed me. I don't doubt that he'll try again once he gets out. "I don't either."

We walk on in silence for a while and I feel the fear start to leave me again. I take Tony's hand. I know it makes him sad that Dad gave me a childhood Tony never could, but he's given me something far more precious now: something Dad and the law could never do.

I feel safe again.

"Thank you," I whisper.